# HOW
# FREAKING
# ROMANTIC

# HOW FREAKING ROMANTIC

A NOVEL

## EMILY HARDING

**GALLERY BOOKS**

New York   Amsterdam/Antwerp   London
Toronto   Sydney/Melbourne   New Delhi

# G

Gallery Books
An Imprint of Simon & Schuster, LLC
1230 Avenue of the Americas
New York, NY 10020

This book is a work of fiction. Any references to historical events, real people, or real places are used fictitiously. Other names, characters, places, and events are products of the author's imagination, and any resemblance to actual events or places or persons, living or dead, is entirely coincidental.

First Gallery Books trade paperback edition July 2025

GALLERY BOOKS and colophon are registered trademarks of Simon & Schuster, LLC

Simon & Schuster strongly believes in freedom of expression and stands against censorship in all its forms. For more information, visit BooksBelong.com

For information about special discounts for bulk purchases, please contact Simon & Schuster Special Sales at 1-866-506-1949 or business@simonandschuster.com.

The Simon & Schuster Speakers Bureau can bring authors to your live event. For more information or to book an event, contact the Simon & Schuster Speakers Bureau at 1-866-248-3049 or visit our website at www.simonspeakers.com.

Manufactured in the United States of America

10  9  8  7  6  5  4  3  2  1

Library of Congress Cataloging-in-Publication Data

Names: Harding, Emily, author.
Title: How freaking romantic : a novel / Emily Harding.
Description: First Gallery Books trade paperback edition. | New York : Gallery Books, 2025.
Identifiers: LCCN 2024035344 (print) | LCCN 2024035345 (ebook) |
   ISBN 9781668082744 (paperback) | ISBN 9781668082751 (ebook)
Subjects: LCSH: Women law students—Fiction. | Lawyers—Fiction. |
   Divorce—Fiction. | LCGFT: Romance fiction. | Novels.
Classification: LCC PS3608.A725328 H69 2025 (print) |
   LCC PS3608.A725328 (ebook) | DDC 813/.6—dc23/eng/20240807
LC record available at https://lccn.loc.gov/2024035344
LC ebook record available at https://lccn.loc.gov/2024035345

ISBN 978-1-6680-8274-4
ISBN 978-1-6680-8275-1 (ebook)

*For Poppy and Henry, forever and ever and always*

# CHAPTER 1

My mom likes to say I was born angry. It's usually something she brings up during holiday meals or to her latest boyfriend, inevitably followed by a tittering laugh, as if it's everything you needed to know about me. And I always pretend not to hear, even as the comment stokes my ever-present annoyance—which, now that I think about it, might prove her point a little.

But honestly, is anyone born angry? Terrified, yes. Who wouldn't be? Thrust into a cold, unforgiving world only to be weighed and probed and manhandled by strangers? There's a reason we all emerge screaming. The first few moments of being a person are horrifying. Still, no one comes out mad about it. Mostly because we haven't learned that being scared and vulnerable are things we can even be mad about. That comes later. Anger comes from experience.

The first time I remember being truly angry was at my mother's third wedding. That's not to say there was anything wrong with the wedding itself; of all her ceremonies it was probably my favorite. Her fiancé, Larry Huffman, paid for us to fly first class from Minneapolis to Cancún, where he and my mom exchanged vows on a white-sand beach at sunset. The night before, at the rehearsal dinner, he even let me order a virgin strawberry daiquiri with one of those little paper umbrellas, which, for a ten-year-old girl with trust issues, was a very big step.

No, the anger came the next day, after I watched my mom walk barefoot down the makeshift aisle on the beach. The sun was setting behind a gauzy veil of pink and orange clouds, sending soft rays of light off the Swarovski crystals in her hair, while a guitarist played Canon in D nearby. And when she reached Larry, smiling so brightly that her rose-colored blush creased along her cheeks, I couldn't help but smile, too. The moment was perfect. The epitome of what love was supposed to look like, what romance ought to be.

The music faded and they clasped their hands together as they began to recite their vows. Larry went first, his gruff voice delivering every word like he was in one of his quarterly board meetings. And then it was my mom's turn.

"I, Denise Nilsson, promise to be true to you in good times and in bad, in sickness and in health. I will love you and honor you all the days of my life."

*All the days of my life.*

It suddenly occurred to me that she had said that before. Those exact words were uttered to Darren Lupinski three years earlier on a hillside overlooking a vineyard in Napa. She wore white to that wedding, too. And just like that, the soft focus on the moment pulled to sharp clarity, the stark lines now vivid and cutting through the gossamer of my romantic fantasy.

For the rest of the wedding, the competing vows swirled in my head. During the reception, while the two of them swayed together on the dance floor to the hotel band's moving cover of

Vanessa Williams's "Save the Best for Last," I sat at the head table and poked apart a piece of pineapple cream wedding cake, unable to reconcile the promise I had just heard with the one from three years before. Because even at ten years old, I knew those two events should be mutually exclusive.

I kept the revelation to myself until later that night. Then, as the band began to pack up and my mother landed drunkenly in the chair next to me, I confided in her. Did she know she had said those same words before? Why did they mean more now than back then? And she laughed. Her head tipped back, the carefully pinned updo now flopping to one side and her pristine dress falling off one shoulder. She laughed and laughed, like life was some inside joke I wasn't privy to yet. As if I were a fool for not knowing. And that hurt so much that the pain transformed into something entirely new: anger.

By the time her fourth wedding rolled around, I was wiser. Even at fourteen, I could see the signs. She met Locke Taylor while she was a receptionist at his real estate development company in Atlanta. Her first week of work, he asked her out to dinner. By week three he had said "I love you." Week six saw him fly her to Paris for the weekend. And after five months, Mom came home with a two-carat diamond on her hand, proclaiming, "This is the one!" They were married in September. She filed for divorce on their second anniversary.

Needless to say, when she called in the middle of my sophomore year of college to tell me about marriage number five, I just sent a card.

It wasn't necessarily that the pain had dissipated. I feel too much too often for that. It's just that anger is such a useful tool against it all. Protection that ensures you're always ready for the pain, that you can fend it off and walk away unscathed. A proverbial suit of armor that I have gotten quite good at wielding, thank you very much.

But despite that protection, pain can still find a way to sneak up and surprise you. Like when your mom moves to Florida with husband number six and forgets to tell you until two months after the fact. Or the first time you open your student loan debt statement and see the interest rate spelled out in actual dollars. Or, most recently, when you get a phone call in the middle of the night relaying information that you feared was coming for weeks: your two best friends, the ones you worked so hard to bring together, are getting divorced.

And suddenly the old scar along your heart that you had worked so hard to protect is ripped back open again, leaving you feeling raw and powerless and duped. A ten-year-old sitting alone in a ballroom somewhere in Mexico.

Sometimes a person has to lean into anger just to survive.

Which is why I've spent this entire elevator ride up to the law office of Hayes, Patel & Asher daydreaming about nailing Nathan Asher's balls to the side of the building.

I'm not literally going to nail his balls to the side of the building, of course. God, I'm not some kind of monster. That said, the moment the elevator doors open on the white marble lobby and reveal a wall of obscenely large gold letters displaying the law firm's name, I feel a twinge of regret that I forgot my hammer.

## HAYES, PATEL & ASHER LLP

It takes a special kind of prick to display their own name in gold in their Midtown Manhattan office. There's probably a person who's been hired just to polish it, too. Their sole job is to make sure each letter glows, maintaining this brazen reminder of the fortune you're about to lose just by walking into this office.

That's the side of falling in love that no one talks about: the money and time required to fall out of it. Marriage is peddled like love's fail-safe, but no one tells you to read the fine print. And why would they? They're too busy profiting off everyone so blindsided by heartbreak and prenups that they forget to notice the price tag attached. And *that* is fucking disgusting.

I stare up at the gleaming letters, scowling at every curve and corner, and imagine their angles forming something else entirely.

## HAYES, PATEL & ASSHOLE LLP

Ah yes, that's better.

"Can I help you?"

The lyrical voice snaps me from my reverie. I look over to the reception desk, a glass behemoth that looms in the center of the palatial waiting room, and the beautiful woman seated behind it.

It takes all my strength not to roll my eyes. Because of course the prick who has his name spelled out in huge gold letters would hire a woman who looks like she just stepped off the runway at New York Fashion Week to greet him after walking by said gold letters every day.

She's smiling at me, a nervous smile, which tells me that despite offering assistance, she isn't yet sure if she wants to follow through on it. I shift my weight as her eyes flit down my body, aware of how I look: unwashed brown curls barely contained by the scrunchie on top of my head, baggy sweatpants covered with coffee stains, tattered sneakers held together by mismatched laces and prayers. I want to scream: *Listen, I know I look bad, but I've spent every waking moment either in class or studying for the bar and it's exhausting, so give me a fucking break!* But I bite back the words as I approach her, my shoulders straight like that might somehow negate the outfit, or at least disguise the rage coursing through my veins.

"That Asher guy," I say, pointing at the gold letters on the wall. "Is he here?"

Her gaze darts down the hallway to my left before coming back to me. "Mr. Asher? I . . . I believe so."

I nod toward the same hallway. "Down there?"

Her eyes go wide as she realizes her mistake. "Is he expecting you?"

"Nope."

I start down the hall, ignoring the protests from the supermodel behind me. It's only a few meager pleas anyway. Then she falls silent, and I can only assume she's calling the man himself, letting him know that a crazed woman, possibly homeless, is making her way past the rows of employees busy at their desks on her way to his office.

I throw open the door at the end of the hall and, sure enough, it's exactly what I expect: a huge sterile space with a glass-and-steel desk directly in the center, covered in papers, with a laptop off to the side. And behind the laptop sits a man in a perfectly tailored navy suit with a phone to his ear.

He doesn't acknowledge me, only listens intently to the person on the other end of the line.

"Thanks, Vanessa. It's fine; don't worry about it," he murmurs into the receiver. Then he hangs up and turns his eyes to me. They're blue—bright blue—and a spike of resentment shoots through me for all the times I ever found blue eyes attractive. "Can I help you?"

Four words have never been so enlaced with patronizing amusement, as if waiting to see what I have in store. As if this is fun.

"Nathan Asher, right?"

"Right." He leans back in his chair and unbuttons the front of his suit jacket, getting himself comfortable.

"You're Joshua Fox's divorce attorney."

He smiles. "Are you Mrs. Fox?"

"No."

His cool demeanor falters, but only slightly. I can see him taking mental stock of me, trying to connect the dots.

"I'm here to tell you that your client is an asshole and you're an even bigger asshole for representing him." I'm standing just a foot or so from his desk now. How did that happen? I had been so concerned with keeping my voice even that I had forgotten to keep a safe distance, one that would make it impossible to take an involuntary swing at his jaw.

"And you are?" he asks.

I ignore him and barrel on. "You realize he's the one who filed for divorce, right? He blindsided her with those papers, demanded that she move out as soon as possible, so why the hell is he the one drawing it out? Or do you even care? The more hours you spend helping him bleed my friend dry, the more zeros on your paycheck, right?"

"Ah, Jillian Fox is your friend." He says it as if this all suddenly makes sense, and he can now mentally disengage. As if he's not the catalyst for this crack in the foundation of my support system, my friends who are my whole life. And just like that, there's a new tear in my heart, bleeding and raw, and I have to shore up my anger again to protect it.

I take a step closer to his desk, my hips flush with its glass edge. "First it was the apartment. Then the dog. Now he wants *alimony*?"

"Is that a problem?"

"Of course it's a problem! Josh doesn't need it! But instead of telling him that, you've fully endorsed the idea. Do you honestly think it's Jillian's responsibility to support your client just because he quit his job to go to grad school, then decided to quit that, too?"

"Yes," he replies. He has the audacity to still look amused, as if this happens every day. God, maybe it does.

I nod with the realization. "Ah, I see. You're not just paid to be an asshole. You're a bona fide, purebred asshole."

"Okay, let's not—"

"No." I hold up my hand. "Don't pretend like there's room for manners in this conversation. Or integrity, for that matter."

That seems to get to him. He leans forward, eyes narrowed. "Excuse me?"

"You already put a price on your integrity, Mr. Asher. Eight fifty an hour, right?" I reply, bracing my arms on either side of his desk. "Well, when you drive home tonight in your luxury car, eat that expensive steak at some fancy restaurant, and then go home to fuck that beautiful woman who wouldn't give you the time of day if not for your penthouse apartment, I hope you enjoy it. That's if you don't choke on the steak first. A girl can dream, right?"

He stands, but I've already turned around, marching back the way I came.

"Hold on a sec—"

I slam the door behind me before he can finish.

The office that only moments before had been a hive of activity is now silent, a dozen sets of eyes following me as I walk down the hall, keeping just short of a sprint until I reach the waiting elevator and press the down button.

# CHAPTER 2

"You did *what?*"

Jillian gapes at me over the plastic take-out containers of tuna sashimi and California rolls spread across the cardboard boxes in the center of the room. It was a bold move, ordering raw fish from a restaurant with a C rating from the city health commission. But Sammy Sushi is also the only restaurant in a twenty-block radius that will deliver Bloody Marys in huge plastic cups before noon on a Sunday. And after a long morning of packing and crying and then more packing, it was an easy choice.

To be fair, we weren't going to cry. While Maggie and Travis sat in traffic this morning on their drive into the city, we had a long call about how we absolutely couldn't cry. Despite the divorce and how it had strained Jillian's finances so much that she was being forced to move into a small studio in Queens, this apartment needed to stay neutral, a place still defined by the good memories we made there. So we agreed to remain stoic and strong.

But then I met them outside Jillian and Josh's building on Barrow Street in the West Village. They parked their truck along the curb and the three of us walked up to where the front door was propped open. Jillian was waiting for us at the top of the stairs, just outside their second-floor apartment. Behind her, the door still displayed the welcome sign she painstakingly painted two years before, back when she was still smiling and saying that she and Josh were fine, *really*. Back when we believed it.

When Josh and Jillian found this place after we graduated Fordham seven years ago, it had seemed so sophisticated, so grown-up. It was an address that equated some sort of unlocked achievement in our game of adulthood, a new center of gravity keeping us together after college. Despite conflicting schedules and nonexistent funds, we would still congregate here on the weekends and on holidays, sure that it would be the foundation for a new era of memories.

Jillian stood in the doorway with a blank expression, her eyes bloodshot and puffy. And without saying anything, we knew that all aforementioned promises of not crying were null and void.

I turn to where Maggie is seated next to me now, cross-legged on the floor with her short black hair sticking out in every direction and Jillian's golden retriever, Tex, curled up next to her. She's given up on packing and is petting Tex with one hand and holding her plastic cup in the other.

"Is this spicy tuna or spicy salmon?" I ask her, motioning with my chopsticks to the congealed pink glob wrapped in rice between us. "All I taste is spicy."

"Bea," Jillian says, refusing to let me change the subject. Her long blond hair is pulled back in a severe ponytail, her full lips pursed in a grim line. Nothing about her appearance has ever been severe before. From the moment I met her during an English literature class our sophomore year, she gave off the ethereal glow of a person created by Disney, as if she awoke every morning in slow motion, dressed with the help of field mice. But now concealer barely covers the dark circles under her eyes, and the pink glow of her cheeks obviously comes from a compact. "You need to tell me exactly what happened."

I abandon the tuna and/or salmon and grab some edamame. "It was nothing. Josh's lawyer is right in Midtown, so I stopped by on my way to class on Friday."

Travis emerges from the hallway, his long unkempt brown hair hidden beneath a Mets cap.

"You don't have class on Fridays," he says, dropping the box by the front door and throwing me a look like he was a dad catching his kid in a lie.

*Shit.* He's been back and forth to the truck so much, I forgot he was listening.

"I thought you were going to stay neutral," I say, glaring at him.

"I am neutral," he shouts over his shoulder as he heads down the hallway to the bedroom again.

"You're doing a good job, sweetie," Maggie calls after him, then takes a long pull from the straw in her drink. "Great lifting."

Next to her, Tex yawns like he's not as impressed.

"Okay," Jillian says, releasing a long breath as she turns back to me. "You stopped by. And then what?"

I push a mess of curls away from my face and try to make my voice sound nonchalant. "I went to his office to discuss Josh's latest request for spousal support."

"Discuss?" she asks carefully.

"Well, *I* wanted to discuss. *He* wanted to be a dick."

"Oh God." Jillian groans.

"You were so upset, Jills, and Josh wasn't picking up his phone—"

"You called Josh?" she cuts me off, eyes wide.

I barely hear her, distracted by the sudden realization that after five phone calls and three dozen text messages, Josh hadn't even replied. "You know, I think that prick blocked my number."

"I think he blocked your number when you publicly castrated him for making out with Theresa Bianco during spring break junior year," Maggie says.

I consider this for a moment. "True."

"This isn't like when we broke up in college, Bea," Jillian replies. "We're adults now, and we're getting divorced. There are motions and injunctions and arraignments—"

"There aren't any arraignments in divorce proceedings," I say, popping an edamame bean in my mouth.

Maggie leans back against a half-filled cardboard box and starts rubbing Tex's belly. "You know, *New York* magazine did a profile on this Asher guy a few months ago. Called him one of the top divorce attorneys in the city," she says. "His picture was . . . not horrible."

My chopsticks hover above a California roll as I recall Nathan Asher. Objectively, Maggie's right. He's not horrible. The opposite of horrible, actually. Thick brown hair—the kind you know would be curly if he didn't cut it this side of short—and a sharp jaw that his stubble had no hope of disguising. His broad shoulders had been draped in what was no doubt an expensive suit, and his arrogant smile could probably charm even the most hardened judge in New York's family court. So no, not horrible. But in the same way a corpse flower isn't horrible; it's quite gorgeous, until you get too close and realize it smells like dog shit.

"They deliver *New York* magazine all the way upstate?" I ask, cocking my head to the side and hoping my sarcasm covers up the misdirection.

"The Hudson Valley is not upstate, you philistine," Maggie replies. The statement is punctuated by a large slurp from her straw.

"I don't think you're using that word right, Mags."

"Bea," Jillian interrupts us, her voice strained. "I need to know exactly what you said to him."

"Well…" I trail off as I try to remember. There had been insults, but what exactly had I said? The adrenaline must have blocked out my short-term memory, so all I can recall is how he looked at me, at first arrogant and smug but changing ever so slightly to betray a bit of surprise. Maybe even offense. "I'm pretty sure I called him an asshole. I definitely called Josh one."

"Oh my God." Maggie cackles as Travis appears from the hallway with another box.

"It's not like I jumped on top of the guy's desk and attacked him or something," I say, but then I pause, remembering. "I might have said I hoped he choked to death on some steak, though."

"Jesus Christ," Travis mutters as he drops the box next to the front door, startling Tex awake. "Jillian, you need to call your lawyer."

My mouth falls open. "Hey! Neutral, remember?"

"I am, but come on, Bea," he says. "You're about to graduate from one of the best law schools in the country. You're taking the bar in just a few months. Why did you think this was a good idea?"

To be honest, I didn't think it was a good idea. I didn't think at all. Objectively, I knew it was irrational, but there was nothing about this situation that instilled objectivity, and I didn't want it to.

I'd known about the growing problems between Jillian and Josh for a while. All of us had. But we also assumed they would work it out, the same way they had since college. Then Jillian left to stay with her mother right before Thanksgiving. Josh blindsided her by filing divorce papers the following week. Suddenly, our once-tight group was being torn apart, but the details were in short supply. The whats and whys of how their once happy union had deteriorated to a point where Jillian had to schedule time to pack up her things from her own home were drip fed over a quick coffee or obligatory weekend call. A sidenote to our lives that were shooting off in different directions. And that hurt so much that anger seemed a much more appealing option than common sense.

That's the bit people always forget. Pain is anger's neglectful parent.

"Josh's lawyer doesn't even know my name, Trav," I say, throwing another edamame bean in my mouth.

"Yeah, but all he has to do is ask Josh about the crazy, curly-haired woman covered in freckles who stormed his office, and you're screwed."

"Oh, stop it." Maggie waves her hand between the two of us like some drunken referee. "I don't care how mad Josh is, he wouldn't sell Bea out like that."

I'm not willing to give Josh that much credit, but it's not worth having that argument with Maggie again.

Travis shrugs. "All I'm saying is we shouldn't get involved or we'll just complicate things more. It's the same reason we told you to stop sending Josh those anonymous STD notification texts, Bea."

"I don't know what you're talking about," I lie, stabbing the last bit of an avocado roll with my chopstick.

"Regardless," he says, his hands going to his hips. He's in full dad-mode now. "You should know better."

I roll my eyes. As much as he loves to dole out unsolicited advice these days, back in college, Travis had no idea what to do with his life and had a litany of majors to prove it. After graduation, when he and Maggie finally started dating and she got her dream job at a hedge fund, his indecision became a full-blown crisis. The struggle lasted a few years, until Maggie realized she in fact didn't want to become a major player in the financial world and decided to take her life savings and buy a dilapidated bed-and-breakfast up in the Hudson Valley instead. Suddenly, they not only had the perfect excuse to move in together, but Travis found his purpose. Now his life is happily filled with drywall, paint tarps, and sanctimony.

"So, what am I supposed to do?" I ask him. "Josh didn't even tell Jillian he was filing for divorce, and now he's treating the whole thing like it's a cash grab, and you want me to just ignore it?"

"Yes." He says it like the answer is obvious. "Listen, I know why you're pissed, Bea. Which is saying something, because you're pissed ninety-nine percent of the time, and I usually never get it. But when push comes to shove, Josh hasn't really done anything wrong here, and—"

Maggie whips her head around to glare at him. "Are you seriously taking Josh's side right now?"

"I'm not on anybody's side!" Travis groans, throwing his arms up. "I'm Switzerland!" With that, he turns back down the hall, stomping toward the bedroom. The dog gets up and follows him, his paws tapping against the hardwood floor.

"Is he okay?" Jillian asks.

Maggie raises her cup and takes another sip. "He's fine."

I want to make a snide comment, but then Jillian closes her eyes and sighs. The sound is heavy and sad.

"This is my fault," she whispers, almost to herself. "I shouldn't have said anything about the alimony."

A pang of guilt hits my chest. It had been a late-night confession, one of those phone calls that rarely happened anymore: Jillian ringing after midnight, trying to pretend as if a call that late was still normal, like everything was okay. And it had been for a few minutes, until I asked about the divorce. The tears had come on so quickly I hadn't heard them at first. Jillian was always good at that. Quiet crying.

I had stayed on the phone with her for more than an hour, listening to all the details about their financial disclosures and Josh's petition for spousal support, and offering advice when I could. By the time she hung up, I thought she was okay. But now, with exhaustion and stress written across Jillian's pale, drawn face, I know she's not.

I lean forward and take her hand, squeezing it tightly. "Hey, I'm sorry. Seriously. But look on the bright side: in the history of New York divorce cases, this can't be the worst thing that has ever happened."

Maggie pauses, her straw hovering at her lips. "That's a pretty big spectrum, don't you think?"

I shoot her a withering glare.

"Okay," Jillian says to herself, lifting her head and straightening her back. "This is manageable. I'll call my lawyer tomorrow morning. That way she'll be ready in case his attorney calls or if Josh decides to freak out about this and—"

"It's fine, Jills, I promise," I say, squeezing her hand one more time before releasing it and reaching for my chopsticks again. "We never have to talk about Nathan Asher again."

# CHAPTER 3

The first thing you learn in law school is that weekends are a myth. A legend told in hushed tones around study groups, or to your own haggard reflection after pulling two all-nighters in a row. Even if you do somehow manage to eke out a few hours on a Sunday to unwind, by the time you disengage your brain from torts and case law so you can ponder abstract concepts like "relaxing" and "self-care," Monday arrives with as much fanfare as a pap smear: horrifying but necessary.

The light at the end of this sleep-deprived tunnel is the third and final year of law school. When you reach the esteemed status of L3 and graduation is just on the horizon, it's safe to take your foot off the gas. Those who are smart decide to relax a bit and enjoy those weekends we've all heard so much about. The really smart ones load up on electives that could be grouped on just a couple of afternoons each week to make that weekend even longer.

I remind myself of this as I'm shoving a piece of toast in my mouth at 7:58 a.m. on Monday morning, scrambling to do something with my erratic curls before I run out the door of my cramped studio apartment. Because I am not smart. I signed up for a public policy seminar at ten o'clock on Monday mornings. That in and of itself isn't so bad; it only takes me thirty minutes to get down to campus from my apartment on 168th Street, so I could feasibly sleep in until nine. So why am I scrambling to get out the door by 8:00 a.m.? Because in addition to being an L3 with a full course load, I'm also a teaching assistant for one of NYU Law's most infamous law professors. There are papers to grade, student emails to reply to, and copious amounts of coffee to drink before I can even step foot in class.

I want to stress that on paper, this all looked very doable. In practice, it is a clusterfuck.

This particular Monday morning my curls refuse to stay clumped together on top of my head, so I set them free. Frazzled ringlets spring out in every direction as I swipe on a bit of mascara in the hopes it might save my reflection, or at least distract from the dark circles under my hazel eyes. The plethora of freckles used to do the job, but there's only so much I can ask of them now.

By 8:09 I'm downstairs, wrapped in my old wool overcoat that's entirely too thin for the freezing weather, and running through the narrow lobby of my prewar building with a computer bag slung on each arm. The front door is propped open, letting in the frigid air as a familiar team of plumbers file in. Idris, the building's super, is in the far corner directing them to the stairwell. I need to remind him yet again that the hot water upstairs still barely gets above room temperature, but I don't have time to stop. Instead, I just yell over my shoulder: "Where the hell is my hot water, Idris!"

He smiles and waves at me like this our usual morning greeting. I only realize once I'm out the door that he's not far off.

~

If I can snag an express train, campus is exactly seven subway stops away from my apartment. Unfortunately, this morning the express train decides to go local after 125th Street, so my thirty-minute commute becomes fifty. By the time I ascend the steps at Fourth Street and round the corner to Washington Square Park, it's 9:24 a.m. I'll barely have time to stop by my office before I need to head to class.

Apparently, on top of being an idiot, I am also a masochist.

The NYU Law campus is really just a cluster of buildings surrounding Washington Square Park, an enclave in the greater NYU sphere. In autumn it's gorgeous, with the historic brick and stone buildings framed by the golds and reds of the park's foliage and the towering arch in its center. Students and locals crowd every available space, and New York feels less like a city and more like a village, albeit one filled with twentysomethings arguing about international copyright law while a man wearing a top hat and monocle walks his iguana nearby.

But right now it's mid-January, which means the park is barren. Gray snowbanks line the sidewalk and the wind whipping down Fifth Avenue makes it too cold to attract the usual crowd. The only people I pass are two fellow students who jog by, looking fresh-faced and chipper in their NYU Law sweatshirts. I make it a point not to look at them as I scurry toward the colonial brick facade of Vanderbilt Hall. Even though I'm only a few years older than almost everyone here, moments like this make it feel like a lifetime.

My phone starts to ring just as I enter the lobby. I reach into my bag, my fingers probing the candy wrappers and bodega receipts. When I find it, I see my mother's face lighting up the screen, and groan.

A phone call from Denise Nilsson can go one of two ways: (a) she needs to complain about something for an extended period of time before hanging up with barely a goodbye; or (b) she requires my opinion on something, which will in no way factor into her final decision.

"Hi, Mom," I answer.

"Do you think I need a neck lift?" she says in greeting.

Ah. So it's option B, then.

"I'm doing great, thanks. How are you?" I say as I swipe my ID through the lobby turnstile.

"I'm serious, Bea. I just walked by the mirror in the hallway and gave myself a jump scare."

She says it like I've seen the mirror in question. In truth, I've never set foot in her house in Fort Lauderdale, let alone the entire state of Florida. I also haven't seen her neck in at least three years, when her sixth (and shockingly, still-current) husband, Todd Whitaker, surprised her with a trip to New York so she could see the new Neil Diamond musical on Broadway.

I make my way to a waiting elevator with a couple of other students. "Don't you think it's a little early on a Monday morning to be contemplating invasive surgery?"

"Oh, I've already been up for hours. Todd and I grabbed the first tee time at the club this morning. It was invigorating. You really should try it," she says as the doors close and the elevator lurches up.

My mom has a habit of adopting the personality of whoever she's currently married to. Golf is only the latest in a long list of hobbies, most of which were discarded in the wake of divorce. After she found out Darren Lupinski was a White Sox fan, she took out a new credit card to buy season tickets. When Locke Taylor revealed that he loved rebuilding classic cars, she suddenly had a burning desire to own a 1968 Ford Mustang. It's a pattern that's existed for decades.

"I'm not sure I can squeeze golf lessons into my schedule right now," I reply. The student standing beside me looks up from his phone in confusion.

"Well, you should," my mom says. "You sound tired."

"That's a prerequisite of law school, actually."

She hums to herself. "I told you three years ago that you were too old for that."

I roll my eyes as the elevator doors open on the third floor and I walk forward down the hall. "Thanks for the reminder."

"I'm just saying." Her voice takes on a tinge of indignation. "Most people go to law school right after college, not years later so they're middle-aged when they graduate."

"I'm twenty-nine, Mom," I say, trying to keep my annoyance in check as I unlock my office door. I say "office," but really it is little more than a large closet with a small window in the corner. There's room for a desk and a chair, though, which is all I really need anyway.

"You know what I mean. Look at that friend of yours. Jared? Josh? He tried to go to grad school, and it ruined his life."

I let my bag drop to the floor and ignore the sting of her comment as my body falls into the desk chair. My mom has never been good with details, let alone the ins and outs of my personal life. Questions about anything other than herself are rare, and when they do come, I've learned the answers are only partially retained. While I had mentioned Jillian and Josh's divorce a couple of times over the past few months, she always had a cursory response, something that implied sympathy but ensured the conversation would move on to how her sink was back-ordered, so the bathroom renovations had been delayed again, or how she was thinking of becoming a Pilates instructor. Maybe that's one of the reasons she was so eager to move down to Florida from Boston a few years ago; her distance is just another excuse to avoid getting bogged down by my life's tedious details.

Still, I'm surprised by the sudden urge to talk to her about the divorce, the alimony, everything that was tearing our small group apart. But before I can say anything, my mother groans.

"Oh God, it's awful. The skin below my chin is just *hanging* there," she says. I can imagine her right now: the phone to her ear as she leans toward the mirror, poking at her jaw.

I sigh. "You don't need a neck lift, Mom."

She hums again, a telltale sign that, while she's listening, she absolutely doesn't believe me. "Well, I have to run. Todd's pulling the car out. We're grabbing brunch with the Davidsons."

"All right," I reply. I have no idea who the Davidsons are, but that doesn't seem like a reason to hold her up. "Keep me posted about any other elective medical procedures."

"Will do!" she says. And then she hangs up.

～

I managed to make it to my ten o'clock class on time, but missed my window to grab a coffee beforehand, which is a tragedy. Professor Callahan is a renowned expert on public health law and social justice, but she also never changes her intonation or inflection, so her course is one monotonous drone for two hours. Without caffeine, it's hell.

I trudge back to my office afterward and grab my mug that has *I Hate It Here* written in big block letters across the side. Josh bought it for me when I got into law school because, in his words: "It reminded me of you." At the time I wanted to throw it at his head, but I can now admit that it is the perfect size to fit a large serving from the coffeemaker in the third-floor lounge and still leave room for milk. I cradle it in my hands as I head back to my desk, somehow already an hour behind on the grading that was supposed to start my day.

But first: email.

There's a sea of them waiting in my inbox from students. Their questions range from the insane to the surprisingly pertinent, but regardless, I'll get to all of them later. Right now, I scan the list for one with "RE: Graduating Law Student Job Inquiry" in the subject line.

There's none.

*Shit.*

I always assumed the most stressful part of post–law school life would be passing the bar, not lining up a job where I would be able to utilize my new skills.

But I'm not going to panic. Not yet. Yes, I sent out nineteen emails to nineteen separate firms right before Christmas. And no, I haven't received a single reply yet. But that was only a few weeks ago. People are barely back in their offices after the holidays, let alone opening unsolicited emails from desperate law students looking for a job. There's nothing to worry about. Not yet.

As if on cue, Blake appears in the doorway, his attention on his cell phone. Frank Landry only hires two L3s to be his teaching assistants each year, and as excited as I was to snag one of the coveted positions that would help pay my tuition, I was equally as annoyed to find out that Blake Sepper got the other. Not that I had anything against Blake personally. It's only that he seemed more interested in gossip surrounding the student body than in doing any actual work. To make matters worse, his office is right next to mine and, as he reminds me biweekly, two square feet larger.

"Hey," he says, leaning gingerly against the doorframe, as if it might wrinkle his blazer.

Blake always struck me as someone who watched '80s movies growing up, just to steal fashion tips from the antagonists. With his blond hair swept across his forehead and his blazer open to reveal a white shirt unbuttoned one too many, he looks like he's a few seconds away from convincing you not to take that quirky girl you like to prom.

When he doesn't say anything after another moment, I sigh. "Can I help you with something?"

"You can start checking our voicemail," he says, his attention still on his phone. "Or at least let me change the message so it doesn't sound like it's just yours. It's full again, and I have people who need to contact me."

I roll my eyes. While we have separate offices, our status as teaching assistants means we're still forced to share one voicemail. It never felt like that much of an issue, especially since I assumed most people used their cell phones anyway, so after recording the outgoing message the first week of school, I promptly forgot all about it, except for when Blake stops by to give me my messages and complain.

"Who needs to contact you?" I ask.

"Faculty. Students. That TA from Kirkpatrick's office. I ran into him last week and I swear he was flirting." Blake finally looks up and waggles his eyebrows at me.

"Why don't you give him your cell number?"

"I need to make him work for it, you know? This way, if he wants to call, he'll have to use the directory and call here so . . ." His voice fades as I narrow my eyes at him and, for a moment, he looks genuinely confused. "What, do you want to talk about actual work or something?"

How this man already has a clerkship lined up with a federal judge for after graduation, I have no idea.

"Go away, Blake."

He shrugs as he pushes off the doorframe, pausing just long enough to say, "By the way, Frank's looking for you."

I snap my laptop shut as I shoo him away and head upstairs.

Frank Landry's office is on the floor above mine, a cave-like room at the end of the hall piled high with papers and books and journals. Some people might find it claustrophobic, but I don't. Despite the harsh fluorescent lights, the piles of books, along with the smell of sandalwood from the cologne Frank has probably been wearing since the '70s, makes it feel oddly homey, like being wrapped up in a warm blanket. That is, until the old man behind the desk opens his mouth.

"Where the hell have you been?" he bellows before I've even reached the doorway.

"It's called class, Frank," I say with a smile, walking in and letting myself collapse into one of the two armchairs parked in front of his desk. "I'm a student here, too, remember? I have the loan statements to prove it."

"You shouldn't be in class. You should be looking for a job," he barks.

I scrunch up my nose. "I feel like maybe that's the opposite of what you're supposed to tell me."

He waves his hand indiscriminately in the air, as if such details aren't important.

There's a running joke among the students that Frank Landry has been teaching here since the law school opened in 1835, and right now, I can almost believe it. His back is bent at an awkward angle, his glasses askew on a wrinkled face that's pinched like he's ready for a fight.

He mumbles something under his breath, then shifts in his seat to grab a folder from the bookshelf behind him. The movement is slow, and when he turns back to face me, I can see the grimace on his face.

"How are you feeling?" I ask.

"I need to get a hip replaced. How do you think I'm feeling?"

He settles back in his seat, struggling to find a comfortable position. I could be sympathetic. I could offer support. But I know that the only thing Frank hates more than discomfort is pity, so I decide to change the subject instead.

"Blake said you were looking for me."

He grunts in agreement. "I need you to send me the syllabus for Alternative Conflict Resolution. And get materials together for the next few weeks."

Alarm bells go off in my head. I'm the TA for Frank's Alternative Conflict Resolution seminar, just as I was in the fall. I wrote the syllabus in August, and he's already told me we didn't need to change it this semester. I had assumed that meant everything else would be the same, too: each week I would meet with Frank to go over reading materials and graded papers before heading to class with him and taking notes. Together, we are a well-oiled machine. "Why do you need all that?"

"Because they finally scheduled my surgery, so I'll be out on medical leave soon."

Something heavy drops in my stomach. It's no secret that Frank needs a new hip. He complains about it regularly to anyone within earshot. It had also been one of the first things he told me when I came to speak with him about the TA position. Partly because my concentration is healthcare law and it offered him the perfect opportunity to bitch about the American healthcare system, and partly because a potential surgery would require him to take sub-stantial medical leave, and pass off the supervision of his teaching assistants to one of the school's adjunct professors.

But as much as I hate the idea of having to acclimate to a new professor midyear, I also never really weighed it as a possibility. From all accounts, Frank had been complaining about his hip for years. Any concern that it would happen during my tenure always seemed negligible.

"When are you going in?" I ask.

"Couple of weeks," he says. I frown and he notices. "Don't look so depressed. You're not the one getting a new hip."

"Yeah, but I am the one who's going to have to help some clue-less adjunct get up to speed on your classes."

He bows his head down just enough to look at me over the rim of his glasses. "You cover one class."

"On top of going to my actual classes. And, you know, maintaining a social life."

He chuckles as if he knows as well as I do that "social life" is used here in the broadest sense of the term. "Speaking of which, one of my former students invited me to this reception thing on Friday for the New York City Bar Association."

"And?"

He continues to glare at me from under his white bushy eyebrows.

I know that glare and I groan, letting my head fall back in defeat. "Are you going to make me do a work thing?"

"You got plans or something?"

I could be honest. I could say, *Yes, Frank, I have Friday nights carved out for three hours of dedicated study time down at the laundromat between the wash cycle and folding.* Instead, I just mumble, "Maybe."

"I can ask Blake to come instead, but that kid is so far up his own ass I don't think he's seen daylight since preschool."

I can't help but laugh.

"You need a job after graduation, Bea," he continues. "This will have a room full of lawyers who might be able to help with that."

I know he's right. And the fact that he knows he's right only makes it worse. While it's no secret that I'm about to graduate, only a select few know the details. Despite a position on the Law Review masthead last year, an internship with a prestigious nonprofit last summer, and a coveted TA position my final year, I still flail at the one extracurricular activity that's required to actually secure a job: networking.

And when I say "select few," I mean Frank.

"Come on, it won't be so bad," he continues, reading my expression. "Make some small talk, enjoy some of their expensive champagne, then head home."

It sounds easy. And if it were anything like the usual professional events Frank drags me to, it will be. At least this one is off campus, which means there's a chance that an attorney from one of the law firms I applied to might show up. Maybe even someone from Land and Associates. My heart does an odd flop at the thought, even as I scowl at its naive optimism. Because really, what are the chances? There are only a handful of firms in the city that deal with healthcare law, and even fewer on the ethical side of it. If you narrow that list down to the firms run by women, you're left with only one: Land and Associates. They're small, but they're also the best. That's why scoring an interview with them is akin to winning the lottery on the same day scientists announce the discovery of the weeklong orgasm. So, the odds that one of the associates, even Marcie Land herself, might attend this event? Close to impossible.

Then again, if they show up and I miss the opportunity . . .

I huff, sending a stray curl away from my face. "Forward me the info."

Frank snorts. "Don't sound so thrilled."

"Excuse me. Excuse me!" a panicked voice calls out from behind me. I turn enough to see a young man leaning through the doorway. His oxford shirt is light blue and starched so thoroughly that it sticks up into his neck as he bends forward to speak to Frank. "Are you still available for office hours?"

"Depends," Frank answers, his tone even and bored. "What's your question about?"

"The outline for Contracts."

"Then no," he replies, turning his attention back to me. "The event starts at eight. Be there on time."

I scrunch up my nose. "Why? No one ever shows up on time for these things."

"Because I want to introduce you to a few people and I'm not staying late, that's why."

I am about to make the completely unfounded claim that I'm perfectly capable of introducing myself when Oxford Shirt Guy leans in further, now almost horizontal in the doorframe. "But it's only 2:57!"

Frank leans an elbow on the desk. "So?"

"Your office hours are until three!"

"Then get here earlier next time."

"But . . . but . . ." The student huffs. "I don't even know when the summary is due!"

"Then read the syllabus like a normal person!" Frank bellows, somehow managing the thunderous tone while barely moving a muscle.

The guy blanches, and I think he might be close to tears as he scurries back down the hallway.

Frank nods to me. "You in?"

I roll my eyes as I stand. "Yeah, fine."

"Be there at eight," he calls after me as I head out the door.

"I heard you the first time," I reply, but then a bit of guilt hitches in my chest and I add, "Want me to bring you up some lunch?"

"Depends. You buying?" he replies.

I don't look back, just flip him the bird and smile as his laughter echoes down the hall after me.

# CHAPTER 4

Despite it being January and one of the coldest days of the year, I have to crack open a window to let in some frigid air while I get ready for the event on Friday. This is nothing new. My building has steam heat, and in addition to sending a delightful metallic hammering sound through the walls at all hours of the day, it deploys hot air without any practical temperature control. Since that's also the case for every apartment on the eight floors below me, that same heat rises and makes my small studio apartment hot. Really hot. The kind of hot that sits heavy in the air and makes your skin sticky and damp so trying to apply makeup is Sisyphean. I finally give up, settling on mascara on my lashes and red stain on my lips before I pile my curls up into a loose bun on top of my head.

"You need to find a new apartment," I mutter to my reflection.

Of course, that's laughable. I might as well tell myself to buy the top floor of the Plaza. Until I pass the bar and get a position that pays me more than my monthly student loan bill, I can barely afford my rent for this place, let alone the security deposit on a new one.

Not that I want to move. Not really. Despite the heat, and the size, and the fact that the building has been clad in scaffolding due to "renovations" since I moved in seven years ago, I love this apartment. Mostly because it's mine, everything from the faded pink sofa I found in the back of a vintage shop in Brooklyn to the queen bed in the corner with the headboard I reupholstered in a fluorescent sixties-era print.

After a childhood spent crisscrossing the country as my mother jumped from one marriage to the next, and then four years of living with roommates at Fordham, I had been adamant about living alone after graduation. When I broke this news to my friends, everyone had rolled their eyes as if I had told them I was going to hunt for a unicorn in Central Park. Which, looking back at my income at the time, wasn't really that far off the mark. Josh had been the only one to outwardly challenge it, laughing and betting me a hundred dollars that I would be stuck with a roommate in Hoboken by the end of the month.

Two weeks later I found the blessed ad buried deep on Craigslist. One typo meant that it didn't come up unless you were scouring every single ad posted in real time or you were searching for studio apartments for more than nine thousand dollars a month. I was the former. I've also been bugging Josh for my winnings ever since.

A loud ding breaks my train of thought—the alarm on my phone chirping to let me know it's six thirty and time to leave.

I fan my blouse in the arctic air one more time, then close the window before grabbing my coat and my bag and heading for the door.

The elevator miraculously appears only a few seconds after I press the button. When the doors open I find Mrs. Seigel already inside, her motorized scooter parked in the center of the car and her attention down on her phone. I squeeze in beside her.

"Hi," I say as I press the illuminated *L* button a couple of times.

"Already pressed it," she murmurs around the unlit cigarette hanging from her lips.

"Yeah, sorry. I'm just in a hurry."

She finally looks up, surveying the outfit under my thin wool coat: the black-and-white-striped shirt, the high-waisted slacks, the stiletto ankle boots.

"Hot date?" she asks.

"No, just a work thing."

She grunts and turns back to her phone. "Too bad. You need to get laid."

I force a smile just as the elevator doors open onto the lobby.

"Have a good night, Mrs. Seigel," I say as I step around her and head for the front door.

The train is delayed, and my heels slow me down on the trek from the subway, but I still miraculously arrive at 408 Park Avenue on time. I look up at the looming limestone exterior as I make my way inside. It's imposing, just like every other building in this neighborhood. The lobby is the same, too: cream marble and polished teak walls. All manufactured elegance amid anonymous buildings and hollow streets.

The security guard at the desk directs me to the elevators that take me up to the party. I take a deep breath as it ascends, ignoring the light jazz overhead and focusing on the task at hand. I have to network. I *need* to network.

Had I known that networking played such a huge part in a successful law career, I'm not sure I would have bothered applying to law school. But instead, after graduating Fordham and working for more than three years at a healthcare nonprofit in Brooklyn— where I was getting increasingly frustrated about the policies that were making said job impossible—Josh suggested that if I wanted to yell about the injustice of it all, I might as well go to law school so I could get paid for it. He said it half in frustration, half in jest, but that didn't matter. The idea took root, spreading slowly in my mind until it had wrapped itself around every other idea I had for the next year.

And how hard could law school be, really? I graduated Fordham with honors and aced the LSATs. I was sure that when I got accepted into NYU Law, it would be a breeze.

I was wrong.

Surprising to literally no one but me, law school is a different game entirely. There's no cheat code that will save you, no amount of preparation that will alleviate the pain. The only thing you can do is keep your head down and work hard. Harder than every single person there. So hard that you barely notice when the days between visits with your friends become weeks, or when your two best friends start drifting toward divorce. So hard that you convince yourself that school is enough to fill the holes left everywhere else in your life.

I hear the din of conversation even before the elevator reaches the twenty-seventh floor. Sure enough, when the doors open on the event space, I see that I'm not the first to arrive. Far from it. The massive room is already littered with dozens of people; the lure of free booze and canapés is apparently too much for New

York's brightest legal minds. The far wall is all windows, affording an epic view of Queens just across the East River, but no one seems to care. They don't seem to notice the waiters who float through the crowd with trays of puff pastry and champagne, either, invisible for the most part to the people bragging and arguing and joking with one another.

I drop my coat off with the waiting attendants, then grab a glass of champagne and take in the crowd, all slightly different interpretations of the same stereotype; the men are in dark suits with either a navy silk tie or a gray one. The women offer only a slightly wider spectrum: suits and dresses that are all expensive and gorgeous, but none that venture out of the black or gray palette.

My eyes snag on Frank, who's sitting at a table on the opposite side of the room. He's talking with two people I don't recognize— probably the people hosting the function. That would explain why he only gives me a cursory eye roll, his universal sign for "not worth it."

*Right*. I nod and turn away.

I wander to the far corner, positioning myself between a large potted palm and the sprawling view of Queens. There are a few odd stares in my direction, as if they're not sure where to place me on their spectrum of importance, but after a few moments they must surmise that it is low, and they move on. Thank God.

A glimmer of hope springs in my chest, the idea that maybe, just *maybe*, I will get out of this scot-free: no condescending questions, no awkward pickup lines. I can meander through the crowd and stealthily look for Marcie Land and not have to—

"Hello there."

Goddammit.

I turn, quickly donning a plastic smile for the man now standing in front of me. In terms of the demographics of the room, he's young, early thirties, probably. And he's not bad looking, but also not attractive in any way that stands out. He looks like a Ken doll with an entitlement complex.

"I'm Ted," he says, smiling back. "And you are?"

"Beatrice." I lean in on brevity, hoping it will shut down any potential flirting. But Ted seems unfazed.

"Nice to meet you, Beatrice. I don't remember seeing you at one of these things before. What firm are you with?"

"I'm not with a firm."

"Ah, that explains it," he says, his smug smile broadening.

"Sorry?"

"This." He has a glass of wine in his hand and uses it to motion down my body. "Don't get me wrong, you're gorgeous. But none of this screams 'lawyer.'"

Anger bristles under my skin, and suddenly it's an effort to keep the smile on my face. "That's funny. I'm about to graduate law school."

I know I shouldn't say it, shouldn't share part of myself with this guy, but I can't help myself.

"No shit." He laughs. "Where do you go?"

"NYU."

His eyes light up, and I realize too late that sharing this information was a mistake.

"What a small world. I'm in the middle of negotiating a huge endowment for them. It's actually part of a much larger trust that we've been wrangling for a couple of years now. Spans a few countries so, you know, it's been a headache, but also really rewarding. I think it was Vince Lombardi that said . . ."

I take a deep sip of my drink and stop listening. The sooner Ted finishes his monologue, the sooner I can extricate myself and sneak off to another corner. Maybe steal a canapé or two along the way. I let my eyes drift across the room, mapping my escape.

That's when I see him. There, just leaving the bar with a drink in his hand, is the corpse flower himself: Nathan Asher.

*Fuckfuckfuckfuckfuuuuuuuuck.*

I turn away so abruptly, Ted pauses his banal story to eye me quizzically. "You okay?"

"Yup," I say. My fake smile feels like an ugly crack across my face, but I don't care. Because this is bad. So bad that my brain is tripping over all the reasons, throwing them at me so quickly my heart feels like it might explode from my chest.

*He's going to confront you! Here! In front of your boss! You could lose your job! He could ruin your reputation in front of a room of people whom you need to beg for another job! Your career could be ruined before it even starts!*

I take a deep breath before I go into full panic mode. Because, I remind myself, there is no reason to panic. He's on the other side of the room. There is no way he saw me. And even if he *did* see me, which he didn't, there is no way he would acknowledge me. As if he would have the gall to just—

"Ted," a deep voice croons behind me. "I didn't know you knew Beatrice."

I turn and there he is, sauntering toward us. He's in a navy suit similar to the one he wore the other day, but now his tie is maroon, and there's a glass of what appears to be bourbon in his hand. He stops and offers Ted the same smile Ted offered me earlier: a simulacrum of something genuine, used to disarm, to charm. I remember how some of my professors who still work in law gave each other that same smile, and I suddenly realize it's probably something unknowingly imbued in the profession, a trait passed down for survival. I wonder if I have it.

And then I blink with another realization: Nathan Asher knows my name.

"Nate!" Ted exclaims, shaking the asshole's hand. "Good to see you, man." Then he pauses, motioning between us. "You two know each other?"

I quickly say no at the same time as Nathan replies yes.

I crane my neck to glare up at him. Jesus, he's tall. Stupid tall. The kind of tall that would require him to bend down, hands on his knees, to make eye contact with me. He'd probably do it, too, a small gesture that would be so condescending. It hadn't happened in his office, but that doesn't mean he wouldn't do it here where there's a larger audience.

Ted laughs, oblivious. "Is it the NYU Law connection?"

An eyebrow arches up Nathan's forehead.

This is it. He's going to tell Ted how we really know each other. There will be a whole scene right here in front of everyone, including Frank, and I'll get fired. God, he'll likely ruin my chances of getting hired at any law firm in the city before I've even taken the bar.

But nothing happens. He just glances down at me and takes a slow sip of his drink. Then he turns back to Ted. "No."

"Ah. Well, Beatrice here is about to graduate, so I was telling her about the endowment I'm negotiating for that place." Ted laughs again, as if we're all in on the same joke. "Trying, anyway. It's been a pain in the ass convincing them to take it."

"Why's that?" Nathan asks in a polite tone.

Ted scoffs. "There are some law students fighting it, as if this kind of cash just grows on trees. I mean, come on. Beggars can't be choosers, right?"

This grabs my attention. I turn back to Ted, my eyes narrowing. "Sorry?"

He waves me off. "It's nothing, just some students petitioning to turn it down because the Haun family made their money in pharmaceuticals or something."

"Opiates," I say. "They made their money peddling opiates."

His expression becomes patronizing. "Well, that's not entirely correct—"

"Yes, it is," I cut him off. "I know because I organized that petition."

He blinks, his Ken doll expression flattening like his brain can't quite process this information and needs to reboot. I'm about to challenge him further, to ask why else he thinks the Justice Department is suing the Haun family in federal court, but then Nathan slaps a hand on Ted's shoulder and asks, "Hey, did you catch up with Jennings? He was looking for you."

Brain reengaged, Ted turns to Nathan. "Oh shit, really?"

Nathan nods, motioning to the far side of the room. "Yeah, he was by the bar with Neil."

"Right. Thanks. Uh, it was nice talking to you." Ted's already a few feet away as he hurls the farewell over his shoulder, not bothering to look back at where he's left us.

I watch him disappear into the crowd before turning to look up at Nathan again. His short brown hair is sticking out in all directions as he surveys the room, like he's run his hand through it a few times. It's at odds with the precise lines of his suit, as if the disjointed mess on top of his head balances out the perfection everywhere else.

"Nice to see you again, Beatrice," he finally says. His voice is deep, an octave lower than the cacophony of conversation around us.

"You know my name." I work to keep my tone bored.

He smiles. "Well, you forgot to introduce yourself the other day. I had to ask Josh when he stopped by my office."

I roll my eyes. Of course Josh sold me out. At this point he would probably supply my social security number and blood type if he had it.

"That must have been a fun conversation," I reply.

"Depends on your definition of fun."

I tilt my chin up. "Why, what did he say?"

"Words. Many, many words."

"What specific words?"

"I believe 'harpy' came up once or twice."

I snort. "Well, at least he found a good use for that classics degree."

Nathan finally deigns to look down at me again, his eyebrows knitted together in something akin to confusion. But it dissolves almost immediately, as if he remembers who I am. How his client fits into a larger ecosystem, this tight-knit group of friends now picking sides, choosing their weapons.

But the realization doesn't cause him to look away, just study me further. His eyes do a slow survey of my face—my nose, my freckles, my mouth—and I suddenly understand why he's such a good attorney. I have no idea what's going through his mind even though it feels like he can see everything going through mine.

"What are you doing here?" he finally asks.

"What are *you* doing here?" I snap. It is not my proudest moment, but I feel on edge, like I'm a specimen in a glass case about to be dissected.

"This is the New York City Bar Association. I'm a lawyer. Do I need to connect the dots for you?" It's the tone of someone speaking to a toddler, like he's explaining why we can't have ice cream for dinner.

"I'm just surprised you passed the bar."

His eyes narrow on me, and suddenly it's the same expression he gave me in his office, that blend of curiosity and disdain. "Have you?"

"Have I what?"

"Passed the bar."

"What makes you think I'm taking it?"

"Because your friend Ted mentioned you went to NYU Law."

Alarm bells go off in my head. Too much information. He has entirely too much information, and I need to deflect. Quickly.

"I thought he was your friend."

Nathan scoffs. "No."

"Then why did you come over here?"

"Because it looked like you were five seconds away from ripping his balls off."

For some reason, the word "balls" coming out of Nathan Asher's mouth sends an odd thrill up my spine, like I've forced him to break some asshole code of ethics. "Well, that's what us harpies subsist on. Testicles and weakness."

He stills, and for a moment it looks like he might smile, but his stern, unreadable expression is battling against it. Finally, he hides his lips behind his glass and takes a long sip of his drink. I watch how his Adam's apple bobs as he swallows, how it's dusted with the same stubble that covers his jaw.

I bring my own glass to my mouth and turn away.

"You haven't answered my question," he says after another moment.

I shift my weight from one foot to the other, doing my best to convey annoyance. "Which was?"

"What are you doing here?"

"Networking."

"Huh." He glances around at the corner where we're situated, at the tall palm I'm practically standing behind. "And how's that going for you?"

He doesn't say it like an insult, just an observation, but there's still that derisive look in his eyes that somehow makes it worse. It's like watching a wolf play with a bunny right before he devours it.

"Is this the plan?" I ask, my voice sharp.

"Plan for what?"

"Me. You clearly know my name. And now you know I go to NYU Law. There's nothing stopping you from contacting the school and telling them what I did. You could even tell that Ted guy and everyone else here, and I'd never be able to get a job after graduation. So, I just want to know if that's the plan." The words come out like a threat. Like I wield some power here instead of just this glass of liquid courage.

That law school smile again. "I was waiting to see if we'd get a repeat performance."

My anger ignites and I open my mouth, ready to demolish my already delicate sense of professionalism, when a hoarse voice calls out behind me.

"Nate!"

I turn just as Frank emerges from the crowd. He hobbles forward with his cane and a rare smile on his face.

I blink as the two men shake hands, and my brain is only half processing what's happening in front of me. Because if this is happening, my entire evening is going so much worse than I initially thought.

"Good to see you, Frank," Nathan replies with a smile, one that seems genuine. "How've you been?"

"My hip is killing me," he growls. Then he notices me and turns, offering me a nod. "You met Bea?"

My mind reels as it tries to find something, literally anything, to say, but Nathan beats me to it.

"Not formally, no."

Frank nods to the corpse flower beside me. "Bea, this is Nathan Asher, the only other TA besides you that I never threatened to fire. Best damn student I ever had. Nate, this is Beatrice Nilsson. She's one of my current TAs. Graduates in May."

For a brief moment I'm one-hundred-percent sure I'm high. Someone slipped something into my drink and I'm hallucinating. That's the only explanation for the scene unfolding before me right now. There's no possible way that Frank and Nathan know each other, that they're friends, because that would be bad. Worse than bad, that would be—

"Bea."

My attention snaps to Frank. He's staring at me expectantly. "What?"

"Nathan asked about your concentration."

My eyebrows knit together. "Why?"

Nathan offers that mocking, superficial smile again. "Because this is called networking, Beatrice."

It's a challenge. Even worse, I take the bait.

"Healthcare rights."

He nods, a cursory action. "Interesting."

I'm so eager to shove that arrogant look off his face that I almost tell him why: that I have firsthand knowledge of how the healthcare industry can destroy people, how multibillion-dollar companies can promise a cure but deliver a curse, right before they wash their hands of it entirely. How it has affected me, because not so long ago it affected his client. But that's too much, too personal, especially for him.

Frank turns to Nathan. "You graduated, what, seven years ago now?"

Nathan nods. I finish my champagne in one large gulp.

"He got published in the Law Review his final year, too," Frank continues. He looks almost proud. "What was the title of that article again?"

"'The Evolving Ethics of Family Court,'" Nathan replies.

"Ha!" I bark out a laugh before I can stop myself. Frank stares at me, and a few people around us turn to look, too, eyebrows raised. The only person that doesn't seem shocked is Nathan. There's that almost-smile on his face again, which sits somewhere between amused and predatory.

"Something wrong?" he asks.

"Oh, just . . . so many things," I say, plastering on my own law school smile again. It's a delicate balance, the appearance of civil discourse. And I hate how he is so much better at it than me.

"You okay?" Frank asks me, frowning.

"Yup." I can feel the champagne churning with my temper; it's a dangerous mix. I need to extract myself before I say something I can't take back. This time, in front of my boss. "I think I need another drink, so if you'll excuse me . . ." I take a step backward.

Frank eyes me a moment longer before turning back to Nathan, starting their conversation again. Neither seems to notice as I take another step back. And then another. In fact, Frank is still talking as I turn and practically sprint to the bar.

# CHAPTER 5

I've drunk too much champagne. Or is it I drank too much champagne? Whatever, I've had too much.

This is not my fault. Well, technically it *is* my fault since I am the one who kept grabbing glasses all night, but I needed it to dull the stark realization that the man I verbally assaulted a week ago now holds my career in the palm of his hand. Because despite the fact that I had been there and watched as Frank and Nathan Asher talked and laughed and reminisced, the reality was still too hard to swallow.

Not the champagne, though. That was fantastic.

But now the bar is closing up and the catering staff have started to collect the empty glasses abandoned around the room. The guests take the cue, practically yelling their goodbyes to one another, promises of calls and meetings that will never happen.

This is why I'm so bad at networking: I can never see past the bullshit. The veneer of professionalism falls away, and all I notice are dozens of lawyers acting like they enjoy one another's company, then drinking so much they end up stumbling toward the exit to head home until they do it all again. Every one of these things is the same.

Of course, I'm thankful for the cover right now as I make my way toward the elevators, trying to avoid the one person who somehow keeps popping up: Nathan Asher.

It was an activity that kept me busy most of the night. As I wandered the party aimlessly and endured numerous mundane conversations with men looking to discuss anything but law, my only goal was to keep a safe distance between Nathan Asher and myself, while appearing to not notice him at all. But just when I thought I was doing a good job, my eyes would snag on his messy hair, his broad shoulders. It didn't help that he stood at least a half foot taller than most of the other people there, a monolith in a designer suit.

I lost sight of him with the first exodus of revelers, but I still make sure he's nowhere in sight before grabbing my coat from the attendant and scurrying to a waiting elevator. I follow a few other stragglers out through the lobby downstairs, keeping my head down as I slide through the revolving glass door.

The cold air hits me like a blow, stealing the breath from my lungs as I walk out onto the sidewalk. Somewhere in my foggy brain I register that it's colder than it was a couple of hours ago, but I don't move to close my coat. Neither do any of the other people leaving with me; they're too busy laughing and talking and trying to find their drivers amid the line of black cars waiting at the curb.

I reach into my bag, fingers already numb as they probe the darkness for my phone. I finally find it, but the screen remains black regardless of how many times I press the button to wake it up. The battery is dead.

Great. Just great.

I throw it back in my bag and blow out a deep breath that swirls into a cloud in front of me before disappearing. There's a line of traffic ahead, but hardly any cabs. The ones that do pass have their lights off; either occupied or off-duty for the night.

I know where the evening goes from here: I'll try to get a cab and fail, because it's Friday night and no one can ever get a cab on a Friday night in New York. That means I'll have to take the subway, transferring three different times before I finally get home to Washington Heights. Then I'll head upstairs to my apartment, flip on all the lights, and turn on another episode of *The Real Housewives of New York City* that I've already seen, but I'll keep on because the sound makes the space feel less empty. Something to make me feel less alone. It's a habit now, and I hate that it became a habit so easily that I don't even remember when the loneliness became too much to bear.

A familiar ache swells in my chest, making those old scars around my heart burn. I'm too tired to battle against it tonight, so I let the pain grow as I walk on the curb, wavering slightly as I watch the thin line of cars pass by.

"I thought you went home." The deep voice comes from behind me, and it only takes a moment to recognize it. The sound of an anthropomorphized corpse flower.

For a second I contemplate ignoring him, but my champagne brain doesn't transmute the message in time to stop my head turning just enough to glance behind me.

Nathan is just a few steps outside the building's revolving glass doors, flipping up the collar of his camel-colored wool coat as he saunters toward the street. Toward me. Had he still been at the party when I left? I hate how foggy my brain is; not quite drunk but definitely not sober, either.

"And I thought stalking was illegal," I drawl.

He doesn't reply, just stops a few feet away and stares at me. The streetlamp above sends hard shadows across his face, accentuating the line of his brow, his jaw. It does something strange to my stomach, a contraction of every muscle in my core, and I quickly turn back to the street.

I half expect him to walk away now. He's gotten his barbs in, and I've gotten the last word; we can retire to our separate corners and lick our wounds in peace. But I don't hear him move. And suddenly I wonder if that's the only thing we have in common: we'd both rather talk to someone we hate than deal with whatever is waiting for us at home.

"Do you need a ride?" His voice is biting, as if he's already regretting the offer.

This time I do ignore him, focusing on the street instead of the towering presence behind me. There are no cars passing now and only a few headlights in the distance, but I still raise my hand high above my head as if I can materialize a taxicab out of thin air by sheer force of will.

There's one last black Suburban parked a little way down the curb, and I can see the driver watching us. No doubt it's Nathan's car and I'll hear his footsteps heading that way any second. He'll get in and pull away, and I'll finally be able to breathe. But there's no sound. There's no nothing.

*That's a double negative*, the sober part of my brain whispers.

I scowl and turn to look over my shoulder again. He's still standing there, his hands in the pockets of his coat.

"What are you doing?" I snap.

"Making sure you get a cab."

"I'm perfectly capable of getting a cab."

A long moment passes as we stare at each other, like we're both waiting for the other to do something.

"You can go now," I finally say, nodding to his car.

He has the gall to almost look offended. "I'm not going to leave you here in the middle of the night. I'll go when you're in a car."

I roll my eyes and turn back around, raising my hand a bit higher. My gaze stays locked on the horizon, where Park Avenue fades and a thin line of traffic drips toward us. I can feel his attention on my back, and I know, I just *know*, he's waiting to make some snide remark. After another minute, the silence becomes too much and I whip around.

"What?"

"I didn't say anything."

"You were *thinking* something."

A beat. "You're not going to get a cab at ten on a Friday night."

Derision drips from his tone, and I narrow my eyes at him. "Wow. That's really constructive. Thank you for that."

His full lips contort into something like a frown, and it's that look from his office again. As if he's somehow both amused and disappointed in me. "What are you going to do if you can't find one?"

"I'll take the subway."

"If you thought taking the subway was a good idea, you wouldn't be trying this hard to hail a cab."

I want to fire back a retort, but the words are cut short as a chill runs through me. That's right, it's cold out. I pull my thin coat tight around my body, as if it will trap some warmth, and focus on the road again.

Another minute passes before I hear him take a step toward me, then: "I can give you a ride."

I let out a biting laugh. "No way."

"Why not?"

"Because I'm not telling you where I live," I say, turning enough to glare at him.

"I already know where you live," he replies evenly. "Josh gave me all your contact information when he came by my office."

I blink as the anger falters in my chest. It's like my warm buzz has been doused with cold water—yet another reminder of all our points of contact, how quickly we've become linked. I swallow and turn back to the street, raising my arm again. Two cars drive by. Neither of them are cabs.

"Beatrice."

I refuse to look at him.

"Beatrice," he repeats. "Let me give you a ride."

I want to fight. I want to unleash every awful word on my tongue and leave his ego in shreds. But I'm tired. So tired that all I manage to do is lower my hand and turn to face him fully. I expect to see that smug grin waiting, the one that tells me that he thinks he won again. But he only stares back. The hardness in his expression softens to accommodate a bit of apathy, perhaps a bit of resignation. We're both tired.

"Whatever," I mumble. And then I start toward the car.

The driver gets out as we approach, opening the back door for us. I slide in first, sinking into the leather seat and God, I hate how good it feels. The heat envelops me, prickling my skin and loosening my muscles.

Nathan gets in beside me, the space just large enough to accommodate his long limbs. He nods to the driver, who's now in his seat behind the wheel, then turns back to me. "Where to?"

I hesitate for a moment before relenting, giving the driver my address uptown. He nods and slides the car into drive, merging into traffic.

Silence descends and the city blocks dissolve as the car turns, cutting across Central Park toward the West Side. I keep my gaze forward, but I can still see Nathan out of the corner of my eye as he unbuttons the front of his blazer and pulls out his phone. The screen illuminates the serious line of his brow as he stares down at it. He is too big for this space. I feel like the world has shrunk, but he's remained the same size.

"So," he murmurs, his attention never leaving his phone. "Healthcare rights law."

I don't acknowledge that he's spoken, just stare out the window.

He continues, undaunted. "Do you have a job lined up yet?"

"I'm applying."

"Where?"

"A few firms in the city."

"Land and Associates?"

My body tenses as my eyes snap back to him. "How did you know that?"

A shrug. "It's the best healthcare law practice in the city. They handled that class action lawsuit against Glazer Pharmaceutical that went to the Fifth Circuit last year. And I know Marcie Land. She's a friend."

It's hard to describe all the emotions that hit me at once. The shock, the excitement . . . then the crushing disappointment. Because I also remember who I'm talking to. And how he has even more leverage over me now.

"Too bad she wasn't there tonight," he continues. "I would've introduced you."

I laugh; the sound is cold and clipped. "And said what, exactly? 'Hi, Marcie, this is Bea. She recently stormed into my office and nailed my balls to the side of the building.'"

He doesn't fight his smile this time. It broadens slowly across his face, revealing a dimple in his right cheek. A fucking dimple. It softens his hard features and sends something electric through my pulse.

"Is that what happened?" he asks.

"It's what would have happened if jail time hadn't been a mitigating factor."

"Well then, God bless the New York penal code."

"Right," I say sarcastically. "Because you have so much respect for the legal system."

He only stares at me, waiting.

"Your essay," I answer his unasked question. "'The Evolving Ethics of Family Court'? As if you have any right dictating *that* to anyone."

"I'm not sure your ethical standards work as the benchmark here."

I scoff. The sound comes off much more drunk than intended. "Give me one good reason why not."

"How about storming into the office of another attorney with the intent of nailing his balls to the side of his building."

My mouth falls open and, in the half second it takes me to snap it shut again, he turns back to his phone.

"God, you really are an asshole," I finally manage to say.

He doesn't look up from the glowing screen as he murmurs, "Because I appreciate irony?"

"No, because you destroy people's lives for a living and think it's a joke."

A muscle ticks in his jaw, but he doesn't reply.

I glare at him, that familiar anger enveloping me like a warm blanket. "You aren't even going to pretend that it's not true?"

"I don't destroy people's lives, Beatrice," he says. "I'm there to help pick up the pieces."

"And divide them up evenly, right?"

"If that's what's best."

"And how do you know what's best?" I ask, turning in my seat to face him fully. "How can you tell what's fair and what's right when you're only getting one side of the story?"

He finally looks up just enough to raise an eyebrow at me. "What's fair and what's right aren't always the same thing."

"Why the fuck not?" My voice is loud enough that the driver's eyes dart to us from the rearview mirror.

Nathan frowns again, that disappointed look. "You're studying to be a lawyer. You know how this works."

I want to blurt out that I know only too well how this works. That I have an expertise honed over decades, starting when I was six and watched my mom launch a vase at my dad's head and scream, "I want a divorce!" The next morning, we were gone. It was a cycle that would be repeated for years: a whirlwind romance, a quickie wedding, a traumatic divorce.

To be fair, some were worse than others. But regardless of the emotional impact on those involved, I was always an afterthought. The auxiliary family member meant to pick up my mother and dust her off. The one who would be fine, who wouldn't remember. And somewhere along the way, that had hardened into a callus around me, protective but also so confining I wanted to scream.

I never do, though. And I won't give this man the satisfaction of starting now.

"You're right," I say, donning my sharpest smile. "Thanks so much for your professional insights, Nathan."

The car turns right as I pivot my body back toward the door, staring at the darkened storefronts flying past through the window. I want to forget where I am, who I'm with, but I can see Nathan's reflection in the glass. He's staring out his window, too, his fingers clasped around his phone, but the screen is dark now.

It's another long moment before he says, "It's Nate."

I whip my head around again. "What?"

"I usually go by Nate." His voice is clipped, like he's annoyed. "The only person that calls me Nathan is my mother."

"Why do you think I care?"

A low, dry laugh. "Never mind."

I narrow my eyes at him. "No, seriously. Did you think you'd give me a ride home and I'd somehow forget who you are? How much we hate each other?"

He drags his gaze back to me, his face devoid of any means to decipher what he's thinking. "I have people tell me to fuck off on a daily basis, Beatrice. That doesn't mean I hate them."

"No, just that you're emotionally dead inside."

"Being able to separate my emotions from my work doesn't mean I'm emotionally dead."

"No, but that smile sure does."

This catches him off guard. "What smile?"

"The one you used with that Ted guy tonight—the one all lawyers use. That fake smile and that fake laugh like you care about what people are saying when it's painfully clear you don't."

That almost frown again, as if I'm the one out of line here. "For someone condemning false niceties, you were more than willing to maintain a civil conversation with me earlier without bringing any of this up."

"Because I was at a work event."

"And who in their right mind would make a scene at someone's workplace, right?"

My eyes widen as a hot flare of anger ignites in my chest. He watches and has the audacity to almost look amused.

"Fuck you, Nathan," I say, turning back to the window.

He leans back in his leather seat, letting out a low sigh. "Are you always this pissed off?"

Another bitter laugh escapes my lips. "Right. I should just smile and ignore the fact that you're sitting here talking to me like I'm five. Or that almost every other man that approached me tonight was more interested in getting me to come home with him than discussing my résumé. Or that I spent the entire subway ride down here tonight aware of every single person that came in and out of the train because I didn't want to get assaulted before I had the chance to feel like shit thanks to my would-be colleagues. Or that if one of those colleagues did decide to give me a job, I'm almost guaranteed to make fifteen percent less than a man doing the exact same thing. And even then, I'll have to smile and be grateful. Because God forbid I be angry, right?"

I expect to see that patronizing expression that's already become so familiar, but the humor has dimmed from his eyes, as if he realizes the rare bit of vulnerability he's just exposed.

"Bea..." he starts, but my name hangs there as his tongue darts out to wet his lips, like he's debating how to continue. I watch the motion, how his throat bobs and his bottom lip glistens. I wonder if it tastes like bourbon. Like caramel and smoke and heat and—

*What. The. Fuck.*

I quickly turn away, forcing my attention out the car window. The champagne is wielding too much power, forming thoughts that have no business in my brain. All I have to do is ignore them for a few more blocks.

Turns out, they don't like being ignored. They poke and prod that small part of me that's bereft, begging to bait him again. Anything to maintain the embers of anger still glowing in my chest.

I need to get out of this car.

We turn down my block and my hand goes to the door handle, itching to pull it and jump out. I can feel Nathan's eyes on me now, too, watching as I sit on the edge of the seat. Finally, the car slows, coming to a stop right in front of my scaffolding-clad building. The driver has barely put it in park before I throw the door open, sliding off the leather seat and stepping out onto the sidewalk. I don't look back as I slam the door shut. I concentrate on my steps, short and quick across the pavement. A moment later I hear another car door, followed by the sound of long, lumbering strides behind me. I try to quicken my pace, but there's only so fast I can walk in these heels, so I decide instead to keep my focus on the front door ahead.

I arrive only a moment before he does, his footsteps stopping just a few feet behind me. I try to pretend he's not there, but my heart is hammering at his proximity, making my fingers clumsy and my ability to find the keys at the bottom of my bag impossible. Another minute passes before it all becomes too much and I turn.

"What are you doing?"

He looks back at the car, then to me, like the answer is obvious. "I'm walking you to the door."

"Why?"

"Because I drove you all the way home and my mom would kill me if she knew I didn't bother to make sure you got inside safely." His voice is deep and gravelly, and I hate how it vibrates through my body, tripping up my pulse.

"You can do that from the back seat!" I exclaim, motioning wildly to where the car is parked along the curb.

Nathan only continues to stare down at me like I'm some sort of morbid curiosity.

I throw my arms up. "And why the hell do you keep bringing up your mother?"

His brow furrows. "I didn't realize I was."

"Right! Sure." I scoff. "You're all about the nice mom anecdotes and the rides home, and the proper manners—"

He shifts his weight and puts his hands on his hips as if he's finally losing patience with me. "Is that a problem?"

God, *is* it a problem? Why has he gotten under my skin enough that I'm standing here, every muscle in my body vibrating with tension? I've confronted countless assholes like him in the past—I'm good at it. But for some reason, this one feels distinctly different, like a jigsaw piece that refuses to fit into place.

"No, the problem is that you can't be patronizing and arrogant and actively work to destroy my best friend, and then decide to be nice!"

His blue eyes widen slightly, and he has the audacity to look mildly annoyed. "Excuse me?"

"You can't be an asshole and then have manners!"

"Well, I guess it's a night of contradictions, then."

I reel back. "What the hell is that supposed to mean?"

"You can't spend three years studying law and then be surprised by how it's practiced, Beatrice."

I bristle at how he says my name, like it's an insult. A weapon to be wielded against me.

"You know nothing about me." I step forward to point my finger in his face.

He leans down so he meets my gaze head-on. "Now you know how it feels."

Something white-hot is rushing through my veins, something so similar to anger, yet more complex. More faceted. I want to yell, but all my words dissolve on my tongue as I glare at him, at the similar fire burning in his eyes. It looks a lot like hate. But there's something else there, too.

And then I kiss him.

It's hard. Lips and teeth and force, no affection, just that deep burning as my fingers thread roughly in his hair. I was right: his tongue does taste like bourbon, a delicious mix of peat and caramel. His arms wrap around my body, holding me close while our tongues wage war. But it's a battle that only pulls us deeper, under the surface of the anger and frustration, into a pool of something pulsing and alive and all-consuming.

"You're such an asshole," I murmur against his lips.

He shifts as if he might lean away to argue the point, but no, that won't do. This kiss is too good. So I pull him back, my hands desperate and clumsy as I grab his coat to force his weight on me, wedging myself between his chest and the building's brick facade.

The scaffold above us creaks as if it's moments away from collapsing, but God, I don't care. Right now, the entire island of Manhattan could be swallowed up by the Hudson and I wouldn't notice. It's only his lips, his tongue, his hand holding tight to my waist while the other goes to my jaw, angling my head exactly where he wants it. A groan escapes my throat and his grip on my body tightens as he murmurs a low *fuck* against my mouth.

I'm about to tell him to shut up and come inside, but then the front door of the building swings open, followed by the sound of a motorized scooter.

We both still, locking eyes for a moment before turning in unison to see Mrs. Seigel riding out of the lobby onto the sidewalk. She's in a nightgown with her bathrobe thrown over her shoulders, and there's an unlit cigarette hanging from her lips. She only notices us as she turns to head down the street, eyeing Nathan, then me, and then smiling.

"Way to go, Bea," she says, pumping one fist in the air as her scooter slowly motors past.

Nathan turns back to me, his forehead creased with confusion, but the reality of the situation hits me at the same time.

"Oh my God." I push his chest away. "Oh my God. Go away."

"Excuse me?"

I'm shaking my head as one hand comes up to cover my face and the other flails wildly for the door before it closes again. "What are we doing? What am *I* doing? Oh my God."

I am a mess. A total and utter mess, and Nathan is just watching with a hint of a smile as I try desperately to maneuver past the heavy front door into the lobby.

"Good night, Beatrice," he calls after me as I head toward the elevator.

"Fuck you, Nathan!"

And then the door slams shut behind me.

# CHAPTER 6

My alarm goes off at seven, sending "Escape (The Piña Colada Song)" echoing across the room from where my phone is charging on the kitchen table. My eyes fly open only to wince at the sunlight streaming in through the window. Goddammit. I forgot to close the curtains again.

I groan, trying to keep my eyes closed as I roll out of bed and stumble toward the small table. With one eye open, I begin batting at the screen, somehow turning the phone off before Rupert Holmes starts singing about making love at midnight. Someday I'll remember to turn my alarm off on the weekends. But not this day.

I trudge to the bathroom—a small closet-sized room that barely has space for its toilet, sink, and bathtub—and turn on the faucet, splashing a handful of cold water on my face before looking up at the mirror where my reflection is waiting patiently to depress me. I hadn't washed my face last night; I had simply fallen into bed and waited for sleep to take me, like that would erase everything that had come before it. Of course, it hadn't. And there's the evidence written across my face: the smoky streaks of mascara under my eyes, the faded lipstick smudged across my swollen lips.

The memories of last night come flashing back in one horrifying moment. Nathan's tall, broad body enveloping mine, my lips navigating his, nipping and pulling and pressing as his hands found my hair, my jaw, my hip, and—

*Ohmygod.*

I sit down on the edge of the tub and let my head fall forward. I kissed Nathan Asher.

I want to blame the alcohol. That would be the easy excuse. *I was drunk! It didn't mean anything!* Except I'm not hungover. I don't even have a headache. Sure, I was tipsy last night, but not enough to usurp my judgment. The champagne had been like a talisman, something to keep in my hand to distract me from his presence. Or at least the small dimple in the corner of his smile.

But it didn't work. I still kissed him.

My hand instinctively goes to my lips, feeling their tenderness. No, I didn't just kiss him. I threw myself at him.

Oh. My. *God.*

I strip and turn on the shower, stepping in before it has time to reach its peak lukewarm temperature. But even under the cold water, the dull ache in my belly remains.

What had I been thinking?

*Getting laid*, a voice that sounds a lot like Mrs. Seigel echoes in my head.

I scowl and lather my hair.

Okay, yes, it has been a while since I've been with anyone. Even longer since I've been in anything remotely close to a relationship. And if I'm being honest with myself—really, brutally honest—

the loneliness of the past year has been almost harder than school. The fractures in our friend group were easier to ignore during class and work and studying, but at night, when it's just me alone in this small apartment, the weight of the solitude feels so much heavier. It makes me sad and angry and frustrated because I don't know what to do with it all.

Maybe that's why I kissed him. I had given him my worst and he rose to the challenge, throwing it right back so by the time we stood in front of my building, there were no more weapons left. Kissing him was just another outlet for the anger, a release valve for the pressure that had been mounting since I first saw him.

That's still not an excuse, though.

I dry off and brush my teeth, glowering at myself in the mirror. And then, as I throw on a pair of old sweatpants and a worn sweater, an entirely new and terrifying thought enters my mind: I have to tell Jillian.

My cell phone is still charging on the table, and I stare down at it for a long minute before finally picking it up. New excuses start flying through my head as I find her number—she's probably busy, she might not be up yet, she could be busy unpacking—but I still press the call button and bring the phone to my ear.

*RING.*

*RING.*

*RING.*

Suddenly it connects, and my pulse spikes in my veins until an automated message begins: "The number you are calling is not available. To leave a message, please press the pound sign."

I press pound. I hear the beep. But for a moment I'm struck dumb, staring straight ahead at the blank wall in front of me, at a complete loss as to what to say.

"Hello . . . Jills. It's me. Bea. Hi. I'm here. And . . . leaving you a voicemail. Because I have to tell you . . . a thing. So . . . this is a voicemail. Call me back. Yeah. Thank you."

I hang up and fall back on my bed, my heart racing even faster, not really willing to ponder how insane that message will sound when she eventually listens to it.

It's another minute before I look at my phone again to see the time: 7:49 a.m. It's Saturday, the day I usually set aside for cleaning and grocery shopping, but I still have to do last night's laundry and make up for all the reading I didn't do because of—

I squeeze my eyes closed, warding off the memory.

Right.

I stand and head to my hamper to begin separating my colors from my whites, and somehow convince myself that everything will be fine.

There's a distinct sort of bliss found at a laundromat on a Friday night. Something akin to nirvana, or at least as close as you can get while wearing sweatpants. The key to this peace is twofold: one, it's always empty except for one or two people coming in to check their machines, and two, the soft lull of those dryers is a perfect white noise machine, drowning out the city just beyond the large front windows. A person can spread their notes and their laptop and all their bar exam study books out across the main folding table without a single nasty look from anyone. It's perfect, the ideal study/relaxation atmosphere.

Unfortunately, it is not Friday night. It is Saturday morning. And that bliss I usually find has been replaced by a room full of people who likely have regular plans on Friday nights and aren't consumed by abject horror at having to wait for a free dryer.

The main folding table is lined with people actually folding clothes, so after I throw my clothes in a washer, I find a free chair along the wall and open the only book I brought with me, *The Bar Exam & You*. I do my best to block out the cacophony of conversation and movement around me, and focus. Still, by the time I pull my clothes from the dryer and drag the basket back to my seat, I've barely made it through one chapter.

I'm folding my favorite days-of-the-week underwear when I hear my phone ringing somewhere in my bag. My heart drops as I reach for it, half expecting to see Jillian's face on the screen. I find Maggie's there instead.

"Please tell me you're in the city," I whine when I answer.

"I'm never in the city. I live upstate now, remember?"

"You said the Hudson Valley wasn't upstate," I reply.

"I just spent an hour driving around trying to find this hardware store, only to have to ask a guy in overalls where I could find the caulk. I get to call it upstate today."

I smile to myself. Whenever Maggie complains about moving out of the city, I know it is more for my benefit than hers. After graduating from Fordham, our group had the next few years all planned out: we would all live in the city, spend holidays together, celebrate milestones, create a real-life version of *Friends*. Then Maggie got her dream job at a hedge fund. The first year there was spent learning that she hated hedge funds and the American banking system in general, then the next three had her saving every paycheck and dreaming of what she would do when she finally quit. The answer came in the form of a real estate listing for an old bed-and-breakfast in Cold Spring. She and Travis put in an offer, and just like that, their lives turned into a Hallmark movie, albeit one that required some serious renovation.

"And did overalls guy know where to find the best caulk?" I ask.

She laughs. "He did. Now I just need to find the tile adhesive, then I can go home and start day drinking."

"We can day drink here, you know."

"Yes, but up here I can do it while pretending it makes me better at retiling a backsplash," she replies. "I'm trying to get the whole kitchen done before we go on vacation."

"Mags, you two don't leave for Miami until next month."

"And?"

"How long does it take to tile a backsplash?"

"Yeah, well, when you're day drinking, it takes a little more time," she says. "So, what are you up to?"

"Laundry."

"Isn't that usually Friday nights?"

I scowl. "I hate that you know that."

"Oh please, at least I can fully appreciate the gravitas of you being there right now. Does this mean you had plans last night? A date? Please tell me there was drunken debauchery."

I try to laugh. It sounds ridiculously forced.

A pause. "Wait, am I right?"

"It's nothing," I say, folding a pair of faded blue underwear that have "Wednesday" printed across the front.

"Oh, it's definitely not nothing," she murmurs. "Spill."

"I told you it's nothing."

"Your voice is doing that high-pitch thing you do when you're lying."

I wince at being called out so thoroughly. "I did something epically stupid."

"Hold on." I hear Maggie shuffling around before her voice finally returns. "Sorry, I had to move a bucket of drywall compound so I could sit down for this. Continue."

"Okay." I let out a long breath. "You know Nathan Asher?"

"No," she says, then pauses. "Wait, maybe? Why does that name sound familiar?"

"He's Josh's divorce attorney."

"Right," she says, unfazed. "The one you called an asshole."

"Yeah, that one."

"Oh God, did you go back there? Is he getting a restraining order?"

I gnaw at my bottom lip. "Not exactly."

"Okay." When I don't elaborate, Maggie continues, "You're going to have to give me something here because I'm lost."

"So, my professor invited me to this event last night, right? Just sort of standing around and networking and stuff to help me in the job search."

"And?"

"It was an event for the New York City Bar Association. So, a huge room full of lawyers."

Something clicks into place on the other end of the line. "Oh shit, he was there."

"Not only was he there, he knows my professor."

"Of course he knows your professor. Don't all lawyers know each other?" she says as if this is common knowledge. "So, what did he say? Was he awful?"

I cringe. "I'm not sure 'awful' is the right word."

Silence stretches out on the other end for so long that I wonder if we got disconnected.

"OH MY GOD, DID YOU FUCK JOSH'S DIVORCE LAWYER?" She screams so loud I have to hold the phone away from my ear.

The woman beside me turns, eyes wide. I force a smile as I bring the phone back to my ear.

There's more shuffling, like Maggie is moving again, then a deep voice speaking in the distance.

"Sorry, sir," Maggie says, her voice slightly muffled as if she's got the phone pressed to her shirt. "I'm just talking to my friend about her questionable moral compass."

I start folding my laundry again, hoping it will recharge my patience. "Please tell me overalls guy didn't just hear that."

She either doesn't hear me or ignores me. "Yes, this caulk is perfect, thanks," she says, her voice still muted by what I can only assume is her shirt. Then there is more shuffling before her voice returns to the call, now in a low, teasing whisper. "You dirty, dirty slut."

"I didn't sleep with him!"

"Why not? Were you wearing your day-of-the-week underwear or something?"

I'm about to fold Tuesday but drop it back in the basket. "No."

"Okay, then what happened?"

"We . . . kissed."

"Did you kiss him or did he kiss you?"

"Mags, I literally threw myself at him."

"But did he kiss you back?"

I pause, my head cocking to the side as I try to remember. I had been so lost in the moment that all I really remember is how much I wanted it. Which brings up a sobering thought: I never bothered to ask if he wanted it, too. He had merely walked me to the door, and I acted like a drunken pendulum, berating him one minute, then launching myself at him the next. Even if he did kiss me back, that doesn't negate the fact that I pretty much ambushed him. Again.

"I think so? We were up against the side of my building and it was . . . there was a lot of . . ." I let my voice fade as my cheeks flush.

"Dry humping."

I cringe again. "We were *not* dry humping."

"Oh, okay, so you were just making out with the man currently throwing kerosene on our friend's life. In that case it's totally fine."

I don't reply, but the guilt hits my chest like a physical blow.

"I'm kidding," she adds a moment later, as if she can see my crushed expression. "But you realize how insane this is, right?"

"Yeah," I say, nodding to myself.

"So, then what?"

"I came to my senses and went upstairs. Alone."

"You just left him there?"

"Yup."

"Wow," Maggie says. There's more silence on the other end as she seems to consider this, then says, "So where were his hands? Did he keep them above the waist or did he get under—"

I pinch the bridge of my nose and try to swallow back my frustration. "That's not really the point, Mags."

"Depends what your point is."

"The point is, I need to tell Jillian."

She scoffs. "That's the last thing you need to do."

"Are you serious?"

"Are you? Bea, her happily ever after is blowing up in slow motion and you think it will help her to know you're sleeping with the guy holding the match?"

"I'm not sleeping with him!" I exclaim.

The woman beside me eyes me again before standing up and moving a few seats down.

"I know, but dry humping the enemy doesn't have the same ring to it," Maggie says.

My head falls back against the cement brick wall. "What the fuck is wrong with me?"

"Stop it. There's nothing wrong with you. He's objectively hot. You're allowed to be attracted to him."

"But I almost invited him upstairs. What would have happened then?"

"He would have run screaming when he caught a whiff of your morning breath?"

I glower at the far wall. "It's not that bad."

"Oh my God, Bea. It's like something died—"

"*Anyway*," I interrupt, pushing a clump of curls away from my face. "It doesn't even matter because it's never happening again."

She snorts out a laugh. "Yeah, but do you want it to?"

"Of course not," I say loudly, as if volume will mask any uncertainty. "He's Josh's attorney. *Josh*. The situation is already a mess, it doesn't need—"

A loud ping rings on the other end of the line, alerting Maggie to a text message. "Hold on," Maggie says. A moment later, she's back. "It's Travis. Can I tell him about this? It's just too good."

"Don't you dare. We need to just forget about this and move on."

She hums. "You're probably right." There's a long pause before she continues. "Did you at least get an orgasm out of it?"

"Okay," I say, shaking my head. "I'm hanging up now."

"Love you!" she calls out as I move to disconnect. "Keep calling me with all your bad life choices!"

I throw the phone back in my bag and begin to refold Tuesday.

# CHAPTER 7

The rest of the weekend is an effort to stay distracted, which proves much more difficult than anticipated. A few years ago it would have been easy; I would've picked up the phone and called Travis to meet me downtown for a movie, or Jillian, so she could drag me to a museum. I would force Josh to go to yoga with me or Maggie to a thrift store. Maybe I would even collect all of them and spend the day abusing the bottomless mimosa policy at Lucky Cheng's brunch cabaret like we had so many times before.

But there's no one to call now. No one just a few subway stops away, to come and offer me respite from my own thoughts. So instead I turn on an old episode of *The Real Housewives of New York City* and hope the women's ill-fated getaway to the Berkshires will keep my loneliness at bay. Then I go to yoga alone, check emails, do more yoga, complete the next three weeks' worth of case law reading assignments, and wait for Monday when I can go to school and be distracted by that instead.

Which is exactly why I'm dressed and walking out the door at seven o'clock Monday morning. My public policy seminar isn't until ten, but in the meantime, there is a pile of assignments I need to grade and about a million emails from Frank's students, wondering what will happen while he's out on medical leave. All very boring, very monotonous, and very good for keeping my brain occupied.

Unfortunately, for the entire subway ride downtown, my brain refuses to comply. By the time I climb the steps up to West Fourth Street, the memory of Friday night is like a new favorite toy, one I keep coming back to, pondering the different ways it could have played out, what could have happened if—

The dull sound of ringing breaks my train of thought. I don't slow my steps as I reach into the various pockets of my bag, pulling my phone out and clumsily bringing it to my ear.

"Hello?"

"Hey, what's up?" Jill's voice stops me in the middle of the sidewalk.

*Fuuuuuuck*, I mouth to the sky, causing an old man to pause and stare in horror at me before he continues down the street. I should have looked at my phone before answering, given myself a moment before being completely ambushed. But now I have been cornered and the only answer I can think of is: "What?"

"Bea?" Jillian says, as if our crystal-clear connection might be bad.

"Oh, hey, Jills," I reply lamely.

"Hey. Sorry, I was avoiding my phone all weekend, trying to forget about the divorce for more than five minutes, so I only just got your message. You okay?"

"Yeah, yes." I continue walking, trying to slow my drumming pulse. "I'm great. Totally great." I am not great. "I just . . . wanted to check in."

"Nothing to report, really. Same old, same old."

"Well, that's good," I say, and wince because of course that's not good. The same old is awful. But my brain isn't functioning properly, and the fact that I'm aware of this only makes it go more haywire.

Jillian laughs as if there's an implied joke in my reply. "So, what's going on with you? Your message said you had to tell me something."

"Oh, right. Well . . . It's nothing really." I take a deep breath. "There was just this event thing on Friday."

"Okay," she says, then pauses. "Did something happen?"

"No. Why?"

"Because your voice sounds weird."

"It doesn't sound weird." It does, in fact, sound weird.

"Bea."

I cringe. "Okay. So, Nathan Asher was there."

Jillian groans. "Is he going to get a restraining order or something?"

"No?" I reply, only realizing after I say it that I'm not entirely sure.

"Why did you say that like it was a question?"

I laugh. It sounds absolutely maniacal. "It was fine! I'm fine!"

"Are you sure?"

This is the moment I could tell her about the kiss. I could tell her everything. But the words get caught in my throat, wrapped up in how much pain it will cause, how she'll see it as another betrayal, maybe the final one that will fracture our small group beyond repair. So I follow Maggie's advice and swallow the words back. Whether Jillian knows or not won't change anything. It's done and it's never happening again.

"I just . . . I wanted you to know that I saw him and we talked and everything is fine."

"Well, as long as it was fine," she says. I can hear her smile in the words. "Listen, I was going to call you today anyway. I have a favor to ask you."

The light changes and I cross the street, ignoring the blaring horn of the taxi that tried to beat me to the corner. The kernel of guilt in my stomach is distracting me, and I know it doesn't matter what she asks—I will absolutely do it. "Sure, what do you need?"

"Can you pick up something from the apartment?"

The tension in my body is replaced by a familiar dread. "I thought we got everything."

"I thought we did, too, but Josh emailed me last night. I guess the cabinet above the fridge still has all my bakeware in it."

"Jills, I've never seen you bake anything in your entire life."

"It's all my grandma's vintage Pyrex. You know, the white with the blue-and-orange designs on the side?"

"I thought you were trying to convince me."

"Bea," she says with a sigh. She already knows I'm going to say yes. She knew before she called because I would kill her before I'd let her go to that apartment again. Even the idea of her having to see Josh, talk to him . . . I can already feel the embers of my anger poking at my chest.

"Okay," I mutter. "I'm downtown, so I'll head there and grab it now."

"You're already at school?"

"I'm researching how much it would cost to hire a hit man to break Josh's legs and it's safer to do it on the school's network."

She laughs. "Well, thank you. For the dishes, not the hit man."

"You're welcome."

"It shouldn't be too much, just one box."

"What do you want me to do with it once I get it?" I ask, readjusting my bag as I turn the corner. The wind whips down Sixth Avenue, sending leaves and debris and my curls into the air.

"Just hold on to it until the next time I see you."

*And when will that be?* I want to ask. But I don't. Because we don't discuss it, the slow erosion of those norms that only a few years ago had felt so solid.

"Okay," I reply.

"Oh, and Bea?"

"Yeah?"

"Be nice."

~

My sneakers crunch along the last remnants of snow on the sidewalk as I make my way down through the Village to Barrow Street. I used to love this walk to Josh and Jillian's apartment, each block crowded by looming oak trees, their bare branches softening the city's hard edges. The further west you walk, the more intricate the architecture, turrets and windows, and carefully curated stoops that make it feel like you're suddenly on a movie set.

Now, as I continue forward, hugging my pathetically thin coat tight around my body, the street doesn't have the same veneer anymore; it feels desaturated. Stale.

Per usual, the front door of the building is unlocked, so I don't bother buzzing up to the second-floor apartment. I let myself in and climb the steps to the front door with the familiar welcome sign still hanging on it. I could knock. Normally, I would. But I see the brass button for the doorbell just there on the wall. It looks brand-new because it is. Jillian installed it to play Beethoven's Fifth every time it's rung, and I also know Josh absolutely hates it, which is why I press it.

Then I press it again.

I press again and again until I hear footsteps inside coming closer. The door flies open and I see Tex first, tongue out and tail wagging like he's happy to see me. And there beside him is a person who is decidedly not.

Josh's dark hair is mussed, his tall frame is clad in sweats, and for a moment the scene reminds me of so many mornings when I would grab him for class. For breakfast. Just to talk. But now it's obvious he didn't bother to look through the peephole, because the minute he sees me his shoulders slump and his head falls back.

"Fuck," he mutters.

Josh has always been good-looking, the kind of guy you look at and just know was voted prom king in high school and regularly dressed up as Clark Kent for Halloween. But right now, that person seems like a faint memory. This Josh is thin, which accentuates the stubble on his square chin. He needs a haircut, too; his black locks are long and flat like they haven't been washed in a while. The divorce is taking its toll.

I push the concern away and offer him a saccharine smile. "Hello to you, too."

"What are you doing here?" he asks.

"Picking up Jill's baking stuff."

He murmurs something under his breath and turns back inside, with Tex following close behind.

I follow him, too, sweeping my gaze across the living room. It looks hollow, even more so than when we left with Jill's things the week before. There's no art on the walls now, no rug on the hardwood floor. It even smells different, the sharp odor of stale Chinese food mixes with the lingering tinge of that vanilla candle Jillian used to burn. The scene would be incredibly sad if I allowed myself to feel sorry for him.

I stay in step behind Josh until we reach the kitchen. It's just as empty, but at least there's evidence that someone is living here. The dining table is still in the center of the room, but Jill's mid-century chairs have been replaced by a lone metal folding one set up in front of a laptop and an array of Chinese take-out containers. Tex's bed is still under the table, too. He's already collapsed into it, with his legs sticking out the sides.

"Where's Jillian?" Josh asks, leaning a hip against the table and crossing his arms over his chest.

"I'm pretty sure you're not allowed to ask that anymore."

There's disappointment in his expression. I recognize it even though his eyes are still sharp and staring daggers at me. Then he nods to a box on the floor by the kitchen doorway.

I kneel down to pick it up. It's heavy and he hasn't bothered to wrap any of the delicate dishes in paper, so they clink together, a warning of their fragility as I struggle to maintain my grip.

Josh watches me, not moving to help. "I heard you went to see my lawyer."

I shift my weight, resting the heavy box against one hip as I raise my chin and pray my expression is blank. "Is that what you heard?"

"That's what he said."

"Well, he also said that you deserve alimony for doing absolutely nothing, so let's take his word with a grain of salt, shall we?"

He scoffs, like he's disgusted. "Why do you have to be such a bitch all the time, Bea?"

My expression hardens and I shrug. My arms are starting to burn with the weight of the box, but I don't dare let it show. "Probably because you deserve it."

"But what else is there?"

My eyebrows knit together. "What?"

"I mean, when you finally decide to stop being a bitch, what's left? You've spent so much time getting angry on behalf of everybody else, expelling so much fucking energy trying to keep our little group together, because you don't have anything else. And you still failed. So after this is done and we're all off living our own lives without you, I'm wondering what's left for you besides just being a bitch."

I stare back at him, meeting his narrowed gaze. The morning sun frames him in a warm glow, softening the hard planes of his face, the vicious line of his jaw. His expression is filled with such vitriol, but in this light there's a sudden hint of the man he was eleven years ago. Back when we met during our first week at Fordham. The memory comes roaring back now: how he tried to kiss me at an off-campus party but I told him to fuck off, only to have him show up again a couple of hours later, right as a guy I didn't know was trying to force me to leave with him. I had been so afraid and overwhelmed, and then there was Josh, appearing like some tall, preppy, semi-drunk guardian angel. He ended up punching the guy so hard he knocked him out. And just like that, we were inseparable—the big brother I never had. He would come to my dorm room at all hours, and we'd talk about school and life and what the hell we were doing about any of it.

He had been there to hold me when I got the call from a Pittsburgh hospital that my grandmother had died. He listened to every rant about my mom's numerous divorces. I was there when he got injured in that football game against Dartmouth, to yell at him when he forced himself back onto the team too soon afterward, just to keep his scholarship. And I helped him when he struggled with the painkillers long after his ruptured Achilles had healed. Along the way we picked up the rest of our crew—Jillian and Maggie and Travis—but to me Josh was always that guy from freshman year, a boy trying so hard to act tough, when really, he was just as scared as the rest of us.

But now, he's a stranger.

"Have a nice life, Josh," I say. And then I turn around and walk out the front door.

# CHAPTER 8

I take a cab back to school. The box of dishes helps me rationalize it: the weight is cumbersome, and its delicate contents need to be protected. But deep down I know I could have walked and it would have been fine.

No, I take a cab because I feel brittle, like someone ripped off my protective coating and exposed my insides to sunlight. Even now, Josh is one of the few people that knows me well enough to do it. And his words hit their mark.

When I get back to my office, I slide the box under my desk and stare at the pile of work waiting for me, hoping it still offers the distraction it promised this morning. But as I press send on yet another email to a panicked student explaining that Tuesday's Alternative Conflict Resolution class is still happening and that an adjunct professor will be announced shortly, I can feel the morning like an abscess in my gut.

*When you finally decide to stop being a bitch, what's left?*

The words rattle around in my brain, hitting the edges with a sharp ding. It isn't the first time Josh has called me a bitch. In fact, I think he's probably called me that more than he's ever used my first name. Still, the word wasn't tinged with its usual good-natured ribbing. There was venom in it now, a truth that hit the most sensitive part of me.

I grab my bag from the floor and dig out my phone. I want to talk to someone, have them distract me from this feeling. I consider calling Jillian, but she already has enough to worry about, so instead I just text to say I have the dishes. She replies a moment later with a thumbs-up. Then I go to my contacts and begin to scroll through the numbers.

I pause at Maggie's name, but I know she'll tell me not to listen to anything Josh says. She might even tell me I'm not a bitch, which would be a verifiable lie, so she can't be trusted to be objective right now. And if I call Travis, he will no doubt tell me I shouldn't have gone there to begin with.

After a minute I let my phone fall back into my bag and stare at the blank wall ahead. I hate this feeling, like Josh opened me up and shoveled out all the bits I try to keep hidden, then tossed me aside, alone and hollowed out. I take a shaky breath. My office suddenly feels too small, too stifling. I need to get out.

I grab my coat and some coffee in a to-go cup from the student lounge, then head downstairs. The sun has finally broken through the clouds by the time I reach the lobby of Vanderbilt Hall, bright enough to give the illusion that winter isn't waiting just outside. That dissolves the moment I open the main doors into the courtyard. It's the coldest it's been in months, and, after the stagnant heat of my office, it feels almost refreshing. I take a deep breath, filling my lungs with cool air that somehow feels like it's bringing me back to life rather than trying to freeze me from the inside out.

The coffee's paper cup warms my fingers as I walk into Washington Square Park. It's fairly empty, but I still meander for a few minutes before finding a bench. I sit down and close my eyes, working hard to ignore the familiar pit of anxiety growing in my chest.

I want to get angry, use rage to ward off this ache, but every reason I come up with to prop up my anger feels flimsy. Am I mad at Josh for pointing out the truth? Or am I mad that it is the truth? That I've spent so long leaning into anger that maybe all my other emotions have been left to atrophy.

I finally settle on being angry about the fact that I can't figure out why I'm angry, which seems to work until I hear my phone ringing somewhere in my bag.

I open my eyes and reach for it. Frank's name is waiting on the screen. "Hi."

"Where are you?" Frank's voice rumbles through the other line.

"In the park, contemplating my life choices."

"Well, wrap it up and get to my office. I have a doctor's appointment this afternoon and I need to get out of here soon."

A bit of anxiety stirs in my chest. Frank is out on medical leave starting next week and, as much as he's looking forward to his surgery, I also know we haven't discussed the broader issue of his absence yet, namely who I'll be left working with.

"Is everything okay?" I ask, standing up and starting the walk back to Vanderbilt Hall.

He offers me a noncommittal grunt.

I frown. "What does that mean?"

"It means I just talked to Nathan Asher. He's headed up to my office right now, so hurry up."

I stop in the middle of the sidewalk as my heart falls through some new hole in my stomach. *Fuuuuuuuuuuuuuuuuuuck.*

"Excuse me?" Frank says.

Oh God, I said that out loud.

"Sorry," I say, squeezing my eyes shut. "It's just . . . Frank, listen. Before you say anything, I need to tell you what happened. I mean, before you tell me what he told you, I want you to know that my actions were completely warranted. And it wasn't assault. Not the first time."

Silence.

"What the hell are you talking about?" he finally asks.

I blink. "Did he tell you how we met?"

"I thought you met at the party."

I push my curls away from my face and brace myself. "Right. Okay. So, we might have met before that? I mean, he didn't know my name at the time, so technically you could argue that yes, we formally met for the first time at the party, but—"

"Spit it out, Bea."

I groan. "A couple of weeks ago I kind of . . . went to his office and confronted him about how he's handling my friend's divorce."

"Confronted?"

"I called him an asshole."

Silence envelops the other end of the line again and all I can hear is my pulse hammering. I know he's going to berate me, and I just want to get it over with. But then I hear a rough peal of laughter.

My brow furrows. "Frank?"

He doesn't hear me. He can't. His laughter is too loud, and then it's muffled like he's dropped the phone.

"Frank." I say it louder.

He comes back, wheezing. "Jesus Christ, that's the best thing I've heard in years."

"But isn't this bad? Don't I have to include it on my character disclosure on the bar application or something?"

"Bea, if every lawyer had to list how many times they've called another lawyer an asshole on the bar application, there wouldn't be any lawyers."

The knot around my stomach loosens a bit and I release a long breath. "Okay, thank God."

"But did you honestly think you'd never see him again? Jesus. This is New York. Everybody knows everybody, especially lawyers."

"Useful information, thanks." Then I pause. "Wait, if he's not stopping by about this, why did you call me?"

"Because starting Monday, Nathan Asher is taking over Alternative Conflict Resolution for me."

My mouth falls open and I stare out across the park while my brain short-circuits. "No."

"No?"

"I mean, he can't. He's not faculty," I blurt out. "He's not even adjunct."

"What the hell are you talking about? Anybody is adjunct if we hire them."

"Then give him Blake's seminar. Isn't that why you have two TAs?"

"Professor Geoffreys already grabbed that one," Frank replies, then he releases an impatient sigh. "It's just for the semester, Bea."

"You want me to work with him for the entire semester?" My voice has gone up an octave, but I don't have the capacity to care.

"Is that going to be a problem?"

God, is it? I don't want to step down. Not only do I need the meager paycheck, but I worked hard for this position. Dozens of people applied, and Frank chose me. Why the hell should Nathan Asher get to influence whether I keep it?

"No. It's fine," I reply.

"Good. Then get up here. He's stopping by right now and I need to talk to you both before I leave today." He hangs up before I can argue.

∽

I practice the conversation in my head on the walk up to Frank's office.

*You are calm and collected*, I think as I march through the lobby.

*You are the picture of professionalism*, I tell myself as I ride the elevator upstairs and step off on the fourth floor.

But then I get to the end of the hall and all my affirmations disappear. They're like scraps of paper reduced to ash under my incandescent rage when I see Frank's office door open and Nathan Asher standing in front of his desk. His back is to me, so he doesn't see me approach. He's too busy listening to whatever Frank is saying. Then he laughs. The sound makes my back teeth grind together, pulverizing the last of my affirmations.

"Ah, there you are," Frank calls out when he sees me, waving me inside.

Nathan turns to look at me over his shoulder just as I reach the door.

"Hello." His voice has that familiar patronizing edge.

"Hi," I say. I don't make a move to sit down. Neither does he.

"I'm assuming I can forgo another round of introductions," Frank mumbles, shooting me a derisive look.

I shoot him one right back.

"All right, then, let's make this quick," Frank continues. "Nate and I have a lot to go over, and I need to get out of here by noon."

"Right," I say, nodding to him. All I need to do is focus for the next few minutes and then I can leave. Easy.

"I filled Nate in on our schedule and how you take notes for me during class. Aside from the seminar, there's also the weekly meeting." He turns to Nathan. "Bea and I usually do that an hour before class, but it's not written in stone if you need to change it."

Nathan leans a hip against the bookcase. The casual pose is at odds with the rest of his polished facade, and the fluorescent light above highlights the imperfections I missed before. The faint scar running the length of his chin below his bottom lip. A deep crease above his left eyebrow, as if he's raised it enough to permanently indent his face. "That works for me."

"Good," Frank says, returning his attention back to the paper in front of him. "Now, regarding assignments—"

"Hold on," I say. "What if I want to change it?"

They both stare at me for a moment.

"Do you want to change it?" Frank asks.

"I want to be part of the discussion."

Frank pinches the bridge of his nose like he's already done with me.

"All right," Nathan says, crossing his arms over his chest. "What works for you, Beatrice?"

It suddenly feels like a negotiation: two lawyers facing off and carving out their demands. I let out a relieved breath and cross my arms, mirroring his pose. This I can handle.

"Frank and I meet every week for an hour, but that's usually because we're also discussing the rest of my workload and the job search."

"Meaning?"

I have to work hard not to roll my eyes. "It's an L1 seminar, Nathan. Do we really need to meet for an hour every week if we're just reviewing materials and assignments?"

"Do you have other plans?"

It's such an innocuous question, but his tone drips with condescension as if he knows, he just *knows*, that I have absolutely nothing going on in my life outside school to schedule around.

"You meet every week," Frank interjects, glaring at me. "You know the material, Bea. And Nate has a day job. You need to be coordinating."

*Damn it*. If I'm honest with myself, it makes sense: I'm far more familiar with the material and how each class is run than he is. But I don't want to be honest with myself. I want to argue, if just to combat the smug look on his face. So I say, "Fine. But only for a half hour."

"All right," Nathan replies. "We can meet at twelve thirty in your office."

I bark out a laugh. "No way."

His brow knits together. "Why not?"

"It's too . . ."

He waits.

"Small," I finally say. My pulse is hammering in my ears and the room suddenly feels very warm.

A small smirk tugs at Nathan's lips, and there's a hint of the dimple.

Frank mutters to himself, then motions to the room around us. "Just meet in here. It'll be empty, and Bea has a key."

Nathan nods. "That works."

They both look to me for approval.

"Just to be clear, this is still Frank's office," I say to Nathan. "And Frank is my boss, not you. You're just my colleague."

Another smirk. "Agreed."

Frank's office phone begins to ring, and he waves a hand at me before reaching to answer. "All right, get out of here. Nate and I still have a lot to get through, and you have office hours."

"Right."

Frank's already talking to whoever is on the other line as I turn to leave. Then Nathan reaches into his jacket and pulls out a business card. "Here's my contact information. I already have the syllabus, but send me any assignments you've graded, so I can review them before next week."

"Great." I pluck the card from his outstretched hand and I look up at him with my best lawyer smile. "See you next Tuesday!"

I don't look back as I leave, measuring my steps as I walk to the stairwell, then down one flight to my office. Only there do I finally exhale, collapsing into my desk chair as the tension in my limbs releases and my body goes limp. My head lolls to the side and my gaze falls on my mug.

*I Hate It Here.*

# CHAPTER 9

"Wait ... what?" Maggie yells into our FaceTime call, her confused expression taking up my entire phone screen. Despite the deafening sound of Travis hammering something on the other side of their kitchen, I know she heard me the first three times, but I still repeat myself again.

"Nathan Asher is taking over my class," I say, poking at the last peanut in my kung pao shrimp. I haven't bothered with a plate, just set up the array of Chinese food containers next to me on the sofa. I had treated myself with delivery tonight, a way to soften the blow of still not having any responses to my job inquiries. The empty inbox is open on my laptop, a glowing harbinger on the cushion beside me.

"So, you're working with the same guy who stuck his tongue down your throat?"

"Technically, I stuck my tongue down *his* throat," I correct her, but my words are swallowed up by a commotion behind her.

"Trav, I think it needs to be higher!" Maggie yells, motioning to where he stands off-camera. "No, higher!"

"Do you need to go?" I ask.

"No, it's just . . . one more inch! Yes, there!" Then she returns to me. "Sorry, trying to get this all done before the Miami trip might have been too ambitious."

Something crashes behind her.

"It's fine!" Travis yells. "I'm okay!"

Maggie rolls her eyes. "All right, so back up. How did this happen?"

I sigh, abandoning my chopsticks and pushing a few curls away from my face. "Apparently my professor was Nathan's professor back when he went to law school or something. They're still friends, so Frank called in a favor."

"Wow." She smiles. "This is the best thing I've heard all week."

"I'm glad you find this so entertaining." I glower at the peanut.

"Well, maybe if you hadn't stormed into his office like a crazy person, then proceeded to get drunk and kiss him, all of this wouldn't be so hilarious."

"Oh, right, like I should have somehow anticipated the fact that I would see him again."

"Of course you should have anticipated it," Maggie says with a snort. "It's New York. You always run into people you never want to see again."

"That's not true."

"Oh really? Remember when I had that one-night stand senior year with that guy we met at that bar in Brooklyn and then two years later he came in for an interview to be my assistant at Westfield Holdings?"

*Damn it.* I do remember that.

"Are you talking about one-night stands with your boyfriend in the room?" I ask, trying to deflect.

"It's fine. He's hanging shelves and not even listening," she says.

"Yes I am!" Travis calls out.

Maggie ignores him. "So, what are you going to do?"

I frown at her. "What can I do?"

"Well, you hate this Asher guy, so I assume you've contemplated resigning?"

It was a good question, one that had been swirling in my mind ever since that meeting in Frank's office. But every time it popped up, I always ended up at the same conclusion.

"I can't. The only way I can afford law school is with this position, so I have to just deal with it."

"Right," she says as if she's considering my options and also coming to the same realization. "Well, at least you can put dry humping on your résumé now."

I glare at her. "That's not happening again. I haven't even thought about it."

She scoffs. "That's such a lie."

She's right, it is a lie. The most blatant, bold-faced lie I have ever told in my long history of lying.

"Whatever," I say, popping the lone peanut in my mouth. "I'll barely see him. We're just meeting before class to review assignments and discuss course material. Which is my job, by the way. So really, I'm just doing my job."

Maggie hums to herself, as if she doesn't believe me at all. "Well, I guess this means we don't have to worry about him getting that restraining order anymore."

"Who's getting a restraining order?" Travis yells across the room.

"Yeah, Bea." Maggie waggles her eyebrows at me. "Who's getting a restraining order?"

I scowl at her. "No one."

Travis abandons the shelf and joins Maggie on camera. "I thought maybe it was Josh this time, since you broke into the apartment and stole his baking shit."

I roll my eyes, suddenly aware of the box of baking dishes sitting on the floor beside the sofa. I had lugged it home earlier that week and promptly forgot about it.

"It's Jillian's baking shit, actually," I reply.

"Well, in his text he said it was his."

"Wait, what happened?" Maggie asks.

"It's nothing," I say before Travis can offer what will no doubt be Josh's version of events. "Jillian just forgot a few things at the apartment, so she asked me to go pick them up."

"Oh God," Maggie groans. "Did you have to talk to Josh?"

"It was fine," I say. "I took some bakeware. He called me a bitch. Then I left."

Travis laughs, and I realize Josh's version of events probably doesn't sound very different from mine.

"Wait," Maggie says, shaking her head. "I'm still confused about what Jillian forgot. Didn't we pack everything up when we were down there?"

I lean over and poke through the contents of the box.

"It's not much. Mostly just a lot of bakeware from her grandma that she was keeping above the fridge," I said, eyeing the Pyrex dishes. "Looks like some cutlery, too, and some fridge magnets. And . . ."

Something small and round catches my eye in the corner of the box. I shift one of the dishes and reach for it, pulling it out and resting it in my palm. It's a light green pill, about the size and shape of a generic ibuprofen, but it doesn't look like ibuprofen. It doesn't look like anything I've ever seen before.

"What?" Maggie asks.

"I'm not sure," I say, bringing the pill up to get a closer look. "I just found something in here."

"What sort of something?"

I hold it up to my phone so they can see.

Travis leans in closer. "Is that a pill?"

"Yeah. I think so."

Maggie and Travis are silent for a minute. I know what they're thinking—it's impossible not to. That's the problem with knowing anyone as long as we have all known each other. We know all the best bits, but we know about the other bits, too.

We never talk about Josh's other bits anymore. To be fair, we never really talked about it at the time, either. After he ruptured his Achilles tendon during a football game junior year, he worked hard to rejoin the team well before his doctors thought he'd be able to. We were all happy for him, even as we ignored his weight loss, his mood swings. We told ourselves it was stress; if he wasn't on the team, he would lose his scholarship. But then he and Jillian broke up. He stopped going to class. It all got progressively worse until the night Travis found him on the floor of their bathroom. A few hours later we were in an ER listening to a doctor explain Josh's accidental overdose and how that injury months ago had led to Josh's addiction to prescription painkillers. Suddenly real life wasn't an abstract idea discussed in the middle of the night from the safety of our dorm rooms but the here and now, punctuated by stark fluorescent lights in a hospital waiting room.

Josh went to counseling for months. And we all did our best to listen and learn and help. Then one day he announced that he was better. Not long after, he and Jillian were dating again. And slowly, the worries of that night faded into the background behind every other worry that life threw our way.

But now, as I stare at the pill sitting in my palm, it resurfaces with crystal clarity.

"It's probably Jillian's," Travis says. "It's all her stuff in there, right?"

"Maybe," Maggie says. "She said she was going to talk to her doctor about getting on something for her anxiety."

I nod absently as I trap my bottom lip between my teeth, an unconscious habit whenever I'm thinking too hard.

Silence extends across the line again before Travis finally sighs. "Will it make you both feel better if I drop Josh a text and ask him about it?"

Relief floods my body as Maggie and I answer in unison, "Yes."

"Fine. But I'm sure it's nothing."

"We know, sweetie," Maggie says, patting his shoulder. "You're probably right."

"Of course I'm right. I'm always right."

I snort. "Sure. Okay."

An earsplitting crash fills the line, and Travis curses as he bounds out of frame.

"Ugh, all right, we need to go," Maggie says. "We're losing shelves."

"Okay. Tell Travis to call me when he hears back from Josh."

"I will," she says. "And tell that new professor of yours that I said—"

I hang up before she can finish.

The pill is still sitting in my palm. I study its dull edges, its soulless shade of green. It's probably nothing, I tell myself as I walk to the bathroom and flush it down the toilet. I almost believe it, too.

But I'm still thinking about it when I crawl into bed that night.

# CHAPTER 10

**BEATRICE**

ARE YOU HERE?

**NATHAN ASSHOLE**

Just coming up.

**BEATRICE**

WE SAID 12:30

**NATHAN ASSHOLE**

It's 12:34.

**BEATRICE**

IF I HAD KNOWN YOU WERE GOING TO BE LATE I
WOULD HAVE GOTTEN HERE AT 12:55

**NATHAN ASSHOLE**

Why are you yelling?

BEATRICE

I'M NOT YELLING

I look up from sending my text to see the elevator doors at the end of the hall open and Nathan emerge. He pauses, his eyes doing a quick survey of the floor before turning to find me at the end of the hall. As he approaches, I notice he's wearing a suit beneath that familiar camel coat, but this time without a tie.

"I wasn't yelling," I say as soon as he's close enough to hear.

His brow furrows as he arrives a few feet in front of me. "Then why were you typing in all caps?"

"My phone screen is cracked right over the caps button, so I can't turn it off."

"Why don't you fix your phone screen?"

I expertly balance my "I Hate It Here" mug and my phone in one hand as I unlock Frank's office door with the other. "Because it's cheaper to type in all caps."

He stares down at me, then at my mug, then frowns before heading inside.

The office looks exactly the same as when we were here the week before. Frank didn't even bother to clean off his desk before going on leave, so the crowded space feels like a still life, everything frozen in time, just waiting for him to return: the piles of papers on his desk, the books thrown haphazardly on the shelves. The warm smell of Frank's cologne has faded, though, and as Nathan enters behind me, a fresh, clean scent of whatever soap he uses replaces it.

There are two chairs in front of Frank's desk. I drop my bag beside one and fall into it. I expect Nathan to take Frank's seat, but he stops next to the chair beside me. He doesn't appear to be in any rush as he places his computer bag on the ground between us and begins to pull off his coat. I try not to watch the motion, but there's no avoiding it. His broad frame takes up the entire view; all I can do is watch how he takes hold of each cuff and pulls it down his arms. Then he lays it against the back of his chair and sits down, his long legs stretched out in front of him.

I had practiced this conversation in my head all morning. I know I have to apologize for the kiss outside my building, obviously, and that alone has planted a seed of annoyance in my chest. Best to just get it out there and move on. But I also have to be clear that I'm apologizing about the assault outside my building and not the verbal assault in his office, which, honestly, wasn't an assault at all.

I'm about to open my mouth and begin my well-rehearsed monologue, but he beats me to it.

"Before we get started, I'd like to apologize."

I blink. It's so far from what I expect him to say that it takes my brain a moment to recalibrate. And even then I'm confused. "What?"

"For what happened after the bar event," he replies. "I'm sorry."

My eyes narrow on him. "Why the hell are you apologizing?"

There's that condescending frown again. "I kissed you without your consent, Bea. You made it clear that you weren't—"

"What?" I blurt out again, louder this time.

"Do I need to repeat myself?"

"Ah, no." I scoff. "No. No, no. I kissed you."

A moment. He blinks, the only clue that it's now his turn to be confused. "Excuse me?"

"This isn't even a question, Nathan. You leaned down to speak to me, at which point I kissed you."

He tilts his head to the side as if he's contemplating the memory. "That's not—"

I hold up my hand to stop him. "We're not debating this. I kissed you. Without your consent, I might add. So, if anyone should be apologizing, it should be me. But I won't, because you kissed me back, so I could argue that there was informed consent—"

"Implied consent."

"Implied consent," I repeat through gritted teeth. I can't believe I'm flustered enough to give him an opportunity to correct me. "So, I'm not apologizing. In fact, I think we need to go back to you apologizing, since you were obviously aware that this current work situation was a possibility and chose not to tell me prior to the events of that night. You withheld information that would have informed my decision-making. That has to violate some of the bar's professional conduct rules, right? I could submit a formal complaint. Or at the very least inform the board of trustees here so they know who they're dealing with. Tell the chairman or maybe write an email to all of them or . . . or . . . something." I'm rambling, and I know I'm rambling by the expression on his face, how one eyebrow slowly arches up until my voice finally fades.

"Are you done?" he asks.

I close my eyes for a moment and take a deep breath, mining the last of my patience. "That really depends on what's about to come out of your mouth."

When I open my eyes again, I find him staring at me, and there's something there in his gaze that causes me to go still.

"I'm sorry, Beatrice," he says. "It won't happen again. I promise."

It feels odd to hear him say "sorry" out loud. It's like the apology somehow solidifies the memory, and now all I can think about is the taste of bourbon on his tongue. My heart does an odd stutter in my chest, and I wave my hand in the air between us like I can somehow bat the words away.

"Fine. Great. Apology accepted. Can we get back to work now?"

"That depends."

"On what?"

He leans back in his small chair, clasping his hands together in his lap. "Frank told me that you rely on the stipend from your TA position to help pay for school. He also said you weren't thrilled with the idea of me taking on his class. If you're thinking of resigning and putting your degree in jeopardy because of this, I'll step down and help Frank find a replacement."

I watch him for a moment, looking for a tell that might reveal some ulterior motive. "Why do you care?"

His lips flatten and he dips his head so he can stare at me from under his brow. "I know you think I'm an asshole, Bea, but I'm not that much of an asshole."

I should feel a wave of relief. There's an escape hatch to this situation, one he's offering up freely. But I hesitate at the thought. Pride muscles in, shouting in my head that he can't force me to reveal a weakness so easily. So I stare at him, in no hurry to reply, and he waits, still meeting my gaze.

"Did you tell him?" I ask. "About what happened?"

*Does Frank know that I kissed you and I haven't been able to stop thinking about it since?*

"No."

The knot of anxiety in my belly releases a tiny bit. That's one good piece of news, at least. Because even without the bruised ego or the irrational need to prove him wrong, I can't ignore the fact that I need this job. I worked so hard to get it, and despite the minuscule paycheck, I have no idea how I'll be able to pay for school—let alone rent—without it. I need to make this work as much as I need to ensure that he never knows how much of an effort it is to appear nonchalant as I ask, "Why would you even want to do this?"

"What do you mean?"

"Well, according to *New York* magazine, you're one of the top divorce attorneys in the city." I reach down into my bag and pull out a bulging binder labeled "Alternative Conflict Resolution." The small color-coded tabs I used to organize the seminar by lesson stick out of the side like a fringe. "Don't you have better things to do on a Tuesday afternoon than teach a basic survey course to a bunch of L1s?"

It's only when I see his eyes flare with some indefinable spark and a sly grin turn up one corner of his lips that I realize I've said too much.

"You read the article?"

*Yes*, I think.

"No," I say.

In my defense, it's not like I went looking for it. Maggie texted me the link right after I told her about the kiss, but I hadn't clicked on it until two nights ago. It was 3:00 a.m. and I had been staring at the same SCOTUS opinion for so long that I needed to think about something else: namely, whatever this was going to be. How Nathan and I were supposed to work together, what the next few months would look like . . . and then reading the article seemed like the natural thing to do. Clicking on the link had felt like research, another avenue to further understand the man sitting across from me.

The website loaded, and then there it was: "Asher to the Rescue." It was a full feature, a supposedly in-depth interview that wasn't really that in-depth at all. Yes, it profiled a myriad of his clients (some rich enough to be mentioned without actually mentioning their names), his sprawling Midtown office (marble imported from Italy! Zero carbon footprint!), and his goals for the future (which was really just the reporter's way of prodding him for more details about his recent promotion to partner), but there was no tangible information about who Nathan Asher was at all. I finished the article with an unsated pit in my stomach, and a resolve to never reveal that I had spent twenty minutes reading about Nathan in the first place.

He's staring at me now, waiting, so I open the binder I've meticulously put together, then close it again with a snap. "How does something like that happen, anyway? Does a reporter just call up your office and say they want to objectify you under the guise of a profile piece?"

His eyebrow quirks up. "You think it objectified me?"

"Nathan, they photoshopped your head onto Superman's body."

"But you didn't read it."

"No," I lie again.

He nods, a flicker of amusement in his eyes. "Okay."

His tone suggests that he doesn't believe me at all, like he can see right through me as much as I wish I could get a mere peek into him.

"Who do you have to pay to get featured like that?" I ask, leaning an elbow on the arm of my chair so I can prop up my chin, as if I'm riveted.

"No one. One of the other partners organized the interview."

"Why?"

"He said it would be good PR for the firm."

"Right. Did they organize the photoshoot, too?"

"No photoshoot. That's my professional headshot."

"Ah. So, the smolder is a *professional* choice."

His glare becomes condescending, and I'm now aware of how he wields that look; it's a mask for those moments when he's uncomfortable. "An inherent trait."

I snort out a laugh. "Should have mentioned *that* in the interview."

"How do you know I didn't?"

*Shit.*

His smile is still absent, but there's a hint of that almost-smile, like he knows it's coming but he's trying to edge. Nathan Asher is joy-edging.

"You didn't answer my question," I finally reply.

"Which was?"

"Don't you have better things to do than take over this class for Frank?"

A slight shrug. "Yes. But when a friend needs a favor, that takes precedence."

The rationality of it catches me off guard. I'm about to retort when a dull ping sounds from my phone. It's sitting face down on the desk, and when I pick it up, the screen displays a text message.

**MOM**

Do you think I should go back to being blond?

Annoyance sparks in my chest. I want to text back a reminder that every time she texts me this, I say no, and yet every spring she does it anyway and regrets it, but then I notice the time.

"Shit," I murmur. "It's almost one."

Nathan looks up at me with the same question on his face as I'm sure I have on mine: *When the hell did that happen?* But he recovers quicker than I do, standing and grabbing his coat.

"Wait." My eyes widen, holding up my still-closed binder. "We haven't reviewed anything yet."

"I went over the syllabus you sent me earlier. It looks good."

"Obviously. I wrote it."

His lips quirk up as he starts for the door. "We'll figure the rest out as we go."

Conflict Resolution is a few doors down at Furman Hall. The large lecture room looks like every other room on the fourth floor: three rows of desks set in half circles radiating out from the lectern up front. When Nathan and I enter, the class is already waiting for us; the room is half full, and the hum of conversation tapers off as their heads turn one by one to the man now approaching the lectern.

I take my usual seat at the end of the back row, so it's impossible not to notice the wave of looks and whispers, the giggles and gawks from the students as Nathan puts down his bag and turns his attention to them.

"Good afternoon, everyone," he says, offering the room that lawyer smile I recognize from the bar event. Everyone falls silent, their attention rapt. "I'm Nathan Asher. I'll be taking over for Professor Landry while he's out on medical leave. I've been practicing family law since I graduated from here seven years ago. Professor Landry was my mentor back then, and I hope I can fill his shoes adequately now. Thankfully, I'll have Beatrice Nilsson to help me."

Nathan motions to me, but only a few heads turn to look in my direction. They already know me; I'm old news. He, however, is fresh meat. "We'll be sticking to the syllabus Professor Landry supplied, which means this week we're discussing Gasley versus Newton. If you'll remember from your reading, Patricia Gasley is suing her former employer for unsafe working conditions . . ."

He continues talking, but as my eyes glide across the room, I realize very few students are actually listening. No fingers typing, no pens scrawling in notebooks. There are only whispers and barely contained grins and mouths hanging open.

I roll my eyes. It's going to be a long semester.

# CHAPTER 11

I refresh my inbox for the ninth time in five minutes. It still says the same thing.

No new messages.

I glower at the screen, finally turning away to stare out my tiny office window. A solitary branch wavers in the wind, but I can see the buds starting to grow along the bark. Small and green and barely visible, but still, a reminder that spring is almost here. My mind goes back to the numbers that have been aggregating in my head: 56 days since I sent out emails to nineteen different law firms; 93 days until graduation; 156 days until the bar exam. And exactly zero job prospects.

I am screwed.

My head falls into my folded arms. I'm vaguely aware that a few curls may have fallen in my mug and are now steeping in five-hour-old coffee, but I don't care enough to move. All I really want is to crawl under this desk and sleep for a thousand years.

Then my phone starts ringing. It's still on silent from class earlier, but I can hear it vibrating somewhere inside my bag. I'm tempted to let it go to voicemail, but then I remember that I sent Travis about two dozen text messages asking for an update on whether he's talked to Josh about the pill or not, and I still haven't heard back from him. If he was finally calling me back, I couldn't ignore it.

But it isn't Travis's name on the screen when I pull out my phone. It's Jillian's.

"Hi," I groan, my voice muffled by the sleeves of my sweater.

"Everything okay?" Her voice is already laced with concern.

"Yup. I'm just going to be unemployed for the rest of my life, then die alone, only to be found two weeks later."

A sympathetic sigh. "I don't think that's true."

I turn my head in my arms so I can see my empty inbox with one eye. "You're right. I'm sure the Fordham bookstore will hire me back. I was one of their star employees freshman year."

She laughs.

"Are we still on for lunch tomorrow?" I ask. "We can grab something near my apartment so you can pick up your dishes."

"That's actually why I'm calling," she says, her voice already apologetic. "Don't kill me, but I have to cancel. I have another interview for that VP of marketing job in Boston. The interview is virtual, but if it goes well, they said they want me to come up in the next couple of weeks and meet the team."

My heart drops. "To Massachusetts?"

She sighs. "It's not *that* far. I would still see you all the time."

"I barely see you now."

"Well, once you get a job at some fancy law firm, you won't have time to see me anyway, so it's fine."

I force a dry laugh as I turn my face into my sleeve again to avoid looking at the empty inbox.

"I am really sorry," she continues. "But I promise we can re-schedule soon. I still have to pick up that box of dishes, right?"

It suddenly occurs to me to ask Jillian about the pill. I haven't brought it up with her and right now seems like the moment. But then what? Travis could be right and it's an ibuprofen or anxiety medica-tion. And even if it's Josh's, there's no reason to think Jillian has any answers. They haven't lived together in months. Telling her will only add to her list of things to worry about. A list that is already too long.

"Right," I simply mumble, pushing the thought from my mind.

"Okay, enough about me. Tell me about the job search."

"I'm going to work at the Fordham bookstore. We just went over this."

She laughs. "Why don't you ask that new professor for a rec-ommendation?"

My head shoots up so fast that the curl that had been in my mug flies out, sprinkling coffee across my desk. "How do you know about that?"

"Maggie mentioned that Frank is on medical leave so you're working with some new guy who is kind of an asshole, but not in a bad way. Whatever that means."

"Jesus," I murmur to myself. Of course Maggie told her. Mag-gie was probably dying to spill the beans and said just enough to alleviate the urge while still keeping the secret. She's as careful as she is diabolical.

"Is it that bad?"

Jillian's voice is so kind and so patient that for a split second I consider telling her that Nathan is the new professor. But that would require telling her everything else that happened before today, so I pull the words back and just say, "Yes."

"Is he at least cute?"

I scowl even as my heart kicks in my chest. "Why would that matter?"

"Because working with someone gorgeous could be fun."

"Well, he's an asshole, so . . ." I don't know what else to say so I scoff, I snort, I make a whole plethora of sounds that I hope equate with jest.

"Well, don't do anything that puts your job at risk, okay? You worked so hard to get into law school, and—"

"Give me some credit, Jills," I say, cutting her off. "Believe it or not, I am capable of being professional."

~

"Bullshit!"

My voice rings through Frank's office, and a woman walking by sends a critical glare at me from the hallway.

Nathan doesn't move from his seat; he just stares at me from under the hard line of his brow. "Why is that bullshit?"

"Because intentional infliction of emotional distress requires *intent*, Nathan."

"Exactly."

I groan as I put an elbow on the side of Frank's desk, avoiding our empty coffee mugs and crumb-covered napkins from the muffins we finished ages ago.

Like every Tuesday over the past few weeks, I had come up to Frank's office with the best intentions—papers graded, case law examples ready. Nathan and I had started our meeting on the right foot. But last week the case had been Southland Corp. v. Keating, which involved a group of 7-Eleven franchisees suing the parent company for breach of contract, which meant Nathan and I spent almost the entire time debating the superior flavor of Slurpee (blue raspberry, obviously). The week before, when we had to detail how Mitsubishi Motors Corp. v. Soler Chrysler-Plymouth, Inc. shaped arbitration in antitrust claims, we ended up arguing about whether you actually needed to own a car in the city (you don't). And today, we should be preparing for a class about DeMarco v. Petrou and residential property disclosure agreements. Instead, I made the mistake of suggesting that the episode of *The Real Housewives of New York City* where the women almost died while on vacation after their chartered yacht encountered rough seas is a good example of negligence since it's clear the charter company knew about the possible weather conditions prior to the trip but never disclosed the information. That's when Nathan asked if I was using the scripted events from a TV show as case law, and now I don't even know what's real anymore.

"It's a reality show."

"And?" He leans back in his chair. I ignore how the small motion unsettles the air, how his smell—leather and cedar and soap—seems to surround me.

"Reality means it is unscripted."

"I think you're severely discounting the role of a television producer."

"I'm not saying that certain elements aren't choreographed," I say, trying to regain my composure. Meanwhile, the man across from me sits with his hands clasped like we're negotiating a multimillion-dollar lawsuit out of court. "But this was a yacht carrying the show's entire cast. Do you think a TV producer would purposely risk their lives like that?"

He shrugs one shoulder.

My eyes widen. This is tantamount to heresy. "These are real people experiencing real events, Nathan. The countess almost died."

A frown as he looks at me like he's just noticed I have two heads. "There's a countess?"

My mouth falls open. "How could you forget the countess? She moved to New York from Connecticut and married into royalty."

The corner of his mouth twitches, like he knows what's coming. Nathan Asher is joy-edging again. "I've never seen the show."

My mouth falls open, but before I can reply with a scathing retort, laughter bubbles up from my chest and bursts out. It's so loud and uninhibited that I should probably be embarrassed, but I'm not. I close my eyes and let my head fall back and laugh. Arguing with Nathan Asher is the most fun I've had in ages.

It's interrupted when my phone starts vibrating somewhere inside my bag. I don't need to pull it out to see that it's the alarm alerting us to the fact that class starts in five minutes.

"That's our cue," Nathan says, nodding toward the door.

The sun is shining in the courtyard as we exit the building and start walking down to Furman Hall, but it's still cold enough that our breath floats in front of us in swirling clouds as we exhale. I pull my coat tighter around my body, trying to ignore the man looming at my side, but it's impossible. Especially when every student we pass seems to notice him, too.

"Any word from Frank?" he asks as we get to the corner.

I nod. "He called yesterday and said they're keeping him for another few days for observation."

Frank's surgery was two weeks ago, and while it went well, an infection developed shortly afterward that required him to return to the hospital until it cleared up. I had gleaned most of this information from sporadic texts and quick phone calls from him that centered around the current state of medicine in this country and his hospital's propensity for orange Jell-O.

"How's he doing?"

"He said if he didn't get a cannoli from Veniero's soon, he was going to set the place on fire."

Nathan smiles and I can tell immediately that this is a rare genuine one. The dimple in his cheek is there. It gives him a boyish look, clear of the harshness that usually tightens his features. "Have you been to see him yet?"

I blink away from his face, pretending the crosswalk needs my attention.

"Not yet. I mean, I will. I just . . . I hate hospitals so . . ." I let the words fade and then I shrug.

"But you're doing healthcare law."

"And?"

I can feel him turn to raise an eyebrow at me. "And you hate hospitals?"

I lift my chin as we enter Furman Hall. The lobby is crowded with students, and I have to raise my voice so Nathan will hear me over the din of conversation. "Last time I checked, you don't have to go into a hospital to sue a pharmaceutical company for helping fuel the opioid crisis."

I stop at the elevators and press the call button before I look up to meet his waiting gaze. There's a line between his brows as he studies my face, like he caught a glimpse of something real there and is seeking out the rest of it.

A pair of elevator doors open and I quickly enter before he can find it.

# CHAPTER 12

I haven't always hated hospitals. When I broke my arm in second grade after falling off the playground at school, the ER doctor gave me a lollipop and a purple cast so by the time I left three hours later, I was actually smiling. And when my mom's fourth husband had a heart attack one night during my sophomore year of high school, I had no problem sitting by his hospital bed for three days until my mom returned from her girls' trip to Las Vegas. I even grew kind of fond of the vending machine across the hall that provided a steady stream of Pop-Tarts at any hour of the day.

No, it wasn't until college that hospitals stopped being something seen in absolutes—a place where people go in broken and come out fixed. Junior year I rode in the ambulance to the hospital with Josh after he was injured during that infamous football game, listened to his screams as they worked to set his ankle. I had been the one to call his mom in California from that sterile waiting room and relay the information from his doctors. It was the same waiting room where I sat with Travis and Jillian and Maggie a year later and listened to a different doctor outline how Josh's injury had led to an addiction to painkillers. How we could take him home, but "fixed" wasn't a term that applied anymore.

At least Frank isn't stuck at that hospital, which is a small blessing. Lenox Hill Hospital is on the Upper East Side on a tree-lined street with neo-Gothic mansions, high-end boutiques, and a never-ending barrage of ambulances arriving out front. I head up there after my Bioethics class on Thursday, stopping at Veniero's on the way. I pick up four cannolis, then trudge down to the subway to catch an uptown 6 train. By the time I walk through the hospital's sliding doors, the anxiety is like a heavy stone in my gut, slowing my steps as I approach the information desk.

The nurse directs me to the elevators, and I head up to the seventh floor. Frank's room is at the end of the hall, and I take my time walking down to it, keeping my eyes on the floor and trying to keep my breathing in check. But the sharp smell of antiseptic is unavoidable—it seeps into the artificial citrus scent of various cleaning supplies. Together they tickle my nostrils, forcing images of rushing nurses, sleepless nights, and barren waiting rooms through my mind.

The door to Frank's room is open, and I pause just outside it. There's a curtain partially drawn around the bed, and I use its cover to give myself a moment to prepare for whatever I'm about to face a few feet away. Despite his age, I've always seen Frank as an immovable force, this permanent thing in a world where everything else seems fluid. In the three years I've known him, I've never seen him look weak. I don't know if I'm ready for it now.

But then I freeze when I hear Frank's laughter, along with another voice, deep and gravelly and familiar.

"They arrived yesterday," Nathan says from beyond the curtain that divides the room and blocks my view.

My heart stutters. I had assumed that if I stopped by during the day it would guarantee a Nathan-free visit. I mean, the man had to work, right? But apparently being a partner in a law firm means you can just leave whenever you want, which . . . yeah, now that I repeat it back in my head, makes sense.

"Daisies?" Frank asks, still chuckling.

"She said they were to celebrate the first time I remembered her birthday."

I don't move from the doorway, just lean in a bit further to listen.

Frank's laughter slowly fades, and it's a moment before he asks, "When was the last time you saw her?"

"Christmas."

"And how was it?"

Nathan sighs. "Good."

"Good?"

A shift of weight. "Better than I expected."

"Well, that wouldn't be hard." Frank lets out another dry laugh.

"She's good, Frank," Nathan says. I can hear a weary smile in his voice. "We're good."

"Are you?"

A shift of weight. "Well, she made it clear she didn't want me sticking around."

"Of course she doesn't," Frank murmurs. "She knows you have your own bullshit to deal with. You don't need to take on hers, too."

"I need a little bullshit in my life," Nathan replies. "I have enough people telling me I'm right all the time."

There's another grunt, as if Frank finds some hidden depth to what Nathan has said. Then, "It's okay to feel mixed up about it."

Another shift in weight, then a sigh. "It's good, Frank."

"You know, one of these days you're going to realize that pretending you're fine doesn't work on me."

Nathan sighs, though the sound of it is mostly lost in the sounds of the hospital around me. "Right."

Silence. Who are they talking about? Nathan's girlfriend? His ex? I lean in further, shamelessly hungry for any scraps to explain what Frank is talking about, but then a nurse appears beside me so suddenly it makes me jump.

"Oh, hello there!" Her voice is loud and chipper and there is absolutely no way that Nathan and Frank didn't hear it from a few feet away.

"Hi," I reply, trying to keep my voice down.

Sure enough, there's a shuffling behind the curtain, as if Frank is moving to sit up as he calls out, "Bea?"

I cringe. "Yup."

The nurse smiles as if she's done a favor. "You can go right in."

"Super. Thanks." I glower at her.

My heart is playing a staccato against my rib cage as I walk forward into the room. It's a carbon copy of the others I passed on my way down the hall: benign wallpaper that's a swirl of pale pink and mint green and white. Framed posters of famous artwork that've been on the wall long enough to fade to a muted effigy of the original. It would feel like a bad hotel room if it weren't for the drone of machines and beeps running like a steady soundtrack from nearby, or the acute smell of hand sanitizer permeating the air.

I maneuver around the curtain dividing the room, to find Frank propped up in the narrow bed. Nathan is in the chair next to him. He looks perfectly disheveled in a way that finally matches his hair. His gray suit is in pristine condition, but his shirt is slightly wrinkled, and his navy tie has been loosened so two buttons can be undone at his neck. There's a hint of that dip between his clavicles, a few chest hairs visible further below it.

But it's his expression that startles me. I don't think I appreciated how hard he works to maintain that air of aloofness until right now. How his surprise peeks through before he can lock down his look of ambivalence. Then he stands like he's going to give me his chair or do something else that his mom probably drilled into him from a young age. I wave the impending offer away, my arm flapping in the space between us awkwardly. "No, no, it's fine. I can't stay. I just wanted to . . . stop by. Say hi. Hello." It's only then that I remember the box in my hand, and I swing it up into the air. "Cannolis!"

"They won't be if you keep swinging them around like that," Frank says, motioning me forward and taking the box from my hands. He sets it down on the table beside his bed, and it's only then that I notice there's an identical box beside it with the same red string tied at the top.

My eyes dart to Nathan, who is still standing across from me on the other side of the bed.

"Oh, did you . . ." I don't know why I can't finish the sentence. The words get tied up in my throat, so I just point at the box dumbly.

He gives me that condescending glare that does nothing to hide how uncomfortable he suddenly is. "You said he wanted cannolis from Veniero's."

"Next time I'll say I want a million dollars and see how I do," Frank says almost under his breath, shifting in his hospital bed again. There's a grimace on his face as he tries to move his leg.

"How are you feeling?" I ask.

"Like I've had a hip replaced." He looks pale and his face is gaunter than I've ever seen it, but his voice is strong—the same deep and biting tone I'm used to. "The infection cleared up, but for some reason I have to stay here another couple of days. Squeeze every last dime out of me, I guess."

"It's for observation, Frank," Nathan says, still standing as his hands come up to rest on his hips. "They can't release you until you've been fever-free for twenty-four hours."

Frank mutters under his breath, a few curses punctuating a monologue that is too low to understand.

"But then you're home, right?" I try to make the words sound encouraging, but my voice is thin, as if I need the reassurance as much as Frank does.

"Then I'm home," he replies. "Course, I'll have a nurse coming by twice a day. And physical therapy. I'll be lucky to be off a walker by summer."

A cold bite of anxiety takes hold of my chest, but before I can press him for more details, a voice calls out behind me.

"Hello, Mr. Landry," a doctor says as she enters the room and pulls back the curtain. She doesn't look up from her clipboard, just walks to the monitors by Frank's nightstand. "How are we doing today?"

"Ready to get the hell out of here," he mutters.

"That's good."

The exchange has the feeling of something that's happened a few times before, but panic still claws at my throat as the doctor begins examining Frank's vitals, studying each blinking screen and how their wires are connected to his body somewhere under that blanket. It feels like my blood is pooling at my feet while my heart races manically to pull it back up into my veins.

I feel a pull then, attention on me from the other side of the bed. Nathan is watching me, his eyes narrow and jaw taut. It's not the derisive look I'm used to, though; he looks like he's trying to work something out. Almost like he's concerned.

"Let's take a listen to your lungs," the doctor says.

Frank grunts again and leans forward.

"We'll leave you to it, Frank," Nathan says, moving around the bed to stand at my side. His hand is suddenly on the small of my back, a light touch that urges me toward the door. "If you need anything, call me. And let me know if they discharge you tomorrow. I'm happy to come pick you up."

Frank waves him off, too busy grimacing at the doctor to notice or care that we're inching out of the room.

I take my first deep breath in what feels like an eternity when we step into the hall. But it's not until we're at the elevator bank that I realize Nathan is still at my side, his hand hovering inches above my back as if I might pass out at any second.

"Thanks," I say, stepping forward to press the down button and give myself a few precious inches of space. "For getting us out of there, I mean."

"It's all right," he says. A moment later, the elevator doors open. He holds one side, nodding for me to go ahead of him, then continues. "I'm not a big fan of hospitals, either."

I examine the taut line of his profile, but he doesn't look at me as the doors close and he leans forward to press *L*.

The ride down is silent until the doors open again, the dull hum of conversations and announcements and the smell of antiseptic welcoming us back to the first floor.

He's still not looking at me as he walks straight ahead, through the hospital's sliding doors, and out onto the busy sidewalk.

"So," he says, adjusting the cashmere scarf around his neck as we stop and face each other. "Are you heading to the subway?"

I nod, a jerky motion.

"Okay." Then he turns and starts down the road in that direction, slowing his steps just enough until I fall in step beside him.

The sky is a watery gray, the sun hidden behind a thin layer of clouds. It's like spring is waiting there, fighting to break through, but the cold still has its hold on the city, forcibly blocking out the warmth. As if on cue, a chill snakes its way under my worn coat, sending a shiver up my spine. I pull it tighter around my body and pretend not to notice how the motion snags Nathan's attention.

"You need a better coat," he says.

I look down at the faded green wool and smooth out the fraying thread along the seams. "I like this coat."

"Why?" It's almost not a question, as if he doesn't expect a rational answer.

I lift my chin defiantly, ignoring how the motion allows another chill to slip beneath the collar. "It's vintage."

"It's falling apart."

"Maybe I like things that are falling apart."

"Is that why you live in that building?"

I blink. He did this a few times in class earlier in the week, too, a sudden redirection in conversation. No doubt it's a trait developed in law school, a way to keep your opponent off-balance. And that's how I end up feeling in his presence, like my center of gravity has shifted and I can't get my footing. "What are you talking about?"

"Your apartment building. All the scaffold."

Half of me keeps forgetting that he's been there, seen my building in all its decrepit glory, while the other half can't seem to shake the memory loose. *Remember how perfectly his body slanted into yours? How warm his breath was as it filled your lungs?* I clear my throat.

"It's not *falling apart*," I say. He gives me a sardonic look, and I roll my eyes. "Okay, yes, it might look like that, but when I moved in, the landlord said they were renovating the exterior and replacing some pipes."

"And how long ago was that?"

I shrug, trying to keep my answer as ambiguous as possible. "A few years."

He shakes his head. "You should move."

"I know this might come as a shock to a guy who owns a cashmere scarf and probably eats caviar for breakfast—"

"I don't eat caviar for breakfast."

"—but there aren't a lot of housing options for a law student with a part-time job and massive student loans."

The line between his brows sharpens. "There has to be more than an apartment that's about to fall down."

"It's not just an apartment, Nathan," I correct him. "It's a *rent-stabilized* apartment."

"No, it's a future EPA Superfund site."

My laugh is so loud that it seems to surprise Nathan as much as me. He turns, eyes wide, and then a smile spreads across his face. It's one of those genuine ones, so uncensored that his dimple cuts deeply into his cheek.

But then my laughter is cut short as a gust of wind whips around the corner, and the dimple disappears. In fact, his entire expression becomes that unreadable mask again as his gaze travels down to where I'm desperately trying to hug my coat closer to my body. The audit is so intense I have to look away, pretend that the window of the bank across the street is somehow interesting.

A moment later, I feel something fluffy and warm around my neck. It takes my brain a moment to connect the dots, and even then, I have to look down at the thick navy cashmere now draped over my shoulders, then gaze up at where the scarf is now missing from his, to register it.

"This is your scarf," I say dumbly, as if this is news to either of us.

"And?"

"And I don't want it."

"Okay." He says it in a way that implies he doesn't believe me, but he doesn't push it. He doesn't make any attempt to take back the scarf, either.

"Nathan, I don't—"

"How's the job search going?"

I narrow my eyes at him. I don't want to give up the fight. But I also can't make myself remove the scarf. It's gloriously soft, insulating my neck and sending a warm flush through my body. Or maybe it's the smell: leather and soap and cedar. So, I just say, "It's going."

He hums, a noncommittal sound. "Heard back from any firms yet?"

"Not yet, but it's a busy time of year. Besides, I have to study for the bar. That's really my main concern right now. If I don't pass, then the job search is moot."

He frowns, a barely perceptible change in his expression that denotes just enough incredulousness. "You'll pass."

I scoff. The bar exam takes place in a convention center on the West Side, a huge hall with harsh lighting where a seemingly endless line of folding tables waits for a thousand would-be lawyers to sit in absolute silence for two days. They couldn't have designed a more intimidating space if they tried. "You don't know that."

We stop at a crosswalk, and he reaches up to itch his jaw. Without his scarf, I can see the column of his neck, the dusting of stubble. "Well, if it makes you feel better, nobody thinks they're going to pass when they walk in that room."

"Except you, I'm sure."

"I didn't," he says. His head cocks to the side as if he's reviewing the memory. "But I think that had more to do with the guy sitting behind me who projectile-vomited on my back, so I almost didn't finish the last essay question."

My mouth falls open. "You're joking."

He shakes his head. "Phones are prohibited in the conference hall, and there's no clocks, so you need to bring your own watch to keep track of the time. This guy didn't realize until the final ten minutes that his watch stopped working an hour into the exam, so he was nowhere near finished."

"Great," I murmur, almost to myself. "Now I have another thing to worry about."

"You'll be fine."

"But what if I'm not?"

"Bring two watches."

I shake my head, but I also can't help my smile. "You're such an asshole."

"You've mentioned that."

I laugh again, and I tug the scarf closer to my body. I'm barely aware I'm doing it, until I notice that Nathan is watching the motion, his smile dimming once again into something unreadable.

"So did you pass the first time?" I ask.

Another nod, this one slower.

I sigh dramatically. "Figures."

"How so?"

"Star law student passes the bar his first try. Goes on to join one of the top firms in the city. Makes partner in under five years."

"But you didn't read that article."

*Shit.* I feel my cheeks warm but wave a hand ahead of me, as if brushing away that minor detail. "You know what I mean. It all works out for you. Perfect law school career, the dream job. That ex-girlfriend is probably a supermodel."

He stops in the middle of the sidewalk as his expression changes, skewing with confusion as he works to keep the lopsided grin on his lips. "Who?"

"Your ex. The one you were talking about back there with Frank and . . ." It's only after the words have left my mouth that I realize I've not only admitted to eavesdropping, but also to caring about Nathan's love life.

He stares at me for a long moment as if I've grown a second head. Then, slowly, something in his mind clicks into place, and his smile softens. "How long were you out there listening?"

I roll my eyes even as my voice goes up an octave. "I wasn't *listening.*"

"Okay." He says it like he doesn't believe me and starts forward again. "Well, we weren't talking about my ex."

"Oh." An odd relief unfurls in my chest as I match his steps.

"We were talking about my mom."

"Frank knows your mom?"

"Not really. They met once at my graduation. But we've talked about her a lot." Nathan lets his gaze skim across the road. A moment passes. "She was diagnosed with MS while I was his teaching assistant."

I stare up at him for a long moment before I find my voice. "I'm so sorry, Nathan."

He glances down at my stricken expression, and his brow softens. "It's okay. She's doing really well right now. There hasn't been a flare-up in a while, and the last one didn't stick around too long. But she was in and out of the hospital a lot before they figured out what was wrong, so I spent more time back home than in the city. If anyone else had been my supervisor, I would have had to quit, but Frank was great about it. Let me have extra time off and do virtual office hours. I graduated because of him."

He turns back to the road ahead. "Anyway, that's why I hate hospitals." His concentration seems to snag on a memory, then he shakes it loose before bringing his attention back to me. "How about you?"

The desire to tell him the truth surprises me. I even open my mouth, ready to share the awful memories of going in and out of them with Josh. But I can't. Maybe if it involved a stranger, if it concerned someone Nathan had no chance of ever meeting—but this involves his client. And revealing the details of Josh's addiction to his attorney . . . the complications of that fall heavy in my gut. So, I shrug.

"Remember that episode of *Grey's Anatomy* when the hospital exploded for like the fifth time? I never recovered."

He chuckles softly, and I can't help but smile, too.

We walk and walk, and somehow the conversation flows so easily and comfortably that I barely notice when we arrive at the subway station. I know this is where I should grab the train—I even see the glowing green globes at the subway entrance around the corner—but Nathan is relaying a story about how he met Frank when he was an L2, so I'm ready to ignore it, to keep walking all the way to Washington Heights.

But then Nathan stops. "This you?"

"Oh, right. Yeah." I nod, working to look like I hadn't noticed.

He nods. Neither of us moves.

"Big plans tonight?" he finally asks.

"Yup," I say, offering him a sharp smile. The last thing I'm going to admit is that I have a date with my flannel pajamas and Netflix.

His expression has that edge I recognize from that first meeting in his office, even as his eyes flit across my cheeks, my eyes, my hair. "Well, I hope I didn't keep you too long. Wouldn't want you to be late."

I nod awkwardly. "Right. Well, I'll see you next week. At our meeting. Our work meeting."

"Right." The corner of his mouth ticks up. "Have a good night, Bea."

Then he turns, already starting down the sidewalk. I watch him disappear around the corner before I head down the stairs and get on the subway. It's not until I walk into my apartment an hour later that I realize that I'm still wearing his scarf.

# CHAPTER 13

I somehow manage to navigate my way up to the fourth floor of Vanderbilt Hall on Tuesday while carrying my backpack, my laptop, my phone, and a bottle of the cheapest red wine they had at the liquor store around the corner. That feat alone would justify the purchase, but as I step off the elevator, I remind myself why I bought the wine in the first place: this morning, buried between the text updates from Maggie and Travis about their long-awaited arrival in Miami, was an email alert. I heard back from a law firm.

Unfortunately, it was a form email telling me that they are in a hiring freeze and not looking to take on anyone at this time. Hence the six-dollar red blend in my hand.

Nathan is already waiting outside Frank's office. His attention is on his phone, brow furrowed as he studies the screen, so he doesn't notice me until I step past him to unlock the door.

He looks up and takes in my frown, then the wine. "You brought lunch?"

I throw him a sardonic smile. "No. After waiting eight weeks to hear back about a job, I got an email from Mitchell and Roch today."

"And?"

I step inside, then fall into my usual chair and hold up the bottle. "I'll give you a hint. This is not champagne."

He sits down in the seat beside me. His expression is pensive, and I know he's searching for the right words to say, so I wave them off before he can find them. "It's fine."

And it is. At least now I can move on from my debilitating anxiety over whether the emails even arrived to their recipients to fully embrace the crippling self-doubt as to why the other eighteen firms haven't bothered writing me back at all.

No, the only thing that really bothered me was how quiet my apartment was after I read the email. I usually have some music playing or the TV on, anything to distract me from the solitude. But this morning I had been so anxious to open the email that I neglected the regular order of things, so silence waited as soon as I closed my computer again. A reminder of how alone I was.

Nathan slips his phone into his jacket pocket and clasps his hands together. He's wearing a gray suit today, but no tie, just a blue oxford shirt. He watches me for a minute, like he's picking his words carefully, then says, "Have you heard back from Land and Associates yet?"

"No, why?"

"Because at the bar event, I said I'd introduce you to Marcie Land."

My mind flickers back to that night so many weeks ago, the memory of our conversation in the car on the way to my apartment.

"No, you said you would have introduced me if she had been there. But she wasn't."

"But she will be at a fundraiser for Safe Harbor this Thursday."

I recognize the name of the charity, but I'm still unwilling to connect the dots. "Okay."

"At the Yale Club. Eight o'clock."

He waits. So I wait. It's a long moment of waiting while we stare at each other.

"And?" I finally ask.

His brow furrows. "Are you being purposely obtuse?"

"What do you mean?" I deadpan.

He narrows his eyes on me as that mix of amusement and derision seeps through his expression. "I'm asking if you'd like to come as my plus-one so I can introduce you."

My heart stumbles in my chest. I should say no. I should laugh and go find a corkscrew so I can open this bottle of wine. Because even though I want to go, even though this is the kind of opportunity I have been dreaming about for months, spending time with Nathan outside of school hours feels dangerous.

But instead I find myself saying, "This would not be a date."

"Obviously," he replies solemnly.

"I arrive alone, I leave alone, and I'm under no obligation to talk to you."

"Understood."

I contemplate another moment, trying to mine more disclaimers. But I finally give up and let my head fall back as I groan, "This means I have to network, doesn't it?"

"You never know," he says. "The Yale Club might have some large potted plants in the corners."

I don't hold back my laugh, letting it make my body shake for a moment before I lift my head again, ready to call him an asshole. But the words dissolve on my tongue when I catch his expression, that almost grin teasing his lips as his gaze travels up the line of my neck to my eyes.

Then my phone starts vibrating inside my bag. The low rumbling sound seems to snap Nathan from his trance and he turns away.

I pull the phone out and see Travis's picture on the illuminated screen. Travis rarely calls on a good day, let alone when he's on vacation. The only reason I can think of now would be an emergency, and suddenly I'm remembering that Travis was going to reach out to Josh about that pill.

"Sorry, I should take this," I say.

Nathan nods, already standing up. "I'll meet you at Furman." He's out the door by the second ring, and I quickly answer.

"What's wrong?" I answer.

There's yelling, laughing, and I swear for a moment I hear a steel drum playing the Cure.

Then Maggie's voice explodes on the line. "BEA!"

"Hey," I reply. "Why are you calling from Trav's phone?"

"He's using mine to talk to my grandma." She laughs, and in the background it sounds like someone is organizing a cheer. "Bea, you will never guess what just happened!"

"What happened?" I ask.

"We got to the hotel and dropped off our bags, and Travis kept insisting we go down to this restaurant, and I was so confused because we ate on the plane, but we went and my parents are here and his parents are here, and then he got down on one knee and asked me to marry him!" Another scream, this one right in my ear, rattling my skull.

"What?" I ask, stunned.

"We're getting married!"

Something heavy falls in my chest. Maggie and Travis have been together for so long, I never thought they would get married. It was one of the consolations I clung to when they'd closed on the bed-and-breakfast. They could buy a house together, move away, but at least they weren't married. Our nucleus would remain intact, safe from further fractures.

"Bea?" Maggie says, raising her voice above the commotion on her end. "Are you there?"

I stare at Frank's cluttered bookcase. It takes me a moment to say, "I just . . . didn't think you wanted to get married."

"Oh, come on, Bea," she says. I can actually hear her rolling her eyes. "Marriage is not a bad word."

I shake my head, trying to swallow down the panic. "I know. I'm sorry. I just can't believe it."

"I know! You have to be a bridesmaid, okay? You don't have a choice!" Another squeal. "I have to go. I love you! I'll text you pics of the ring!"

"Bye, Mags. And congrats—" But she's already hung up.

I should really head to class—I'm already a few minutes late— but I don't. Instead, I take my time walking around the block, trying to smother the unease roiling my stomach, the amalgamation of all the worries and anxiety that have been building for weeks. The loneliness, the job search, the pill still rolling around the corners of my brain like it did in that box. Maggie and Travis's engagement is another marker of how much has changed in the past few years.

By the time I make it back to Furman Hall and the lecture room on the fourth floor, there's only ten minutes left of class. I could go in, but I don't want to draw attention to myself. Still, as I lean against the wall in the hallway where I can see into the room through the door's glass window, I realize I don't want to leave, either.

Nathan is standing in front of the class, leaning his long frame against the lectern and listening to a question from one of the students in the front row. He's taken his suit jacket off and pulled up the sleeves of his shirt to reveal his forearms, the muscles dancing under his skin as he spins a dry erase marker between his fingers.

He's good at this. A month ago I wouldn't have dared admit it, but as I watch him nod and smile and answer, there's no denying that he's got everything needed to be a good professor: patience and kindness and intelligence and—

*Stop it*, a voice hisses in the back of my mind.

I shake my head and begin to turn away, but just then he looks over and meets my gaze through the door. I thought I had done a good job shoring up my defenses, but with that brief look—just a half second before he breaks eye contact and continues addressing the class—I know he can see right through me.

There's commotion in the hallway as doors to other classrooms open. A moment later the door to our lecture room opens, too. Students filter out and conversation fills the air as they turn toward the elevators and stairwell.

I should leave. Go back to my office, open that wine, and finish grading last week's assignment. But then I hear my name.

"Beatrice."

I look up. Nathan's standing in the doorway, watching me intently. It's that impassive expression I'm used to, but there's a hint of concern mixed in there, too. Then he nods to the stairs and starts walking with the confidence of someone who knows I will follow.

And I do.

*Damn it.*

# CHAPTER 14

The Washington Arch looms ahead of us, casting a long shadow on the center of the park and framing Fifth Avenue's straight path uptown. I didn't know where I was expecting Nathan to take me when I followed him out of the building, but it wasn't an empty bench in Washington Square Park. Yet that's where we are. And thanks to the cloudless sky and a temperature just above fifty degrees, the rest of NYU seems to have had the same thought. The park is crowded with students lounging on every available surface, talking and laughing and occasionally playing guitar. There's even one guy with a lute.

But Nathan and I sit in silence. It stretches out for a few minutes before he finally speaks.

"What's wrong?" His voice is low, a deep, smooth sound.

"Nothing."

This is a lie, of course. There's so much wrong I'm having a hard time keeping track of it all.

He sighs. "There's something on your mind."

God, how did he notice that? *Why* did he notice that? It's unnerving how he seems to know me so well, and I don't have the defenses to combat it.

"It's nothing."

The corner of his mouth twitches. "Okay."

I roll my eyes. "I hate when you do that."

"Do what?"

"Convey your skepticism without actually saying anything except, like, one word."

"Okay."

Oh my God, he did it *again*.

I let out a frustrated groan. I'm too tired to prop up this anger and it depletes, leaving my body feeling thin and fragile. "It's nothing, Nathan."

He stares at me, waiting for me to continue.

"Fine, okay." I push a few stray curls away from my face. "Two of my best friends just called to tell me they got engaged."

"Is that bad news?"

"No, it's just . . ." My tongue trips over the words. How do I explain it? I had felt like the glue between our group of friends for so long, defined myself by that role. And now it was all falling apart. "Travis and Maggie have been together for years. They love each other and spend all their time working on renovating this house upstate that will never really be renovated, but they don't care because they love doing it. Things are good. I mean, they're *living* together. That alone is a serious commitment. So I don't understand why."

"Why they're getting married?"

"Why *anyone* gets married."

He sighs, and I already know his tone will be sarcastic before he even says, "Well, Bea, when a person falls in love with another person—"

"Oh my God," I say, working to suppress a laugh. "I'm not saying the *act* of marriage. But why take the risk? Why change something that's already working? You make this huge promise to another person when loving them is easy, but no one tells you how that love could just as easily end with a fight about who gets the silverware or how to divide up the sofa."

Nathan leans back, his legs stretched out and his clasped hands resting between his hips. "Sometimes arguing about a sofa is the easiest way to quantify those feelings without admitting that they're still there."

"Tell that to the sofa."

He smiles, and I see a hint of his dimple. It sends a flutter through my body.

"I just don't get it," I continue, flitting my gaze away from his face to where my sneaker kicks at some dirt. "Love is hard enough without chancing a legal mess."

He lets that sit in the air for a moment. "Not all divorces are acrimonious, Bea."

I know what he's really saying: *they're not all like Josh and Jillian*. But even if we both understand the intimation, neither of us acknowledges it.

"I've seen your office, Nathan," I say with a smirk. "You don't pay that rent with amicable splits."

Silence again. His expression is pensive, like he's caught something buried beneath my words and he's examining it, dissecting its layers. Then he leans forward, his elbows on his knees as he seems to study something at the far end of the park. "I almost got married once."

My pulse trips as my brow pinches with confusion. "Are you serious?"

He nods.

"What happened?"

"Life got hard," he says with a shrug. It's another moment before he continues. "I met Rebecca my second year here. We were both doing pro bono work with the same nonprofit. She was brilliant and gorgeous and had the same goals I did. It all just sort of fell into place. We moved in together after just a few months, started planning a future. Then my mom got her MS diagnosis . . ." The words drift off as he seems to get lost in a memory. Then his back straightens and he scratches his jaw. "My parents took out a second mortgage to pay for her treatment, and it still wasn't enough. She had to quit her job sooner than expected, and bills started piling up. They never asked me for help, but they would have lost the house if I didn't. So, after graduation, I turned down the position I had lined up with the nonprofit I'd been working with and started at a private practice instead. It was long hours, stressful, and every weekend I was heading up to see them. It was a lot."

"Is that why you two broke up?"

That muscle in his jaw ticks again. "It contributed to why we broke up."

I let out a long breath and lean back. "Life always gets hard."

His head cocks to the side as if he's considering. "My parents made it look so easy, though. After the breakup, when I went home to see them, I almost felt like I had disappointed them somehow. Then, one morning, I volunteered to take my mom to a doctor's appointment. I wanted to give my dad a break, but he still insisted on coming. And after she went in and we were in the waiting room, I asked him why he had been so adamant. I mean, none of this was easy. He deserved a break. And he just sort of shrugged and smiled and said: 'Love's not supposed to be easy. But if you're lucky, it's simple.'"

*Not easy, just simple*, I think as I let out a long breath.

Nathan turns back to face me, a soft smile teasing his lips. The sun streams down through the branches of the surrounding trees, casting shadows across his face. It highlights the sharp lines of his jaw, the different shades of blue in his eyes.

"What's really bothering you, Bea?" he asks, like he knows the heart of it. He just needs me to say it out loud.

And I think about the years I had spent holding on to love for the people around me, how much I gave to make sure they were happy and safe—only to still be here, in the same place, as they all moved on.

"I feel like I'm getting left behind by everybody I love," I whisper. I hate that I say it even though I don't think I could have kept it trapped inside me any longer.

"But you still love them," he says.

I nod. "Yeah."

He reaches up and tucks a curl behind my ear. "Then it's simple."

Silence. I know I should say something, offer up some wry response, but I can't muster the strength to do anything but maintain his gaze. It feels like he can see everything, all the raw and scary bits, all the scars deep down that I have hidden away. It's a look that leaves me feeling exposed and vulnerable. But for the first time I don't hate it. I don't hate it at all.

# CHAPTER 15

I glance up at the clock above my office door.

4:49 p.m.

That means Marissa Bishop and Jessica Delgado have been sitting across from me dissecting every requirement for their arbitration analysis assignment for forty-nine minutes.

No one told me that a major part of the job of a teaching assistant is to double as a therapist. We listen, particularly in the beginning, when first-year law students are eager and overwhelmed, when even the smartest ones find themselves second-guessing their efforts. I did it, too; after spending three straight days awake studying for my Civil Procedure final, I had stumbled into my TA's office convinced that I would fail, and did she happen to have any information about joining an art commune somewhere? She talked to me for almost an hour, and I left with clear instructions to drink some tea, take a nap, and calm the fuck down. It was the best advice of my life, and I try to keep it in mind every time a student knocks on my door, needing someone to listen.

Except for right now. Because right now it's blatantly clear that Marissa and Jessica don't need anything other than intel about Nathan Asher.

"Does Professor Asher ever stop by campus on days other than Tuesday?" Jessica wonders.

It's the third time she's asked, and I've already told her no twice, so all I can muster now is, "Why don't you just ask him on Tuesday, okay?"

"Is he doing office hours this week?" Marissa interjects. She's biting back a smile, and I know her question has nothing to do with the case study.

"He has a day job, Marissa."

"Oh, I know," she says, resting an elbow on my desk. "I would get married just so I could hire him when I get divorced."

Jessica's eyes light up. "Then we'd get to see him in those suits, like, all the time."

Marissa nods. "With his tie loosened just a little bit—"

"Okay, my office hours are officially done," I say, hoping it distracts from the sudden flush in my cheeks. "You have two weeks before your papers are due, so you can come back if you have more questions, okay? And, Marissa, if I hear that you started another betting pool over who Nathan calls on first in class again, I'm taking a letter off your grade. I'm serious."

Marissa mumbles something as she picks up her bag and walks to the door. Jessica follows close behind, and I can already hear them whispering between themselves as they start down the hall. I want to tell myself that they're reviewing my stellar advice about the assignment, but I suspect they're still contemplating Nathan's tie.

I close my laptop and glance back up at the clock.

5:01 p.m.

*Damn it.* I try to mentally calculate the commute to the Safe Harbor Benefit. If the A train is running on time, I can make it home by five thirty, but I still need to shower and change and do something with my hair—and what was the address of this place again? I'd have to look that up. But first I have to get out of my office before any more students show up.

I grab my laptop, then shove my arms into my coat. A moment later I'm at the door, digging through my bag for the keys to lock it.

"Where's the fire?"

Blake's voice drawls behind me and I close my eyes, willing my patience to stay intact for the next sixty seconds.

"Home. I have plans tonight," I say, turning around to find him leaning against the wall beside me, his attention on his phone as always.

"Yeah. I know."

I pause. "What?"

"You and Nathan Asher. The Yale Club thing."

My back straightens as if I've been spotted without my camouflage for the very first time. "How do you know about that?"

"Not by choice, trust me. " Blake sighs. "Can you tell him that you share that voicemail with other people? He left a message that was like two minutes long, talking about harbors or something, and it took up all the space. Or, better yet, you could actually check the voicemail once in a while."

I narrow my eyes at him. "Why didn't he just text me?"

"I don't know. Maybe take your phone off silent after you leave class."

"Oh, right," I say, suddenly remembering how my phone was buzzing from the bowels of my bag during Marissa and Jessica's visit.

He hums, finally looking up from his screen to give me a sly smile. "What's going on there, anyway?"

"Going on where?"

His glare becomes pointed. "You and Nathan."

"It's nothing. He's . . ." My voice fades as I try to pinpoint my next words.

"He's what?"

The question lands like a lead weight in my brain. Who is Nathan Asher to me, anyway? My colleague? That feels too thin. My former friend's divorce attorney? Even as that label forms, it dissolves, leaving an odd chill in its wake. No, he isn't that. He hasn't been that for a while. So, is he just the guy I made out with once? It's objectively true, but also seems laughable now. These are all facts, yes, but they're also facets of something else, something greater that's formed without me even realizing it.

Nathan Asher is my friend.

How the hell did that happen?

I blink and realize Blake is staring at me expectantly, waiting for an answer.

"He's temporary," I reply.

Blake hums. "All the good ones are."

I roll my eyes and push past him. "Go away, Blake."

Then I head down the hall.

～

I walk through my front door at 5:42.

Not horrible, I rationalize as I frantically strip before jumping in my lukewarm shower. I already laid my clothes out for tonight, and I can probably get away with minimal makeup. All I have to do is get ready as quickly as possible and mentally review all the research I've done about Marcie Land and her firm. No problem.

Except that when I dry off and start getting dressed, Blake's inquiry still sits in the center of my brain.

I shouldn't let it get under my skin. Blake is a gossip; he lives for finding out secrets before anyone else, which means he probably goes looking for secrets that aren't even there to begin with, especially about the dating life of new, seemingly available professors.

Except that Blake hadn't asked if Nathan was seeing anyone. He asked about Nathan and me. That could easily lead to assumptions, rumors being whispered by any student who walks by Frank's office and sees us together. Maybe they had already.

The solution is obvious, of course: I should just stop meeting with him before class. We never discuss anything related to work anyway, so it would in no way hinder his ability to do his job. But the idea sends a shot of panic through my chest. Because I don't want to stop.

When did I become so dependent on it? When did those afternoon conversations begin to actually mean something? My pulse stutters as the next inevitable thought echoes past the others: what if it doesn't for him? I'm almost embarrassed that I haven't thought about it before. After all, I'm the one who shows up there week after week, too. What if he only tolerates it? What if he's humoring me?

I try to ignore the thought as I throw on my coat and rush to the door. *Keep it professional*, I remind myself. It's the only thing that matters. It's the only way to make it through this unscathed.

~

I pull my phone from my clutch as I emerge from the subway at Forty-Second Street and check the time.

8:12 p.m.

*Shit*. I'm twelve minutes late.

I quickly send him a text to tell him I'm close, then slip my phone back in my bag as I wait for the light to change. As soon as it turns green, I bolt across the crosswalk toward the club's entrance on the corner.

Nathan might wait five minutes, maybe ten, but I can't imagine that he'd stick around past that. I'm still practically sprinting as I approach the front of the Yale Club, though, holding on to the thread of hope that I'm wrong.

There's a group of sharply dressed people congregating in front of the club, along with a steady stream of pedestrians walking by. My gaze slides over all of them, looking for Nathan's imposing height, his familiar mussed hair.

I find him standing by the far window. His hands on his hips and a line of worry between his eyebrows as he looks down the street. The wind is sending his short hair in every direction, tousled and chaotic and in perfect opposition to the clean lines of his coat.

It's hard to quantify my reaction. There's relief, overwhelming relief that he's here. That he waited. But there's surprise, too, because he appears to be searching the crowd with the same anxiety that I felt tightening my chest just moments before.

Then he turns his head and meets my gaze. He smiles, and everything else in my mind bottoms out.

His lips have settled into a lopsided grin by the time I stop in front of him.

"You waited," I say before I can stop myself.

"Did you think I would blow you off?" he asks, his voice low, like he's trying to act offended.

"I was hoping you blew me off," I reply, shifting my weight from one foot to the other and failing to dampen my own smile.

We stare at each other for a long moment, and I can almost feel something shift. A click of a new lens that changes the perspective ever so slightly. His gaze travels across my face, studying the light dusting of blush on my freckles, the subtle red tint on my lips. I suddenly feel self-conscious.

"I should have worn more makeup," I blurt out. His brow furrows, like he's been snapped out of his train of thought, but I barrel on. "It's just impossible with freckles because if you wear too much it looks like you're trying to cover them up and you can never really cover them up, so then you just look like you're wearing too much makeup, you know?"

"No."

I roll my eyes and am about to reply with a cutting remark, but a gust of wind cuts me off. It sends a spike of cold down my spine.

Nathan notices. His gaze snaps down to my old wool coat, then to my neck. It's only then that I remember that in the rush to leave my apartment, I hadn't only grabbed my coat, I had grabbed a scarf, too. His scarf. It's wrapped tightly around my neck, a soft barrier against the chill.

He stares at it for a moment, and I half expect him to ask for it back. But he doesn't. He swallows, then looks away, nodding to the door. "Let's get you inside."

The warmth of the Yale Club envelops us as soon as we enter. Not just the temperature, but the wood-paneled walls, the smell of pine in the air as we make our way through the crowd in the foyer. I take off my coat and his scarf and give both to the waiting attendant. Nathan does the same, then turns around, pausing as his gaze snags on my clothes.

"Oh God, what?" I ask, my tone only slightly panicked as I look down at my cream-colored sweater. It's cropped so it just grazes the high waistline of my blue pencil skirt. The outfit looked great back in the mirror in my apartment, but now I'm not so sure. He's staring down my body, his expression unreadable. "Is there a stain on it or something?"

"No. No, you look . . ." His voice fades without finishing the thought. Then he clears his throat and nods to the staircase. "We're upstairs."

I hesitate, but his hand finds the small of my back, urging me forward. It's barely a touch, but I can still feel it in every nerve ending, like an electric charge has passed from his body to mine.

There are a pair of double doors at the top of the stairs that open to a sprawling reception room. It's already half full, dark suits and black dresses and the din of conversation wafting through. A few heads turn as we enter; I know some of the gazes are for me, but most are for Nathan.

I steal a glance at him as well. I don't think I've seen this suit before—its blue is more vibrant than the navy ones I'm so familiar with—but it's cut in a similar way, accentuating the broad lines of his shoulders.

I look away, working to keep my tone as even as possible as I say, "So what is this event, exactly?"

"You're telling me you didn't google Safe Harbor before showing up?" he asks, grabbing two flutes of champagne from a passing waiter and offering me one.

"Oh, I absolutely googled it," I say, taking the glass. In fact, I had googled it almost immediately after he invited me. "Safe Harbor is one of the largest family shelters in the city, operating five buildings that not only house four hundred families, but also provides job training and childcare to their residents. This benefit is one of a few throughout the year that accounts for a majority of their private funding." I mentally pat myself on the back for remembering the details.

"Then why are you asking?"

"Because Google didn't explain why a bunch of lawyers would spend their Thursday night being altruistic."

He smiles, then takes a sip of his champagne as he lets his eyes scan the crowd. "Well, it's a good cause, and Marcie can be very . . . persuasive."

I pause. "This is her event?"

Nathan nods. "She's been on the board of Safe Harbor for a while now."

"I . . . I didn't know that."

"She doesn't publicize it," he says. "It's a personal thing. Her family ended up relying on Safe Harbor more than a few times while she was growing up. When she was in a position to give back, she did."

I tilt my chin up to look at him. "How do you know all that?"

"I told you, she and I are friends."

"Yes, but *how* are you friends?"

"I used to do pro bono work for Safe Harbor."

My eyebrows knit together, and I know he can see me struggling to make the pieces fit.

"What?" he asks.

"I'm trying to connect point A to point B."

He shrugs one shoulder. "Most of the women there need help leaving bad situations, keeping their families together, just getting a break. And I practice family law. It's *why* I practice family law."

I pause as the memory of our walk after we left the hospital comes back to me. "Wait. Is Safe Harbor the nonprofit where you were going to work after law school?"

He nods.

"So why don't you work with them anymore?"

His back straightens ever so slightly, and some of the openness in his expression dims. It's almost like I can see the mask snap into place, shielding some unseen vulnerability. "I'd like to, but after I made partner, the priority was to grow the firm. I had to focus on our clients, and that doesn't leave a lot of free time for anything else."

"Like taking over an L1 seminar for a friend, right?" I say, a wry smile on my lips.

He pauses, as if he hadn't noticed the fallacy of his argument until now. Then his posture loosens again, and he smiles. "Right."

I glance around the room, the growing crowd of New York's elite. Nathan said he not only did pro bono work with Safe Harbor when he was in school—it was where he met his ex-girlfriend, Rebecca. I wonder if she's here now, one of these statuesque women clad in an expensive black suit and pristine makeup, if Nathan is keeping an eye out for her, too.

"Well, that's too bad," I finally say. "But I guess it's hard to find time to help people when you have to maintain your hourly rate, and your corner office, and your penthouse apartment—"

"I don't have a penthouse apartment."

"Shut up, I'm not done." I wave him off and continue, keeping track by counting on my fingers. "And the magazine spreads, the designer suits, the expensive dinners, the caviar for breakfast . . ."

He shoots me a disappointed look, but one tinged with amusement. "I still help people, Bea. Maybe not in the same way, but I do. I've even had some clients get back together."

I roll my eyes. "Oh, come on."

"I'm serious."

"Name one client that got back together with their ex, Nathan."

"Vanessa Goodridge. She and her husband were in the office to sign their divorce papers and ended up having sex in the bathroom."

I blink. "No."

"They were so loud the receptionist had to take a mental health day."

It takes a moment for my brain to process this. "How does that even happen?"

"From what I understand, Mr. Goodridge was trying to be romantic, so he sent her an apology text right before the meeting, along with an explicit photo."

My mouth drops open. "Like a dick pic?"

He nods.

I cringe. "Ew."

A wry grin starts at one corner of his mouth again. "What?"

"I know this might come as a shock to you, Nathan, but most women don't find a photo of a penis romantic."

A woman walking past us turns to look at me, her eyes wide. I don't acknowledge her, even as Nathan offers her an apologetic smile.

"What constitutes 'romantic'?" he replies once she's out of earshot.

"That completely depends on the woman."

"Okay. What about you?"

I scoff, even as a rush of heat bursts through my body. This conversation is veering into dangerous territory.

*It's all dangerous territory*, a nagging voice says somewhere in my brain.

"I don't know," I blurt out. "A working water heater."

He pauses. "You find utilities romantic?"

"No, but that's the point. If someone went to the effort of getting the hot water fixed at my apartment, it's because they know I really want a hot shower, and *that's* romantic."

"So if someone bought you a dozen roses, you'd give them back?"

"I'm not saying it's not a nice gesture; it's just . . ." I sigh, motioning vaguely in front of me. "Flowers and chocolate and jewelry, it's all bought for the sole purpose of being romantic, and that automatically defeats the purpose." His blue eyes are studying me so intensely that my mouth snaps shut and I need to look away, take a moment to formulate my thoughts. "If something is really, truly romantic, it isn't self-referential. You know?"

"No."

I pinch the bridge of my nose, already regretting this conversation. But it's too late to back out now, so I keep going. "Okay, take my mom. She's been married six times."

Nathan's eyebrows bob up. "Six?"

I nod. "And every one of those husbands made these grand gestures: vacations and jewelry and cars. And yeah, my mom loved it. But there wasn't much more to it than that. Because none of that actually represented love, just the appearance of it. Which is why she's on husband number six. But then you have my grandparents. They were married for sixty-two years and met when my grandmother's Buick broke down. It was one of the coldest nights on record, and she had to get it towed to the closest garage, which just happened to be my grandfather's. But she didn't fall in love with him because he fixed her car. In fact, after he was done and told her how much it was going to cost, she was so pissed she stood there berating him in front of all his employees."

"Imagine that," Nathan murmurs with a smirk.

I ignore him. "Then, halfway through her tirade, he just walks out. Like, turns and leaves the room. Obviously, when he comes back a minute later, she's even angrier. Calls him the worst names you can think of before she just storms out. And there, parked right in front of the garage, is her car, running with the heat on full blast. He had left in the middle of her meltdown to go turn on her car so that it would be warm for her when she was done yelling at him. He didn't do it to get her in bed, he probably didn't even think he would see her again. But he still did it. *That's* romantic."

Nathan narrows his eyes at me. "I'm pissed that you're making sense right now."

I shrug. "Romance exists. It's just so hard to define, we stopped trying and told ourselves we can buy it instead."

He seems to think about it for a minute, taking a sip of his drink as he looks out across the room. "I still think Mrs. Goodridge enjoyed that dick pic, though."

My laugh is so loud that a few people nearby turn their heads to look at us. Nathan doesn't care; he's smiling down at me, his eyes dancing with amusement.

I want to ask him how he does it—how he turns off this person who smiles and listens and jokes and becomes that other person who doesn't mind taking money from heartbroken people who need someone to listen and care. But it feels too close to that place that we somehow agreed not to go. An unspoken truce that keeps this working relationship in play.

So instead I just let my laughter fade and shake my head. "You're an asshole."

We forget about Mrs. Goodridge then. In fact, we forget about almost everything. The room feels like it falls away as the conversation flows, the push and the pull that seems to settle naturally when we're together.

We're halfway through our second glass of champagne when Nathan's eyes fixate on someone behind me.

"There's Marcie," he says.

I turn to see Marcie Land standing just across the room. I don't know how I missed her before. She's almost as tall as Nathan, and her long dark hair is the only thing that mutes her bright orange-and-white silk caftan. Two men in suits are talking to her, but she looks bored; she's glancing away from them as they talk, her eyes skimming the crowd until they find Nathan, and she smiles. A moment later she's saying something to her companions, then she turns and starts moving toward us.

"Oh God." I whip back around to face Nathan, eyes wide. "Distract me."

He frowns. "What?"

"I need you to distract me."

"Why?"

"Because if I'm distracted by something really dumb or offensive, I can't get nervous, and you're really good at saying things that are dumb *and* offensive, so . . ." I shrug like the conclusion here is obvious.

He seems to be mulling it over as he glances past me to where I know Marcie is approaching.

"Something to distract you," he murmurs.

"Yes."

He leans in close to my ear. "What do you think would have happened if your neighbor hadn't interrupted us that night outside your building?"

I'm struck dumb for a moment before a wave of rage rolls under my skin. He watches as it blooms across my face, smiling that goddamn smile that is so annoyingly perfect I want to scream.

"I can't believe you just went there, you smug—"

"Nate!" Marcie's voice cuts me off as she arrives between us and embraces Nathan in a hug.

"Marcie," he replies as she pulls away.

"What are you doing here? You never come to these things," she says, sweeping her dark hair behind her shoulder. Marcie is well over sixty but carries herself as if age is an abstract concept, something that doesn't apply to her.

"I have to show up sometimes, or how would you know to miss me?"

She laughs. "I assure you, love, I don't miss you regardless." She sees me then and does a quick audit of my face, as if she's trying to place me in her memory. "And who's this?"

"Marcie, this is Beatrice Nilsson. She came into my office recently and tried to nail my balls to the side of the building."

My mouth falls open and my eyes dart to Nathan. He only stares back, a hint of amusement dancing in his eyes.

There's a moment of silence, then Marcie's head falls back as she laughs.

"That is the best thing I've heard all night," she says, cackling. "Beatrice, you're officially my new favorite person."

Relief loosens my chest and I offer her a smile. "It's just Bea."

"Bea," Marcie repeats. "Well, I'm glad Nate found a woman who gives him as much shit as he deserves."

Both Nathan and I shake our heads, motioning vaguely between one another.

"Oh, no. No, no," I say with a scoff.

"Bea is a colleague," Nathan continues. "And about to graduate from NYU Law. She's the TA for that Conflict Resolution course I took over for Frank."

Marcie turns to me again. "You're a teaching assistant for Frank Landry?"

I nod. "For the past year."

"My lord, you deserve an honorary degree just for that," Marcie says, and laughs again. Then she turns back to Nathan. "How's that going, by the way?"

"Good," he replies. It's an answer that reveals nothing.

"Good? I would have run screaming after the first day." Marcie rolls her eyes. "Teaching is *not* for everybody."

Nathan smiles that lawyer smile, a mask to hide whatever the hell he's really thinking. If he's embarrassed or if there's something else that prompted it. Regardless, I find myself opening my mouth.

"Nathan's fantastic at it."

They both turn to look at me. Nathan betrays a half second of surprise, while Marcie smiles.

"Is that so?" she says.

I know I've already said too much, but I also can't seem to stop. "I just mean, most of my professors are there to do a job and leave, but Nathan really listens to his students. And he teaches in a way that helps them understand the concepts in a practical way. He's doing an incredible job."

Marcie's smile broadens as she steals a glance at Nathan. "Well. Can't say I'm surprised."

I feel Nathan's eyes on me, but I don't turn to meet his gaze. I'm scared of what I might see.

"So, tell me, Bea," Marcie continues. "What's your concentration?"

"Healthcare rights. I graduate in May."

Her eyebrows bob up at that. "Do you have anything lined up after that?"

"I'm still exploring my options," I say, hoping the words mask my desperation. "I'd like to stay in New York and join a private practice. Somewhere I can get some experience with pharmaceutical litigation."

Marcie nods, an absent gesture as she seems to assess me again. "Looking to make the fuckers pay, then."

I let out a nervous laugh. "Something like that, yes."

The corner of her mouth turns up in a cagey grin. That must have been the right answer. "When do you take the bar?"

"July."

"If I don't press charges," Nathan says offhandedly.

I shoot him a sharp smile. "The judge would agree with me."

Marcie laughs again, delighted. "Hold on to this one, Nate."

He looks down at me, and that half smile appears from behind the lip of his champagne glass just before he takes a sip. I've seen that smile before, but this time it sends a rush of heat to my cheeks, and I have to dart my gaze away. It lands on Marcie. She studies my face for a moment, then glances between us, as if trying to decipher a code that she might have missed before. When she doesn't seem to find it, she brings her attention back squarely to me. "We should get together and talk some more. I'll get your information from Nate and have my office reach out."

My mouth falls open, but it takes a moment before words come out. "That would be amazing, thank you."

Marcie nods even as she looks past me, smiling and waving at someone who just arrived.

"Fucking Simonsen," she murmurs under her breath. "All right, I have to go talk to him so he doesn't follow me around like a goddamn puppy all night. It was nice to meet you, Bea. We'll talk soon. Nate, finish your drink before you sneak out of here. It's expensive."

Then she kisses his cheek and is gone.

Nathan and I watch her leave, and the hum of the surrounding conversations disappears under the weight of the silence between us. It's a long moment before I look up at him again. His eyes are on me, too, but the usual sharp edge of his expression is gone, and a specific kind of warmth has replaced it. I try to say something, assign words to the conflicted thoughts running through my mind. But I only stand there with my mouth agape and my brow furrowed.

He finally cocks his head to the side and throws me a lifeline. "Want to get out of here?"

# CHAPTER 16

I'm going to eat food with Nathan Asher. Not dinner, I remind myself. I refuse to call it dinner; dinner is too much like a *date*, and this is most definitely not a *date*. This is food after a business appointment.

That's the mantra I repeat in my mind as we walk down Forty-Fourth Street, our steps in time with each other. I'm in four-inch heels, but I still wish they were higher, then I could pretend we were on an even playing field. Of course, I could be wearing six-inch platforms and he would still tower over me. It's like nature's ensured he'll always have the literal upper hand.

"This okay?"

Nathan's deep voice snaps me from my train of thought, and I look up to see that he's stopped in front of a diner. It's one of those twenty-four-hour places that looks like it's been at this corner in Midtown since the fifties and hasn't changed since opening day. Through the window I can see fluorescent lighting, sterile Formica tables, and cracked pleather booths. It's devoid of any ambiance whatsoever. In other words, perfect.

"Yeah," I say, shrugging one shoulder as if I don't care one way or the other.

He holds the door open and then follows me inside, past the long counter to a booth near the windows. I slide in one side and take off my coat as he slides in the other, bending his tall frame to fit. His white shirt stretches across his chest to accommodate the movement, and I'm suddenly hit by the memory of how that body so easily enveloped me that night against my building.

I cross my legs and clear my throat, praying the red light from the neon OPEN sign above hides the flush in my cheeks. But now my body is too still, so I grab one of the menus at the end of the table and look down the long list of food. Or at least I pretend to look. I'm too distracted to read anything. I finally give up when the waitress appears, and after Nathan orders a cheeseburger, I just say, "Make that two."

She nods and Nathan thanks her, eliciting a coy smile from her stern face. At this moment, I can see why he's good at his job, why people are so eager to hire him. When his eyes are on you, it feels like you're the center of the world.

And when she leaves, he turns them to me.

"So," he says.

"So."

"You think I'm doing an incredible job?"

I roll my eyes. "Listen, I was just—"

He smiles. "No, I appreciate the endorsement."

Is that what I had done? I hadn't even realized it as it was happening, I had just jumped into action, the same way I always did when I felt like someone I cared about needed support.

*Someone I cared about . . .*

Ohmygod.

"It wasn't an *endorsement*. I just . . . approve of the job you're doing on a professional level."

"I think that's the definition of an endorsement, Bea."

I let out a long breath, sending a few curls bouncing away from my face. "Whatever."

He chuckles to himself, the sound so low it barely registers except for the vibration it sends through the air and into my bones.

*Keep it light*, I remind myself. *You only have to fill thirty minutes and this will be done.*

"Why are you a lawyer?" I ask, and almost wince.

*Jesus. Way to jump straight in there.*

A wry smile tugs at his lips. "Well, my mom was a paralegal when I was a kid. She always brought her casework home, and I would help her with research and organizing files. It was probably more to keep me busy when I was younger, but in high school she got me a job at her firm. It was mostly personal injury, and I was just answering the phone, but that was enough to sell me on it. I decided on family law after I started interning with Safe Harbor."

I nod, slotting the bits of information into my brain for future reference. "What does your dad do?"

"He's a chemistry teacher at my old high school."

"And where's that?"

The waitress walks by and deposits two waters without a word. I grip the cold glass in my hands as Nathan offers her a nod and takes a sip of his before answering.

"Great Barrington. Western Massachusetts."

My eyes widen, a rare giddiness flaring in my chest. "Do you know Dorinda?"

"Who?"

"From *Real Housewives*! Dorinda!"

His expression is blank.

"You know, *The Real Housewives of New York City*," I say, motioning in the air between us like it helps illustrate my point. "She's from Great Barrington! Or maybe she just owns a house there? Anyway, there was this one episode where all the housewives went up there for the weekend, and . . ."

My voice fades as his face contorts with confusion.

My shoulders slump, defeated. "Never mind."

"Okay," he replies, taking another sip of his water. "What about you?"

"What about me?"

"Did you grow up in New York?"

*Shit*. I hadn't considered how he might turn the personal questions around on me. I try to mask my sudden apprehension as I casually shrug one shoulder. "No. I was born in Connecticut but I moved around a lot growing up."

"And why's that?"

I pretend something in the corner of the room catches my eye. I study the empty space as I work to somehow fortify that part of me that suddenly feels dangerously exposed. The chink in my armor. "After every relationship, my mom wanted to move. So obviously, given five divorces and just . . . innumerable breakups, we moved a lot. There was Minneapolis, Atlanta, Dallas, Chicago, and then we moved to Pittsburgh my senior year of high school. I moved to New York for college and I haven't left."

I shrug, as if that punctuates my point, and hope that he'll come up with some inane question or provocative comment to fill the silence, but he doesn't. He just stares at me, his expression unreadable. I know he can fake a smile; I've seen him do it. The small talk, the pleasantries. And God, I want to see that skill now, if only to provide me with some cover. But instead, he just gives me that steady eye contact, his eyes slowly narrowing, and then: "Like the countess."

I blink. "What?"

"From *Real Housewives*. She moved to New York from Connecticut, too, right?" He looks genuinely interested, even as that corner of his mouth begins to tick up again.

I smile. "I didn't marry royalty, though."

"Well, there's still time," he says, and brings his water to his mouth, hiding his grin behind the rim of the glass. Still, I can make out the dimple there in his cheek, so beautiful that for a split second I think I could get addicted to making it appear.

It hits me then: I like him. And I hate that I like him. I hate that this person who is ruining the lives of people I love is someone that I like, someone I could've fallen for. And if it wasn't for Josh and Jillian's divorce, maybe I would have. Maybe he would have spoken to me at that bar event and I wouldn't know enough to hate him. But I have to. And I need to keep reminding myself of that before I get in too deep.

*Too late*, a voice whispers in my head.

I ignore it.

Our food arrives a few minutes later. The waitress doesn't look at me as she puts my plate down; her attention is on Nathan.

"Do you need anything else?" she asks him.

He shakes his head and thanks her as I shove a fry into my mouth.

Conversation blessedly moves on to other topics then—school and work and favorite restaurants and least-favorite books—and for a while I forget to try to quantify whatever it is that we're doing here. It's comfortable, and I don't even remember to check the clock as he presses me about my future plans, and I dig further about Marcie and his work with Safe Harbor. In fact, I don't even know what time it is when the waitress reappears, taking our empty plates away.

Nathan asks her for the check and then turns back to me, a smile tugging at the corner of his lips.

*I want to kiss him again.*

The thought lands squarely in the center of my brain. It's like a splash of cold water on the growing warmth in my chest. A reminder that I shouldn't be here right now. And I definitely shouldn't be enjoying that look on his face as much as I am.

I work to maintain my blank expression, to disguise the fact that the thin thread keeping my composure together is fraying. And I absolutely, positively can't let it snap. So I do the only thing I can think of: try to make him feel as off-kilter as I do.

"Why did you invite me tonight?" I ask.

"Because you wanted to meet Marcie."

"But why introduce me to Marcie?"

His gaze skims across my face. I know he can feel the challenge; it's laced in my tone.

"It's simple. I know her and you wanted to meet her."

*Simple.* The word lands heavy in my brain, along with the last time he said it to me. *Not easy, just simple.*

"But why do you care?"

He was about to take the last sip of his water, but the glass hovers near his lips as he looks at me. "Excuse me?"

"I just mean . . ." My voice stalls and I try to pinpoint the exact words I want to say. "You don't have to care. You don't even have to be here right now. I'm a pain in the ass and your job would probably be a lot easier by not dealing with me, so why bother?"

"You're not a pain in the ass, Bea."

I snort out a laugh, but I can still feel my cheeks warm.

"What?"

"Come on. I know I'm a lot."

His brow furrows as if he has no idea what I'm talking about. "What does that mean?"

"I just . . ." My tongue darts out to wet my lips. "I'm too much. I feel too much."

"It's better than not feeling anything at all," he says. His voice is deep and gravelly.

"Except people don't see it that way. They see that I'm too angry and too opinionated. I'm abrasive and let my emotions get the better of me, and that's a lot for people to deal with, so—"

"Who told you that?"

I sigh, working to make my tone light, like I'm joking. Like this isn't the most honest I've been with anyone in my entire life. "Everyone has told me that."

His blue eyes narrow on me. "You're not a lot, Bea. You care about the people in your life. You defend them and you don't try to be anyone other than yourself. If anybody has a problem with that, it just means they've learned somewhere along the line that those things are faults. That's for them to work out, not you."

I try to prop up a wry smile, but it's fragile, a flimsy defense that's only moments away from falling.

"Don't do that," I say.

He blinks. "Do what?"

"Act like we're friends or something."

"Aren't we?"

I roll my eyes. "We went over this in Frank's office when you took the job, Nathan. We're colleagues."

The air seems to still around us as he studies my face for a long moment, like he's trying to pinpoint exactly what caused the subtle shift.

"Right." He nods absently to himself, like he's considering. "And what about when the job is over?"

"Then we're nothing. I mean, you'll still be the asshole who's actively working to tear my friend's life apart, right?"

That unreadable expression I remember from his office is on his face now, like he's seen my defenses go up and he's suddenly donned his own invisible suit of armor. It's such a slight change I think the average person wouldn't even notice it, but I do. It's uncomfortably familiar.

Except I know how my armor developed. I recognize how years of transience and disappointment required its fortification. Where did his come from?

I don't ask. The question feels too dangerous, a Trojan horse whose answer could reveal too much, leave both of us too exposed.

"And I have a very strict 'no asshole' policy in my life, so . . ." I shrug as if my pulse isn't thundering in my ears.

"Oh really?"

"Yup."

He throws me a sharp smile, so similar to the one from his office the first time we met that my heart drops.

"You didn't seem to have a problem that night outside your building."

A deafening silence falls. The words hit a vulnerable part in my chest, the one that still feels guilty for that kiss. But despite how much I had worried about it over the past few weeks, fretted and stressed and chastised myself, I had never assumed he would use it against me as if it was nothing but leverage.

"Like I said," I reply, mirroring his lawyer smile even as my voice shakes. "Asshole."

I watch as he slowly registers my reaction, how the regret flashes across his face, and his gaze softens.

"Shit," he murmurs, his head falling forward. "I'm sorry, Bea—"

I shake my head as embarrassment engulfs my chest. God, I'm actually thankful for it. Grateful for yet another reminder of why I shouldn't be here. "Have a good night, Nathan. And fuck you."

I grab my coat and scarf and launch myself out of the booth, hitting the edge of the table so our empty glasses clatter against the Formica surface. I don't apologize and I don't wait for him to say anything. I head straight for the door and walk out into the cool night air.

My pace is brisk as I head toward Fifth Avenue. It's colder than it was when we arrived, but I barely feel it. My anger is still too hot beneath my skin.

What was I thinking?

I already crossed a line tonight by going to Marcie's event, but this? There aren't any excuses for this, no justification for sitting down and eating food with that man. Nothing except temptation, and that only feeds my resentment. Because even now I can feel that itch of regret for leaving. And that's even more terrifying.

I continue forward as I pull my phone out and use my app to request a car. It's four minutes away and I have just pressed the accept button when I hear the heavy footsteps behind me. A wide, lumbering gait that makes my heart trip at the same time as I hear his voice.

"Bea, wait."

I don't.

He reaches my side, and it's almost comical how he has to slow his steps to match my quick pace. "I'm sorry—"

"Go away."

"Jesus," he growls, running a hand through his thick hair. Then he reaches for my elbow, a soft but firm grip. "Will you stop?"

I whip around to face him, pulling my arm away. The buildings around us are dark except for the lights of a dry cleaner across the street. It sends hard shadows across his face, his stubbled jaw.

"Is this all a joke to you?"

His hands go to his hips. "Come on—"

"No, I'm serious. Do you feel like less of an asshole when you make me feel like shit?"

He lets out a long sigh. "Of course not."

"Then why did you invite me to come tonight?"

"I just . . ." His voice trails off, and it's silent for a minute before he continues. "I was just trying to be nice."

"Being nice won't make me forget who you are!" I say, forcing a sharp tone that ends up sounding dull and hollow.

He stares at me from under his brow, his mouth a grim line across his face. In the shadows, his eyes look obsidian, so black and so dark they're startling.

"Then what the hell will, Bea?"

I don't have any words to answer him. I try to keep my chin high, my shoulders squared, but I still feel that thread fraying, my regret over the last ten minutes turning into something else entirely as bits of my armor fall to the ground.

Then he takes a step toward me. My heart jumps to a thunderous pace, but I keep my eyes locked with his as he takes another step. Then another. He's within inches of me now, and his expression has a new, hard edge to it.

"You're an asshole," I whisper. It's my last line of defense, words that I desperately want to be true, even as my body reveals the lie.

"I know," he murmurs. His voice is so deep and strained it's like he's begging for the same thing.

Then he takes another step. He is almost flush with my body now; the edge of his jacket skims against my chest. It's too close, and my body is too honest. I know he can hear the quiver in my breath, he can see the throbbing pulse point in my neck. And the only rational part of my brain still working is telling me to touch him, to pull his body to mine and do something about this ache.

I can see that same desire there in his eyes, too. A hungry tinge to his expression as he slowly dips his head down, enough that his lips hover above mine.

"You promised not to kiss me again," I breathe.

He stills, and our warm breath intertwines for a long moment.

"Then I won't," he murmurs.

But he doesn't move away. A moment later I feel his hands gently slide through the open front of my coat. They take hold of my hips, his thumbs brushing against where my sweater meets the waist of my skirt. It's a slow, lazy motion that belies the strength of his grip, the firm but subtle pull of my body to his.

I don't fight it. I can't. All I can do is lean into his touch as his hands move up so his thumbs are just under my sweater, brushing against my bare skin.

He leans in, too, resting his forehead against mine so we are both looking down at where his hands hold my body, as they continue to drift slowly upward. God, I want to look away, but I can't. Every problem that existed just a few minutes ago has disappeared from my mind, and all I can think about is how his thumbs barely graze the underside of my bra, how his fingers wrap around my rib cage like he's afraid I might bolt.

His breath is growing hoarse, but then so is mine. Labored and deep, intermingling between us. And even though he's not kissing me, everything about this moment feels so much more intimate.

Then a loud voice cuts through the air. "Beatrice?"

Our foreheads are still resting against one another as we turn to look. A tan-colored car is parked on the curb. The driver hangs out the window, his expression impatient.

"Are you Beatrice?" he asks.

It takes me a moment to straighten my back, to find my voice. "Yeah. Yes."

"You ready?"

"One second," Nathan says to the driver, and then he turns back to me, his face still so close that I can feel his breath on my cheeks.

"I need to go," I say.

"No you don't."

I want to agree with him. I want to stay and let his hands explore every inch of me. And that thought scares me so much that I take a step back. "Yes, I do."

A muscle in his jaw ticks as his grip on my body loosens and I slip out of his arms.

I start toward the car but within a few strides he's there first, opening the door for me. I slide into the back seat, working hard to keep my eyes off him. Unfortunately, I fail. My gaze travels up to his blue eyes, and my heart tumbles again.

"Thanks for inviting me tonight. And for dinner," I say, forcing a smile onto my lips.

He smiles back, tight and small. "Anytime."

Neither of us move as a million other words tumble through my head, but none of them leave my tongue. Finally, he closes the car door and knocks his fist on the roof, a signal for the driver to go. And he does, propelling us down Forty-Fourth Street so quickly that I don't have time to look back and see if Nathan's watching me leave.

# CHAPTER 17

I spend Friday refusing to think about the not-kiss. Not while I'm brushing my teeth or in the shower, not while I reorganize my closet or when I clean the fridge out for the second time. Because it was, by definition, not a kiss. Technically, it wasn't anything at all. Which is great, really, because last night was just business. That's what I tell myself as I separate my colored laundry from the whites. I went to the event to meet Marcie and nothing else about the night mattered.

But even as I lug my laundry bag and backpack out of my apartment to head to the laundromat, I know I'm not being honest with myself. Yes, I had wanted to meet Marcie, but there was also the thrill of who had invited me. A deep-seated need to spend time with him outside of school, spar with him, coax that damn dimple from his cheek. And somewhere in the back of my brain, I also know that will probably never happen again.

No matter what his motivation last night, I made it clear with Nathan where I stand. Or at least, where I want him to think I stand. I could have asked him to come home with me—I'm pretty sure he was hoping I would—but when I stepped away, he had simply watched me go. He hadn't pressured me to stay. He hadn't even really asked. Every fight felt like foreplay, and maybe he assumed it would end in the same inevitable way. When it didn't, he simply moved on.

That's probably it. In fact, he's probably out with someone else right now. Images of him laughing with her, kissing her, bringing her home to his bed flood my mind, and I'm suddenly uncomfortable. Blindsided by something that should have been a given. Of course Nathan is dating. He's just not dating me.

That sobering thought keeps me company as I ride down the elevator.

The weight of both the laundry and my books and my laptop has me hunched over as I waddle through the lobby. My landlord and Idris are there arguing with a few construction workers, but I ignore them, shuffling out the doors and up five blocks until I reach the laundromat.

It's barely five o'clock, so the sun is still up when I reach my destination. I drop my bag on the linoleum floor, reveling in the pastel colors of the large room, how the late-afternoon light softens the harsh glare of the fluorescents above. For the next few hours, at least. It's empty, too, except for an older man who's seated in the corner waiting for a dryer to finish, and so blissfully quiet that I let out a relieved sigh.

I can't even remember the last time I was able to sit down with a book and absorb the text without any distractions. And yet, as soon as I have a washer running and settle down in one of the plastic chairs with my bar prep book open in my lap, my leg bobs up and down. My highlighter plays a staccato on the pages. I try to focus on the words, to make sense of anything written out in front of me, but my mind keeps finding its way back to Nathan, like he's somehow rewired my brain for his purposes alone.

I groan, abandoning all appearances of studying as I begin moving my wash into a nearby dryer. I'm halfway through when I hear the dull ring of my phone from my pocket. I don't recognize the number. I'm tempted to ignore it, let myself truly embrace this solitude, but decide to answer on the third ring.

"Hello?"

"Hi, may I speak with Beatrice Nilsson?"

My eyes narrow. "Speaking."

"Hi, Beatrice. This is Scott Becker at Marcie Land's office. How are you?"

My stomach drops to the floor as I freeze, one hand on my phone and the other preventing a mountain of underwear in the washing machine from cascading out onto the laundromat's tiled floor.

"Good," I manage to eke out.

"Great. Sorry for calling at the end of the day, but Ms. Land wanted to see if you're available for lunch next week. She has time available next Wednesday."

I open my mouth, but it takes a moment before anything comes out.

"Okay," I say.

"Does one o'clock work for you?"

Does it? I have class that morning, but it's done at eleven and my office hours don't start until three.

I swallow. "Yes, that works."

"All right, I'll email you the restaurant information now. She'll meet you there."

"Great. Thank you," I croak, keeping the phone to my ear after he hangs up.

I'm still staring into the dark depths of the open washing machine as I process the last thirty seconds. I am going to have lunch with Marcie Land herself. This is really happening.

A broad smile spreads across my face, and I look back down at my phone again.

*You have to call Nathan and tell him.*

My brain produces the idea like it's obvious, but my fingers still pause above the illuminated keyboard. He's probably getting ready to go out right now. He's probably on a date. The last thing he wants to hear about is a phone call I got from his friend's assistant.

I scroll past his number in my contacts to my mom's, but I don't stop. If she doesn't understand why I'm in law school, she can't be trusted to exude the right level of happiness about the potential of a low-paying, entry-level job after graduation. I continue down the list until I come to Maggie. I press call, then let it ring and ring. I'm finally connected to her voicemail.

"Hey, Mags, it's me," I say, and only then remember why she's not picking up. "Shit, you're still in Miami. Okay, well, when there's a break in celebrating your future marital bliss, call me! I have some news about a job interview thing that's not really a job interview but, whatever. Bye."

My momentum falters a bit until I find Jillian's number and press call. It's only as it's ringing that I remember Jillian went to Boston this weekend for that in-person interview. She's probably out with her prospective boss right now.

"The number you are calling is not available. To leave a message, please press the pound sign."

I hang up.

Silence swallows me back up again, with only the steady tumble of the dryers to keep me company. I stare down at my expression reflected back in my phone's darkened screen, my excitement dwindling away, eaten up by loneliness. It stokes that ever-present anger in my chest, the resentment and fury over how hard I worked to create this small, tight-knit family, and how it's all falling apart. I want to talk to someone, but I also can't think of one person left who I want to talk to.

Actually, that's not true.

I unlock my phone and find his name again in the contacts.

**NATHAN ASSHOLE**

My finger remains poised above the call button for a long moment. Finally the screen goes dark and I can see my reflection again. The stark openness in my face, the sadness in my eyes.

I shake my head and put my phone back in my pocket. Then I start throwing the rest of my laundry in the dryer.

For the next few hours, I pretend to study until all my clothes are clean and dry. I don't bother folding them, just shove them all back in the laundry bag.

Forget the bar. Forget lawyers and divorces and friends and responsibility. I need to go to bed.

The walk back home is long. I barely look up from the sidewalk as I cross street after street and maneuver around people dressed up and ready to go out for the night.

I don't look up at the front door of my building as I approach, either, which is why I don't see the padlock until I already have my key out, ready to try and enter. But even while I'm staring at the thick chain wrapped around the door handle, the impenetrable lock keeping it in place, it doesn't click. My brain is not computing. That's when I finally look up.

The sign is taped on the center of the door.

# VACATE
## DO NOT ENTER

THE NYC DEPARTMENT OF BUILDINGS HAS DETERMINED THAT CONDITIONS IN THESE PREMISES ARE IMMEDIATELY PERILOUS TO LIFE.

THESE PREMISES HAVE BEEN VACATED AND REENTRY IS PROHIBITED UNTIL SUCH CONDITIONS HAVE BEEN ELIMINATED TO THE SATISFACTION OF THE DEPARTMENT.

VIOLATORS OF THIS COMMISSIONER'S VACATE ORDER WILL BE SUBJECT TO ARREST.

I read it. Then I read it again. Then I stare at it for another minute, my jaw slack until the synapses finally begin firing in my brain and I yell, "What the fuck!"

# CHAPTER 18

**BEATRICE**

ARE YOU BUSY RIGHT NOW

**NATHAN ASSHOLE**

No. Everything okay?

**BEATRICE**

YES JUST WONDERING IF YOU KNOW ANY TENANTS
RIGHTS LAWYERS

**NATHAN ASSHOLE**

Why, what happened?

**BEATRICE**

NOTHING

> EVERYTHING IS TOTALLY FINE

> I JUST NEED A LAWYER PLEASE

**NATHAN ASSHOLE**

Why do you need a tenant rights lawyer at 10 on a Friday night?

**BEATRICE**

> ITS NOTHING

> MY BUILDING MIGHT BE CONDEMNED

> BUT IT IS OK

> I JUST NEED A FUCKING LAWYER

**NATHAN ASSHOLE**

Jesus

Hold on.

I throw my phone back in my bag and collapse on the bottom step of a random building's stoop. It's down the street from my apartment, and after pacing the block a half dozen times, I decided it is the perfect place to sit down and feel sorry for myself. I should have known something like this would happen; the building is barely habitable as it is. But I was lulled into a false sense of security by the low rent and easy commute.

The next thirty minutes are spent combing the city building codes and calling every number offered on the city municipal website. They're all closed at this hour, but I still leave messages for any office that has voicemail. Then my phone starts to ring and Nathan's name appears on-screen.

"What?" I whine into the phone.

"Where are you?" His voice is so deep I feel like it makes the phone vibrate in my hand.

My head falls back against the laundry, and I close my eyes. "I already told you. I'm at my building. Do you have a lawyer for me or what?"

"I'm at your building and I don't see you."

My head shoots up and I open one eye to look down the dark street to my building.

There, standing under the streetlamp, is Nathan Asher. He's in his coat, but it's been thrown over a hooded sweatshirt and jeans. It's startlingly casual, but there's still no mistaking that it's him.

"Motherfucker," I murmur.

"What are you—"

I hang up before he can finish. His hair is messy and pushed back from his striking profile as he shakes his head and looks down at his phone, like he's going to try to call me again.

I struggle to lift my laundry bag, then my backpack. The weight of both has my body bent over at almost ninety degrees as I shuffle toward him. Embarrassing, yes, but hopefully it also distracts him from what I'm wearing—oversized sweatpants that puddle around tattered sneakers, and a Poughkeepsie Fun Run 1996 sweatshirt with no bra.

I stop a few feet in front of him, dropping the laundry bag onto the sidewalk between us. It makes a sickening thud, like there's a dead body hidden inside.

"Is that your landlord?" he asks, staring down at it.

"God, you're hilarious. So funny," I reply, my expression flat. "I'm so glad I texted you."

He tamps down his smile. "All right, what happened?"

"I was at the laundromat for a few hours, and when I came home that sign was on the door."

"You were at the laundromat on a Friday night?"

I roll my eyes. "Love the judgment from a guy who had nothing better to do on a Friday night than come up here to listen to me whine about mine."

His smile broadens again, revealing the dimple and, *ohmygod* I can't deal with this right now.

"Stop smiling. I'm homeless."

He ignores the comment and nods up at the building. "Have you called your super yet?"

I nod. "Apparently a pipe burst, but that's only one issue on a long list of things that got an inspector out here. Now we can't legally enter the building until the issues are addressed. The super says they'll be working all weekend, but he also said the landlord is telling him that he's not responsible for putting any of us up in a hotel, which sucks because even if I fight it, I still need a place tonight and I literally have no money, so—"

"When did he say they'd have everything fixed?" Nathan asks, cutting me off.

I scoff. "'Everything' is a relative term here, but he said they should have enough fixed to get us back in the building by Monday. Which is fine. I have my laptop and my books and literally all my clothes right here, so I'll just keep trying to get ahold of my friends to see if I can go stay at their place in Cold Spring."

"The friends who got engaged?"

I nod. "I left a couple of messages. They're still on vacation, so that's probably why they're not picking up. But I'm sure I can stay at their house. I just need to know the code for the security system. And get a key. So . . . yeah. I'm just going to go to Grand Central and wait for them to get back to me and then I can jump on a train."

"And if they don't get back to you tonight?"

My eyes are everywhere but on his face as I try to think of something, anything to say, other than the truth: I have no idea.

The silence is broken by the high-pitched whirl of a motor approaching. We both turn to see Mrs. Seigel on her motorized scooter coming down the sidewalk toward us. She's in a bright yellow dressing robe with an unlit cigarette hanging from her mouth and barely looks up as I shuffle toward her.

"Mrs. Seigel! Did you see the notice on the door? Do you need any help?" I ask, my voice an octave higher than usual.

She throws a glance up at the building. "Nah. I'm good."

I blink. "But . . . what are you going to do?"

The old woman scoffs. "I'm going to stay at my boyfriend's."

Then she hits the gas, rambling down the sidewalk toward the corner. I watch her go, my shoulders slumping as the silhouette of the motorized scooter turns down Broadway. A moment later, Nathan steps up to my side.

"Want to grab a drink?" he asks.

I let out a long breath, defeated.

~

I let Nathan put my laundry bag in the back of his waiting Uber, but the backpack remains in my arms. It's precious cargo; my books and tablet and laptop feel like a buoy right now, the only things keeping me moored to reality tonight.

I tell myself Nathan understands. After all, he's my colleague. This is all just a professional courtesy.

But that mantra dissolves as soon as I sit down in the back seat. The car smells like cedar and leather and something clean, and it takes my brain a minute to recognize why that's so comforting. It's because Nathan smells like cedar and leather and soap. I want to ignore it, but the moment the realization forms, it seems to grow, enveloping me and prodding memories awake, even as I try to pretend they're not there at all.

I can feel Nathan's eyes on me as the car slides into traffic, so I take out my phone, hell-bent on looking busy. And to be fair, I am; I lose myself in searches for New York City building code and tenants rights groups, so I don't even realize we've come to a stop twenty minutes later until the passenger door next to me swings open again. There's a uniformed doorman standing there, smiling down at me as I stare back dumbly. Then I turn to Nathan.

"Where are we?"

"My building."

My eyes widen. "Excuse me?"

"My—"

"No," I say, grabbing my backpack and ignoring the hand offered to me by the doorman as I stumble out. "No way."

Nathan murmurs something under his breath as he gets out on his side. Then he comes around the car to where I now stand on the sidewalk, clutching my backpack to my chest.

"I'm not going up to your apartment," I say, lifting my chin up defiantly.

"I didn't ask you to come up to my apartment."

"Then why the hell are we here?"

"We're going to drop off your bag and your laundry with Tony," he says, nodding to the doorman. "He can hold on to them while we grab a drink and wait for your friend to get back to you. Unless you want to drag all of this to a bar."

He's looking down at me expectantly, his hands on his hips, and I'm tempted to do just that: bring my laundry and my study materials and set it all right on top of the bar just to spite him. But even as the thought strikes me, it feels perfunctory. These small challenges and thinly veiled aggressions that were once habit now feel like hollow gestures.

"Whatever," I say.

Tony takes the cue and picks up the laundry bag to put on a nearby brass trolley. He has to use both hands and lift with his knees; even then, he struggles under the weight of it. Then he turns to me and smiles, his hand outstretched and waiting for my backpack.

*Oh God.* I hesitate, biting my bottom lip as I slowly offer him the tattered canvas bag as if it were my firstborn.

"Please be careful with that," I plead, watching him lift it onto a hook in the center of the trolley. "Everything I need for school is in there. It's my whole life, and if it goes missing . . . you know what, I'll just take it, it's fine—"

I move to grab it back, but Nathan reaches me first, placing his hands on my shoulders and turning me in the opposite direction.

"Leave it," he says.

I force out a laugh. "Right. It's only my entire future, no big deal."

"I get it. But it'll be fine, trust me."

"That's the thing, Nathan. I don't trust you."

I don't mean it. Even as the words rolled off my tongue, I knew I didn't mean it at all. But it's an old habit, words wielded as weapons, and I use them before I can think better of it. Now they're out and all I can do is watch as they hit their mark.

Nathan lets out a long breath, shaking his head as silence settles between us. When he looks back at me from under his brow, his blue eyes almost glowing, something in my chest constricts.

"Do you want to get a drink or not, Bea?"

I swallow. "Yes."

"Okay. Where do you want to go?"

I let my eyes dart to the buildings around us, finally resting on a bar across the street.

"There."

And then I'm crossing the street before he has time to reply.

Nathan doesn't seem to care that Chaps is a gay bar. He follows me inside, through the clusters of people standing under the rainbow streamers and disco ball, to the long oak bar. There are two empty stools waiting for us, and I zero in on them immediately, sliding onto one and letting out a contented sigh. Nathan stands next to the other and leans against the bar's polished wood.

It isn't busy yet—at least, not as busy as it probably will be in a couple hours. Still, there's a good crowd milling around the dance floor, despite the empty stage and DJ booth, laughing and chatting and swaying to some synthesized pop music playing overhead.

I'm studying the drinks menu when the bartender appears and drops two coasters in front of us. He smiles at Nathan.

"Hello there. What can I get you?"

Nathan points in my direction, and the bartender turns to me. His smile falters and something that looks a lot like pity contorts his features as he gives me a once-over.

"I need a drink," I say, putting my elbow on the bar and resting my cheek in my hand.

"Sweetie, it looks like you need the whole bottle."

He's not wrong. "What's the strongest thing you can make?"

"A martini is just a fancy name for a glass full of vodka, so why don't we start there."

"Bless you," I say solemnly, sure that this man in a pink mesh shirt has just achieved sainthood.

He turns back to Nathan. "And what about you? Are you looking for something strong, too?"

Nathan smiles and shakes his head. "Just a beer. Whatever you have on draft."

The bartender gives him a playful frown and turns away, grabbing a bottle of vodka. I watch him go, then turn back to Nathan. He's still leaning his weight against the bar, the long line of his body relaxed.

"You could totally get his number," I say.

Nathan replies with a lazy shrug.

I roll my eyes. "Oh, that's right. I'm sure you're used to it."

"Why would I be used to it?"

"Please, you know you're gorgeous." I don't mean to make it sound like he has a terminal disease, but it still comes out that way. "You probably have people throwing themselves at you on a daily basis."

"And you don't?"

I scoff.

He shoots me a look. "I'm serious."

"Nathan, I spend every waking minute in class and talking other law students off a ledge. When I'm not doing that, I'm sitting at the neighborhood laundromat dressed like this, studying for the bar. What do you think?"

A line appears between his eyebrows as he stares down at me. The disco ball spins lazily overhead, sending darts of light skimming across his face, illuminating the different shades of blue in his eyes.

"Do you really want to know what I think?"

My heart plummets. Thankfully, I'm saved from having to answer when the bartender returns and places our drinks in front of us. "A martini for the lady and a draft Harp for Paul Newman."

My mouth falls open. "Oh my God! He *does* look like Paul Newman!"

The bartender bows his head as if I had paid him the compliment.

Nathan shakes his head and pulls out his wallet. "Keep a tab open."

He takes Nathan's credit card and gives him a wink. "No problem, Hud."

I laugh and take a sip of my drink. When I set the glass back on the bar, I realize that Nathan's gaze is on my lips. It sends a hot rush across my skin and panic bubbling up in my chest. We're already walking a thin line tonight, and I need to claw back control of the situation, so I do the only thing I can think of: go on the offensive.

"What's going on here?" I ask, nodding to his clothes.

He blinks, and I feel a moment of pride at catching him off guard. "Excuse me?"

I motion my hand vaguely down his body. "This."

He looks down, then back up at me from under his brow. "The sweatshirt?"

I nod.

"Do you have a problem with sweatshirts?"

"No. I've just only ever seen you in suits. This is like seeing you out of uniform."

Nathan hides his smile behind the rim of his pint glass as he takes a sip. "Well, next time you call and need help, I'll remember to change before leaving."

I scoff. "I didn't need help."

"Bea, you told me your building had been condemned."

I swat the words away as if this is a minor detail. "I was handling it."

"Yes, it looked like it was all under control."

"It was getting there," I reply.

He takes another sip of his beer before answering. "Well, you did me a favor."

"Oh, really?"

"I needed an excuse to put my laptop away, or I would have been up all night doing work."

"The demand for mutually assured destruction never stops, huh?"

He tosses me a knowing look.

I laugh again, but the sound is lost in the growing cacophony of conversation and music around us. "I guess I don't have room to talk. I was studying and doing laundry."

"Yeah, I was wondering about that."

"About what?"

"It's Friday night. I thought you would be out with someone."

"Like on a date?"

"No, like a bank heist," he says dryly. "Of course a date."

The comment throws me off-balance, and I open my mouth, trying to find my footing again. "Well, yeah. I mean, I could have been on a date. But right now I'm busy with school and studying and the job search, so . . ." I can feel my cheeks flush, and I dart my eyes away from his. "It's not like I'm not having sex. I'm having sex. Like, a lot of sex."

My voice is so loud and full of such manufactured conviction that the man sitting beside me turns and cringes.

"Okay." Nathan nods, working to tamp down his smile.

"Yup. Sex with like . . . you know . . . people . . ."

I'm floundering. Totally and utterly lost in a sea of lies and embarrassment, and Nathan is watching, unwilling to even throw me a life preserver.

"What about you?" I finally ask, then take a long sip of my drink.

"What about me?"

"You must be out there," I say, waving my hand indiscriminately around the room.

Nathan looks around, pursing his lips like he's considering it. Then he turns back to me. "Not at the moment, no."

"Why not?"

"I've been busy with work. Like, a lot of work," he says, mimicking my tone from a moment before. "So much work with . . . you know . . . people."

I half-heartedly try to suppress my laugh and fail miserably. "Fuck you."

He smiles back, the dimple appearing on his cheek.

I'm about to ask him why he isn't out there sleeping with half of Manhattan when a dull ping pulls our attention to my phone. It's lying face down on the bar, but the light from the screen seeps against the wood.

I want to ignore it, to stay in this pretend world where Nathan and I are friends who get drinks and laugh at each other's stories, but I know we can't. Maggie could be responding, so I reach for it and read the waiting text.

"Is that your friend?" Nathan asks.

I let out a long breath and drop my phone back down on the bar. "No. But New York City needs my help to get out the vote this November, so that's nice."

It almost looks like he's relieved, and that sends a rush of excitement through my veins. But why? I want Maggie to get back to me. I want to go up to Cold Spring and have a comfortable place to sleep tonight. But I also don't want to let him go. Not yet.

"Marcie's office called me today," I admit instead.

He cocks an eyebrow at me. "And?"

"She wants to have lunch next week."

"Why are you making it sound like bad news?"

My eyes go back on the line of liquor bottles behind the bar as I shrug. "I don't know. I guess it feels a little like cheating."

"Cheating who?"

"I don't know." I sigh, scrunching up my nose. "Like I'm cheating the *system*."

"Using personal connections isn't cheating the system, Bea. That is the system."

"That doesn't mean it's fair."

"The world isn't fair." His voice has taken on that same patronizing edge from that night he drove me home from the bar event. He seems to remember, too, because his expression softens before he asks, "Do you want to work for her?"

"Of course I do."

"And do you think you would be a good addition to her team?"

"Absolutely."

"Then that's all you need to worry about."

I roll my eyes. "But won't everyone know? No matter what I do, they'll say, 'Yeah, that Beatrice Nilsson is smart, but you know the only reason she got in here, right?' There will always be an asterisk next to my name."

"Pace yourself, Bea. You could still bomb this lunch."

My eyes widen, and I let out a laugh so loud that the people sitting on either side of us turn to look. But I don't care; I let the sound roll out of me, a cathartic release of all the anxiety trapped inside my body.

"Asshole," I breathe.

He barely hides his smile as he takes a long sip from his beer.

One drink rolls into two, which rolls into three, and I have no idea how much time passes, but suddenly the music is loud, too loud to hear what we're saying to each other. It doesn't stop us from trying, though, yelling and laughing over the pounding soundtrack. Bodies crowd around us at the bar—even more undulate together on the dance floor nearby—but I barely notice. My attention is locked on Nathan.

He's telling a story, leaning in as if it will help, but I still can't hear a word. I pretend to listen, though, because it means he will stay there, so close that I can smell the sharp bite of his cologne.

It's making my mind swim. Or maybe that's the vodka. I have no idea, but I suddenly can't remember the details surrounding why I need to hate him. I can't even remember hating him at all.

His story is reaching an intense conclusion when the music fades and a voice booms through the PA system.

"Welcome, welcome, welcome!"

A drag queen walks on the small stage behind us, her green sequined dress reflecting the spotlight and her red wig tall enough to almost touch the ceiling.

"It's midnight, so you know what that means!" she announces into her microphone. "Trivia time!"

The bar erupts in cheers, and suddenly the bartender is back, passing out sheets of paper and pencils. He offers Nathan a wink when he drops them in front of us, then keeps moving down the bar.

"You know the rules," the drag queen continues. "Best team name gets you a free round of drinks. Most right answers gets my respect. And also a round of drinks. Everyone got it?"

A collective sound of agreement comes up from around us as Nathan turns back to me. I already have the pencil ready and the paper under my splayed hand.

"Are we playing trivia?" he asks, brow furrowed.

I shoot him an incredulous expression. "Of course we're playing trivia."

"Okay," he says, picking up his glass and taking a sip. "What's our team name?"

I scrunch up my nose and think for a moment. "Oedipus and the Motherfuckers."

It looks as if he's about to spit a mouthful of beer across the bar, and he has to put his glass down. I watch him, biting back a smile.

After he finally swallows, he cocks an eyebrow at me. "Where the hell did you come up with that?"

"It was always our trivia team name in college," I say. He waits for more information but I just shrug. "Like I told you before, Josh was a classics major."

We fill out the team name as the drag queen onstage announces that the game is beginning. Conversations dull around us, all eyes looking up at her.

"Okay, first question: What reality megastar grew up in Connecticut before moving to New York and marrying into royalty?"

I turn to Nathan slowly, a smug smile on my lips. "We're totally going to win."

# CHAPTER 19

We lose.

In the end it's not even close. But it's not a complete washout; after that first question about *The Real Housewives*, we get one other question right, which kicks us up from last place to second-to-last. More importantly, we win for best team name, so after our round of free drinks, we decide to celebrate with pizza.

Eighth Avenue is almost empty except for a few lone cabs careening uptown as we stumble out onto the sidewalk. It's late enough that the restaurants on either side of the street are closed, but Nathan starts walking downtown anyway, claiming there's a pizza place still open a few blocks ahead. I keep my steps in sync with his, and when the cold begins to breach my sweatshirt and a shiver ripples through my body, he wordlessly takes off his coat and wraps it around my shoulders.

I'm about to protest, to give it back, but before I can open my mouth, he says, "Shut up," and keeps walking.

The pizza place is right where he promised, on the corner of Fifteenth Street. The fluorescent lighting makes it positively glow, its small white interior on full display through the windows before we even enter.

A blast of heat welcomes us as Nathan opens the door for me. I audibly moan, but I don't care. It feels so good and it smells even better. Like bread and grease and melting cheese. The alcohol had worn off a bit during the walk, and the buzz has been replaced by a gnawing hunger, which now demands at least a whole pie. Maybe two.

There's a group of women in short dresses and heels already halfway through a cheese pizza when we walk in. They're huddled around one of the tall metal tables, talking at full volume in the way you only do when you're thoroughly drunk. The minute they see us, they fall silent. Their eyes follow Nathan as he approaches the register, orders a few slices for both of us, and pays.

We get our food and head to a table in the far corner, but I notice the women's collective gaze is still on him. He has his back to them, so he can't see their eyes raking down his body, the whispers and the giggles.

I turn my attention back to him, too. There's no question that Nathan is gorgeous, but under these harsh fluorescent lights, the fact is even more evident, illuminating the details that I normally work so hard to ignore. The gray flecks in his eyes that are usually invisible beneath the blue. The distinct line of the scar along his chin that's obvious even under his stubble. His light brown hair rumpled from where he ran his hand through it during the quiz. Even his body seems accentuated, the size of it as he bends down to take a bite of his pizza, the width of his shoulders as he leans one elbow down next to mine as he chews. It's like the universe has decided to bypass my judgment and put him on a pedestal where I can do nothing but stare.

He stops chewing and cocks one eyebrow up his forehead. "What?"

I roll my eyes, like that will disguise the flush in my cheeks. "You chew with your mouth open."

He grins like he knows I'm lying but can't be bothered to figure out why. "Do you want another slice?"

I do and so does he, and at some point the women leave, but I don't notice when. I don't even know how long we're there. Only that the conversation rolls on and on and we've eaten almost an entire pizza before we finally leave.

We walk side by side along the pavement, and I suddenly feel a bit more sober. I'm not sure if it's because of the carbohydrates currently swimming in my stomach or the fact that the night is drawing to a close, but I suddenly remember that I have no idea where I'm going to sleep tonight. Or what I'm going to do tomorrow. Or for the rest of the weekend. I momentarily consider a hotel, but the thought flies out of my mind as soon as it appears. Yesterday I had to check my bank balance before going grocery shopping; there's no way I can afford one night in a hotel, let alone a whole weekend. I don't even want to have to think about my credit card debt right now.

Of course, I could always head up to Maggie and Travis's. There's a good chance they have a key hidden outside the house somewhere. But if they don't? That means sitting outside a train station in the Hudson Valley until morning. With all my books and my computer. And a twenty-pound laundry bag.

There's also Jillian. I know she would have me, no question. But she's still in Boston on that job interview. Even if she were home, her studio in Queens is barely big enough for her, let alone a houseguest. It reminds me again that Josh is only a few blocks from here, all by himself in that empty two-bedroom apartment. No way I'm staying there. Bastard.

But none of that is center stage in my mind right now. No, that space is currently being occupied by the man walking beside me, his clean white Nikes in sync with my tattered Converse.

I don't want the night to be done. Not yet. And I don't want to think about why that is, to examine the details that will only make me anxious. No, I just want to stay in this limbo, this wonderful, blissfully naive half state where my slight buzz muffles the alarm bells in my mind. I don't have to analyze the whys or the hows or what happens next. We can just be here. And that's enough.

But we can't stay in that place because after just a few more minutes we're outside his building again. I pull his coat tighter around my body, a feeble attempt to keep out the wind whipping down Eighth Avenue and try to avoid his gaze.

"Well, I guess I should grab my bags," I say, nodding to his building.

"Did your friends get back to you?" His eyes narrow with that familiar skepticism. He already knows the answer.

I shrug, not really up for admitting the answer is no. "It's fine. I can hang out at Grand Central and get on the next train."

Then I smile, like it will soften just how pathetic the rest of my night will be, but his expression stays flat. "It's one a.m., Bea."

"So?"

"So she's not going to get back to you until the morning."

I sigh. "Well, what else am I supposed to do?"

"Stay here."

A heady mix of panic and heat pulses through me, and all I can do is laugh—a tittering, maniacal sound that causes his forehead to furrow.

"No," I reply.

"Why not?"

"Because . . ." My voice trails off as every possible answer runs through my brain at once.

When I don't reply with anything, his lips become a hard line, like he's insulted. Or worse, hurt.

"You can have the bed and I'll sleep on the couch," he says, like he's read something from my expression. "When you get in touch with your friends tomorrow, you can head up there. You don't even have to say goodbye."

My heart is still racing as I scoff. "I would say goodbye. I'm not a *complete* monster."

He frowns as if he isn't so sure.

I let out a soft laugh. "Asshole."

"Yeah, we established that."

He's staring down at me, and I'm staring right back. After a moment, I realize that we have been standing there for a while without saying anything at all.

"All right," I say with as much manufactured exasperation as I can muster. "Show me this penthouse apartment, then."

Tony has an elevator waiting for us when we enter the lobby, and he promises to bring my bags up in just a few minutes. I want to know exactly when and how, but Nathan just says thank you and presses the button for nine. We're silent as the elevator rises, its cables and gears churning above us as it makes its slow ascent. And thank God, because it masks the sound of my pounding heart that's probably audible in the cramped space.

A moment later there's a soft ding and the doors open to a warmly lit hallway. Nathan starts forward and turns right, walking down to the apartment at the end.

The door is metal and the sound of his key in the lock seems to echo in the space beyond it. I want to make a snide comment, something about the size or sheer luxury of this place, but then the door is open and Nathan nods for me to enter. I keep my mouth shut and walk inside ahead of him.

It's dark except for the city skyline illuminated in the enormous window on the far side of the room. The lights from a hundred different buildings expose the large space, the sofa in the center dividing it in two. There's a long dining table on one side, its glass top reflecting pinpoints of light from the window onto the walls and ceiling.

I make it to the center of the room before Nathan flips on a lamp, revealing the tobacco-colored leather of the sofa and the crowded bookcases facing it. The walls are stark white, punctuated by tall black-and-white art prints and a massive TV. The sprawling kitchen is to my right and open to the rest of the room. It's white, too: white marble, white cabinets, white appliances. The entire place is immaculate, but there are signs of life here and there. The haphazard way books are stacked in the bookcases. A bouquet of peonies with a card sticking out the top in the center of the dining table. The expensive-looking espresso machine marred with coffee stains on the kitchen countertop.

I turn as Nathan makes his way around the room, turning on a few more lamps.

"Not the penthouse," he says.

"Not far off, though." I let my hand glide along the leather sofa as I wander to the window.

He chuckles, that deep sound that's barely a sound at all, just a vibration in his chest. Then he walks to a door between the kitchen and the hallway.

"I don't think there's much in the fridge, but help yourself to whatever you can find," he says, opening the door to reveal a linen closet.

"I'm good," I say, pretending like I'm looking around the room and not watching the span of his back as he reaches up and grabs some sheets and a blanket from the top shelf.

I pivot back to the window a little too quickly when he turns around. I can hear his footsteps, the heavy, even gait that eventually stops next to the sofa. There's a rustling of fabric, and I look over my shoulder to see him unfurling a sheet across the cushions.

"So . . ." I say, but my voice trails off.

I want to continue with: *This is the place that Jillian's divorce bought.* But I don't. I can't. It feels unfair to lay that at his feet when I've been so willing to ignore it up until now. If it came out it would only be to push him away, to reforge whatever flimsy boundaries I had been trying to keep up. The role of enemies suddenly feels so forced, while nothing else with him ever has.

So instead, I just ask, "Why are you helping me?"

He tucks one corner of the sheet into the corner of the sofa and sighs. "Because as much as you may hate to hear it, you're my friend."

I don't hate hearing it. In fact, my heart trips over itself with the words. I try to mask it, though, adding a bit of sarcasm to my voice as I tease, "Do you make out with all your friends?"

"No." He throws a blanket on top of the sheet. "And we agreed not to do that again."

"Doesn't mean you haven't thought about it."

His expression becomes skeptical. "You haven't?"

"Nope," I lie.

The corner of his lip twitches. "Okay."

I suddenly feel warm, every inch of my skin aware of his proximity. And whatever alcohol is left in my system gives me the courage to press him further.

"What have *you* thought about, exactly?" My tone is teasing and light, covering for the fact that I'm so hungry to know; that I'm struggling to maintain control of a situation that has me so wildly out of my depth.

His head falls slightly and his hands let go of the bedding to rest on the arm of the sofa. I can see the tension in his muscles, his arms and shoulders taut as he shakes his head and murmurs, "Don't."

My eyebrows knit together. "Don't what?"

He looks up. His gaze is serious. "I heard you when you said you didn't want anything to happen between us. I saw how upset you were when I even mentioned it the other night. So just . . ." He sighs and rakes a hand through his hair, frustration contorting his features as he seems to work to find the words. "Don't make it harder for me just because you can."

I blink. "Excuse me?"

"Come on, Bea. You're my friend and I—"

"You think I'm making this harder for *you*?" I interrupt. Irritation is suddenly bubbling in my chest, the perfect vessel to funnel everything hot happening inside my body. "I didn't force you to take Frank's class. I didn't invite myself to meet Marcie or to have dinner afterward. I'm not the one that came uptown tonight without being asked to."

"I know." His expression softens as he puts his hands on his hips. "You're right, and I'm sorry—"

"I'm not looking for an apology," I reply, taking a step toward him before I can think better of it. "I could have ignored you, or stepped down from my TA position, but I didn't. I'll take responsibility for that. But don't try to make me feel bad about it, like me standing in your apartment right now is all my fault."

"I'm not saying it's your fault," he says, his voice stern and demanding, like we've suddenly entered a courtroom. "I'm saying that you have the power here. You set the ground rules and I'm trying to follow them."

My arms fly out at my sides. "When the hell did I set the ground rules?"

"Are you serious?" He takes a step toward me. There are mere inches between us now, but neither of us seems to notice. "You set them every time we talk. You're always reminding me who we are to each other. Every day you make it clear where I stand with you. What you want."

I'm buzzing with fury, not because he's wrong but because he's uncomfortably right. He hasn't been privy to my private thoughts; he doesn't know how much all of my words have been about so much more than pushing him away. It's about self-preservation.

But I'm still in self-preservation mode, so I lash out in the only way I can.

"Oh really? Okay, what the hell do *you* want, Nate?"

His entire body stills as his gaze flicks to mine and stays there for a long moment. Then I realize what prompted the reaction: I said his name. Not Nathan. Nate. He had asked me to call him that ages ago and I never had, even when I knew he was becoming my friend. I'd never given him that. Not until right now.

The air in the room shifts, suddenly heavy and electric. I want to take a breath, but my lungs refuse. His eyes are so intense that the anger burning in my chest bottoms out into something much more substantial.

He lets out a long breath and whispers, "Bea—"

A knock on the front door slices through the air and cuts him off.

His eyes stay locked with mine for another moment before he runs a hand down his face, then turns to walk down the short hallway. A minute later, Tony appears with a brass luggage trolley carrying my bags. He smiles and nods to me as he carefully puts the backpack on the dining table, then leaves the laundry bag on the ground beside it.

"Thanks, Tony," Nathan says, offering a tight smile as he walks him back out.

I stand there listening to the unintelligible hum of their conversation for a minute or two before I hear the sound of the door closing, the lock sliding into place.

Nathan appears again, his hands in his pockets. That burning that had been in his eyes only a few minutes before is gone. I recognize the defenses he's put back up, the internal armor that's so similar to my own.

"It's late. Let me show you the bedroom and you can get some sleep."

I don't know what to say, so I remain silent as I follow him through the living room, down another hallway to the bedroom. It's big, especially by New York standards. By the window there's an armchair and a haphazard pile of books next to it. In the center of the room there's a king-size bed that sits low to the ground in a modern wood frame. It's flanked by matching nightstands, the kind with thin wood legs that look like they were stolen from the set of *Mad Men*.

I turn to say as much, expecting to find him beside me, but he's still standing in the doorway. He hasn't stepped foot in the room.

"Bathroom is right through there," he says, nodding to the door in the far corner. "I think I have some extra toothbrushes under the sink."

"Thanks." My voice sounds thin.

"Do you want me to bring your bags in here?"

I shake my head, wrapping my arms around my waist even as I lift my chin proudly. "No, it's fine. I can just sleep in this."

"Okay." His gaze travels down my body before he finally turns. "Night, Bea."

The door closes with a small click, and I find myself standing there staring at the pattern in its wood grain as I listen to his retreat down the hall. His steps are heavy and slow, growing fainter until the sound finally disappears all together.

And then it's just silence.

# CHAPTER 20

It's another minute before I take off his coat and lay it across the nearby armchair. I peel off my sweatpants and shuffle to the en suite bathroom in just my sweatshirt, brushing my teeth with one of his spare toothbrushes like I'm on autopilot. Then I'm in bed, *his* bed, staring up at the lights and shadows of the city dancing on the ceiling as if it can distract me from the fact that I'm surrounded by the smell of soap and cedar and *him* buried in these cool sheets, wrapped around my limbs. My skin is buzzing, a low voltage throb just under the surface that makes every nerve ending too sensitive, too aware.

I kick off the sheets, flopping my body to one side, then the other. But I can't get comfortable. I'm awake now, the effects of the alcohol completely burned away as my brain spins, trying to figure out just how we got here.

But that's not really the question, is it? Because I know deep down that it was inevitable from that first kiss. We tried so hard to fight against gravity pulling us together that, like quicksand, it just swallowed us up more quickly. The only thing we have to show for the battle is a friendship that only complicates this whole thing more.

And maybe that's it. If we had met at a bar, I would have gone home with him. I would have already been in this bed and found excuses to get out of it. I wouldn't have gotten to know him because I wouldn't have had to, and that would have made it easier to let it go. But instead, the struggle to keep those battle lines drawn, to ensure that we stayed on opposing sides of Josh and Jillian's fight, only means that I left the rest of myself exposed, suited with the wrong armor so now I'm just naked, vulnerable and seen and completely out of my depth.

My mouth goes dry with the realization.

This is bad. Very bad.

I sit up, my skin hot despite the chill in the room. There's no chance of sleep now, no possible way my body will relax.

I need a glass of water.

Of course, there are no glasses in the bathroom. I rifle under the sink, peek into the medicine cabinet. Nothing. I even try to fit my mouth underneath the tap, but it's too shallow and I only succeed in getting the front of my hair wet.

*Damn it.* I'll have to sneak out to the kitchen.

I make my way to the bedroom door but stop in front of it. How long have I been lying here trying to fall asleep? Twenty minutes? A half hour? He's probably asleep by now, right? Or at least close enough that he won't hear a pair of footsteps tiptoeing into the kitchen.

I listen at the door just to be sure. There's only silence on the other side. Still, I wait another long minute before opening it. Then I carefully make my way down the hall, tugging at my oversized sweatshirt in an attempt to hide my underwear as my bare feet softly land on the hardwood floor. The kitchen is open out to the living room, but even before I make it there, I see that the entire room is dark.

Slowly and so, so carefully, I inch into the kitchen and take a glass from the shelf above the sink. I fill it with water, then turn around, taking a sip and looking out into the dark living room.

That's when I see a pair of eyes on me.

"HOLY FUCKING SHIT FUCK!" I scream, almost dropping my glass.

My vision adjusts enough to the darkness, and I immediately recognize that it's Nathan. He's sitting up on the sofa wearing just a pair of boxer briefs, and his bare chest is exposed, shadowed by his elbows that rest on his knees.

"You okay?" His voice is a low murmur from the other room.

I take a deep breath. "You scared the hell out of me."

"I didn't do anything."

I shoot him a biting look. "Besides sitting here in the dark like a serial killer?"

A moment, then he replies, "I couldn't sleep."

His expression is flat, his voice low and even, but there's something in his eyes that stops the quip that's about to leave my tongue. A raw and desperate edge that stills me.

"Me, either," I admit, then lift the glass of water to my lips and take a deep sip.

When I bring it back down, he's still watching me.

"You want some?" I offer.

"Yeah," he says, raking a hand down his face. "Thanks."

I turn back to the sink and fill the glass back up. My hand is shaking under the tap, and I can hear my pulse in my ears, a low and steady rumble as I turn the water off and walk out to the living room.

I stop in front of him, his legs planted wide just a foot or so ahead. He doesn't say anything as he takes the glass and brings it to his mouth, and I stay quiet as I watch him down the contents, the bob of his throat as he swallows, the shape of his lips around the glass's edge.

When he's done, he places the glass on the side table without looking back up to me.

Silence swallows us up again. God, why is this so awkward?

"Listen," I finally manage to say, but then stall when his eyes come back up to meet mine. I feel like he can see right through me, like he knows exactly what I'm thinking and feeling and God, I almost wish it were true so I wouldn't have to find the words. "I'm sorry. For earlier."

He lets out a haggard breath. "No, you shouldn't—"

"Shut up and let me say this," I cut him off. He stills, his whole body taut, and I have to take a deep breath before I can continue. "I don't think you're an asshole."

Nothing in the room moves except my pulse, which can't seem to keep up with my heart.

"I mean, I *do* think you're an asshole, obviously. But not because I hate you or anything." A nervous laugh laces through my words, but it fades quickly. "Of all the things I feel about you, hate is definitely not one of them."

He's watching me from under his brow, such an intense stare that I let my gaze drift to the wall behind him so I can breathe.

"I'm usually really good at this, you know. I'm the one who knows right from wrong. There's no gray area for me. But with you . . ."

My voice fades, and I shrug.

He doesn't offer me a reprieve, doesn't fill the silence with any sort of encouragement or support. He just waits.

For the first time, doubt hits my chest, fear that I've really done it this time. I've tested his last nerve and he's done with me. I realize at the same moment how much that would hurt.

And if this is it, if he's really over this, over *me*, then fuck it. I have nothing else to lose.

"With you, I know what I feel but I can't. I know what I want but I also know I shouldn't."

A moment passes. "So, what is it you want, Bea?"

"I want . . ." My tongue darts out to wet my lips, as if it will somehow buoy my courage. Then I say the simplest thing that comes to mind: "I want you to kiss me."

His eyes narrow like this isn't a good thing, and, oh God, I might have completely misread this situation.

"I mean, if you want to," I continue hastily. "I'm not assuming you do, I'm just saying that I'm not opposed to it. To be honest, I was never really opposed to it, so don't feel like you have to keep that promise or anything, because it's not—"

I'm still rambling when his hands come up and slowly wrap around my calves. His palms are big and warm and any words that were on my lips completely dissolve.

"Where do you want me to kiss you?" he murmurs, his eyes still locked with mine as his thumb begins to move back and forth across my skin.

There's a bite to his words, like there's resentment there beneath an aching need. Like he holds it against me.

I know that feeling. The conflicted core of whatever it is we're doing. But I also know that other feeling, the one I see reflected in his eyes as he looks up at me: that there is something greater than resentment or reason driving us off this precipice.

When I don't answer, his hands begin to slowly skim up my bare legs, grazing the sensitive skin behind my knees as they travel up, stopping on my thighs.

"Here?" he asks.

When I don't answer, he leans forward, brushing his lips against the skin above my knee. It's so slight, so soft, it could barely constitute a kiss, but I don't have time to consider before his hands are moving again, up up up, beneath my sweatshirt, his thumb skimming the bottom edge of my underwear.

"Or here?"

*Oh God.* My eyes flutter shut as he leans forward again, his hot breath caressing my thigh just before his lips graze it.

My voice hitches as those hands continue up. His fingers gather up the hem of my sweatshirt so it cinches around my waist.

"Or . . ." He stills and there's a long pause before he continues. "Are these days-of-the-week underwear?"

*Ohmygod. Ohmygodohmygodohmygod.*

My cheeks are suddenly burning as I try to push him away, but he holds me in place, his grip tightening on my hips.

"It's laundry day," I hiss. "So don't you fucking dare—"

My words evaporate as he tugs me toward him and kisses the faded letters that spell out Tuesday on the pink cotton. I feel his hot breath through the fabric and can't help the sound I make, the hungry moan from deep in my throat.

That seems to sever the last bit of his restraint. His fingers spread around my hips and pull me down, their hard grip hauling me into his lap so I'm straddling him. His face is so close now, his lips grazing my own, his labored breath infused with mine.

"Or here," he says.

I lean in to close the distance, but he pulls back, not far, but just enough that my lips miss their mark, hovering above his.

My brow furrows and he meets my confused expression with a dark gaze.

"You have to say it, Bea," he murmurs.

My heart thunders in my chest as I roll my eyes. "Oh my God, just kiss me alre—"

The words are cut off as he bends forward, his mouth covering mine as our tongues slide together.

It's like that night outside my building; I don't know which of us is in control, only that the kiss is equal parts passion and fury, our lips moving in sync as we nip and suck and taste. My hands are in his hair before I'm even aware of it, gathering the thick strands between my fingers, holding tight as if he might disappear.

His arms wrap around me, forcing my curves into the solid planes of his body. But it's not close enough; I want to get closer, I *need* to get closer, to get rid of these clothes and feel his skin against mine.

He groans, breaking the kiss and leaning back just enough to shift his weight, lifting my body so I'm suddenly falling back into the sofa. Then his body is over me, around me, the delicious weight of him heavy between my legs. I arch into him, desperate to get close again as his hands grip my sweatshirt, yanking it roughly up and off my body.

The cold air hits my skin and sends a shiver down my spine, but then there's only heat as he presses against me again, his lips on my neck, my collarbone, my chest. My arms are around his shoulders, so broad it's like I'm cocooned by him. His heat and weight and size has me trapped and God, I love it.

"Do you know how much I've thought about this?" he murmurs as one of his hands finds the apex of my thighs, tracing over the soft cotton. "Jesus, Bea . . ."

Then his fingers push my underwear aside and sink inside me. I gasp, arching my back, pressing myself into him only for him to use his other hand to push me down, hold me in place as his fingers begin to move, curling them just enough to hit that spot over and over and over again. Soon I'm writhing, aching to break free. And then . . .

My climax hits me like a wave, crashing and consuming and pulling me under before I even knew it was there. I let out a strangling sound only to have it swallowed up by his mouth as he kisses me hard.

"Your sounds," he growls against my lips. "I knew I'd love your sounds."

But I want *his* sounds. I've spent weeks pondering them; the moan he makes when he's undone, the grunt when he loses control. Just thinking about it has my hands raking down his stomach, feeling the ridge of his muscles underneath my nails until I feel him under my palm.

He hisses, his head coming up to look at where my hand is pressed against him through his briefs. Then he looks up, meeting my eyes. His eyes are so dark and hungry that my breath catches. "Bea . . ."

I know what he's asking. I know he's giving me an out. But I don't want an out, I want *him*.

"Please tell me you have a condom," I whisper, bending up to kiss the corner of his lips, his jaw.

His lips meet mine again, hard and unforgiving, and I meet their challenge, my tongue demanding more as my legs move to wrap around his hips. Then my mouth moves down to lick up the column of his neck and he leans over, reaching to the side of the sofa. When he sits up, he has his discarded pants in his hand. He grabs his wallet from their back pocket and pulls out a foil wrapper.

I roll my eyes and groan. "Of course you have one in your wallet. I bet you have—"

His mouth cuts me off, another deep kiss that eviscerates any words that had been there on my tongue.

"Shut the fuck up, for fuck's sake," he growls against my lips.

I laugh, but it dies as he stands, as I watch him shed his boxer briefs. He's silhouetted by the light in the kitchen, but I can still make out the hard lines of his body as he slowly rolls on the condom.

He doesn't notice my attention until he's done. He's still for a minute, and I can tell he's taking me in, too. His gaze travels over every inch of me, like he's committing me to memory. And maybe he is. Maybe he knows that this moment is fleeting. There's a dull ache in my chest at the thought.

Then he moves, a knee on the sofa as he reaches down and tugs Tuesday down my legs before he comes back down to hover over me.

"You asked me before what I think about when I think about that kiss?" he murmurs, bowing his body above mine as he grabs hold of my hip with his hand, lifting me to meet him. "I think about what would've happened if we weren't interrupted. If you had invited me upstairs. What you would have let me do to you."

He pushes his hips forward just a little, as if to test me. I gasp.

*I do, too*, I want to say, but I can't. I'm overwhelmed, not just by his touch, but the feeling that has exploded in my chest, the relief that's been released into my veins. I've been holding back for so long, battling against every instinct that told me I belonged right here, with his hands bracketed around my hips and his body between my legs. The realization that I almost missed it, that this was so close to never happening at all, sends a sharp spike of anxiety to my chest.

A question follows the thought: *What if this doesn't happen again?* But it's hazy, already dissolving before it's fully defined as he slowly pushes into me.

The air leaves my lungs in one long moan. I feel so full, so painfully full, like if he moves he will break me in two, and God, I want him to. I don't ever want to get up from this sofa and lose this feeling.

He's still for a moment, then eases out slowly, only to slide back in. His head falls against my shoulder as he does it again, so achingly slow that I feel every inch. It's so good. It's too good.

"I know, I know," he whispers, and I realize I must have said it out loud. That I'm mumbling, a string of incoherent words as his pace increases, a steady rhythm.

I can already feel the delicious tightening of my muscles again, the growing ache deep in my belly, and I want to chase it even as I want to prolong it, hold on to this lush tension forever.

"Oh my God . . . Nate . . ." I hiccup over the words.

He lifts his head so his lips skim my jaw and his eyes meet mine.

"Say it again," he murmurs.

So I whisper it. "Nate."

He smiles and then his mouth is on mine, demanding and hard, as his thrusts become faster, more savage and urgent. I raise my hips to meet each one.

The room echoes with the sound of us moving together. His grunts and my soft cries. The rhythmic creaking of the sofa. He whispers into my skin—telling me how beautiful I am, how long he's wanted this—punctuating each confession with his tongue, his teeth. Then his fingers move lower, tracing the line of my neck, my rib cage, my stomach, until they reach that apex between my thighs. His thumb begins to move there, slowly at first, then pressing down with urgency and oh . . .

I

Am

*There*.

This second explosion detonates deep in my body, and I cry out, closing my eyes and letting it rocket through me, an electric current pulsing through every nerve.

My body is still humming when his thrusts become jagged and fast, prolonging my ecstasy as he holds me tight and forces my body to meet his brutal pace.

I arch up to kiss his jaw just as he groans, his hips offering one last rough push before he collapses on top of me.

My fingers trace the sheen of sweat on his back as I loop my arms around him, holding him tight while his breathing slows. His lips find my neck, kissing my pulse point.

I know there are a million things I should say. But I also don't want to, not yet. I want to hold on to this perfect moment for just a little bit longer.

But I can't because Nathan finally stirs, raising his body up to rest on his elbows and lifting his head to look down at me. His expression is soft and pensive, but there's uncertainty there wrinkling his brow, too. A hint of doubt.

And that awful fear snakes its way under my skin again.

"What?" I ask. My voice sounds small. Scared.

"It's nothing," he murmurs, glancing down to where my underwear lies next to the sofa. "It's just . . . I could have sworn today was Friday . . ."

My mouth falls open. "Oh my God. You're such a fucking ass—"

A smile curls just as he shuts me up with a kiss.

*Asshole.* I say the word in my head and repeat it and repeat it as his tongue parts my lips. Because he is an asshole for so many reasons, I remind myself. But the incantation fades as the kiss deepens, until I don't even remember to say anything at all.

# CHAPTER 21

Sleep yields slowly as Rupert Holmes sings about piña coladas from my phone somewhere nearby. I'm suddenly aware of the morning sun trying to sneak between my eyelids, and I want to turn away from it, steal a few more minutes to dream, but my body won't listen. It's restrained by a heavy weight across my back, an arm that tightens as I begin to stir. I lift my head and open one eye. I'm greeted with a broad chest dusted with brown hair.

*Nathan.*

The night comes back to me in an instant. The bar, the argument, the sex.

Ohmygod, the sex.

For weeks I had been so careful, worked so hard to keep everything I felt for him at bay. And then all he had to do was look up at me with those eyes and I was done. All my efforts were forgotten in the hours that followed, and I hadn't even cared, because even in the frenzy of it, I knew it would be over in the morning. And now morning was here too soon.

I hadn't expected the soft rock about getting caught in the rain, though.

I push my hair away from my face and look around the room for the source of my alarm. We're still on the sofa. My sweatshirt is on the ground, and Nathan's clothes, which had been folded so neatly beside him before, are now strewn across the coffee table.

My gaze finally finds my phone peeking out from under his shirt, just far enough to be out of reach. I try to shift slowly, move my shoulders to the edge of the cushions so I can get to it, but his body stirs at the same time.

He lifts his head and does a quick survey of the room, the floor, our clothes, then brings his gaze to where I'm still sprawled across his chest. I can see the night falling into place for him, too; the instant it all comes back to him.

"Morning," he says, his voice gravelly with sleep. A warm smile starts to tug at his lips. I'm barely aware that I'm mirroring it, only that relief flows through me and my body relaxes a bit. His smile is magic.

But before I can say anything, before I can even attempt it, consciousness fully arrives and I slap my hand over my mouth.

*Ohmygod.* My breath.

His eyebrows pinch together. "What?"

I shake my head and add a shrug as if that will somehow make me look relaxed, even though I'm obviously panicking, moving quickly to stand up and get away from him. It's only when I'm on my feet that I realize I'm naked, and there's no distracting from my horror as I desperately reach down for my sweatshirt.

"Bea." He says it slowly, his arms coming out as if he's trying to calm a rabid puppy. But it's no use; I'm frantically pulling the sweatshirt on as I walk backward, hitting the wall before turning around and rushing down the hall into the bedroom, then the bathroom.

I slam the door shut behind me and the sound echoes through the apartment, but I don't care. I'm clawing at the countertop for my toothbrush and the toothpaste.

The water is running, and my mouth is full of minty foam when I hear his knock outside the door.

"Bea."

I freeze.

"Open the door," he says, his voice deep enough to rattle the door. "Please."

I furiously brush, trying to finish as quickly as possible as he continues.

"Listen, I'm sorry," he says through the wood, "if you're regretting it or if you're embarrassed but . . ." He sighs, and there's a thud like he's let his head fall against the door. "Talk to me. Don't shut me out and bolt, like that was just some—"

I suddenly realize how this looks: refusing to talk to him, running from the room, hiding in the bathroom.

*Fuckfuckfuck.*

I throw the door open without thinking about it, the toothbrush in my hand and foam still lining my lips.

"I dow weewat at," I say around a mouthful of toothpaste.

His expression skews with confusion. "What?"

I roll my eyes and hold up a finger—the universal sign to wait—and turn to the sink. I spit into the drain, then turn to face Nathan again.

"I don't regret it. I just . . ." I squeeze my eyes closed before I continue. "I have really bad morning breath, so I needed to brush my teeth."

Silence for a long moment. I open my eyes a crack and see him still staring down at me, his brow furrowed.

"Oh." A moment passes. Nathan's gaze slides off my face to the countertop behind me. "Should I . . ." He nods to the sink, and I turn to see his toothbrush there waiting.

I turn back to him, my eyes a bit wider. "Okay."

We stand there for another moment before he moves forward, sidestepping where I'm blocking the doorway, and heads to the sink. I begin brushing again, watching him out of the corner of my eye as he squeezes toothpaste on his brush and begins to do the same.

We watch each other in the mirror as we brush and brush and brush; it's the only sound filling the small room. After I finally rinse, I lean against the countertop and wait until he's spit out his mouthwash.

"I really didn't want to make this awkward, and I think I just failed spectacularly," I say.

His lips quirk up in a smile. "Bea, I think it stopped being awkward the minute I woke up and found out you have 'the Piña Colada Song' as your alarm."

I nod. "Right."

He turns to face me fully. I'm working hard to look relaxed, but my bottom lip is trapped between my teeth, and he's watching it like he knows what that means, as if he's aware that this is a tell. Then he reaches up and wipes a bit of toothpaste from the corner of my mouth with his thumb.

"We need to talk about this," I say.

"What do you want to talk about?"

"Oh, I don't know, the fact that I just had sex with my co-worker who also happens to be the opposing counsel in my friend's divorce?"

"And?"

"And?" I repeat, incredulous. "This has to violate some professional ethics or something, right?"

"I don't think there's a rule against it."

"But that doesn't make it okay. I mean, you work for Josh and I know Josh and . . . there's issues, and we haven't even touched on the fact that we work together and you know my boss and . . ."

He crosses his arms over his chest. "What's the concern here?"

I take a deep breath. "Just because there's not a clear-cut rule doesn't mean it's right. It might not be a professional violation, but I'm willing to bet you're not going to tell Frank about this, right? Or Josh?"

He only stares at me.

"Exactly," I say. "And I can't tell Jillian. Because I know it would hurt her. I know this is wrong the same way you do."

His brow becomes a hard line across his face. "I never said this was wrong."

"Then what is it? What are we doing here? Are you seriously saying that this is fine? That we should pretend this is going somewhere even when we both know it can't?"

The words hurt even as they pour out of my mouth. But I know it's true as much as he does, even if right now I have a hard time thinking it could be anything other than something substantial. Something real.

But that was last night. It's morning now, and reality requires our attention.

Nathan moves forward, closing the space between us and planting a hand on the counter on either side of my hips. "Then what do you want, Bea?"

His expression is hard, almost angry. And I get it. This feeling, it's completely foreign and terrifying and I feel just as frustrated as he does. We both fought ourselves into the middle of this maze, and now that we're here, we have no idea how to get back out unscathed.

"I don't know," I say.

He stares at me for a moment longer, his gaze sliding to my lips. "Then what about just this?"

"Just what?"

"Here. This weekend."

I let out a breathy laugh. "Nate—"

"Stay here. With me. We give this thing until Monday. Let it run its course."

"And then what?"

"And then it's done. That's it."

My smile fades as I study him, searching the depths of his blue eyes for a tell, something that gives away an ulterior motive. He remains still for the survey, as if he knows I won't find anything.

"Okay. What are the terms?" I finally say.

"Is this a negotiation?"

"Yes."

The corner of his mouth twitches. "All right. Both parties agree to stay here until Monday morning, though either party can leave at any point if they deem it necessary. Neither party will have any obligation to continue the aforementioned relationship after the termination date."

I roll my eyes. "How romantic."

He offers a lazy shrug. "I hear romance is a social construct anyway."

Laughter bubbles up from me, but it fades just as quickly. Then I'm staring at him again, biting my bottom lip. He sees it and something flares in his eyes, as if he's just realized that I'm considering this.

"Come on, Bea," he says, leaning forward so his face is just inches away from mine. "Give me the weekend."

We're so close that I can see the flecks of color in his eyes again, how the blue is streaked with deep shades of gray.

"Okay," I say. My voice is so low it's almost inaudible.

"Okay?" he repeats.

I nod once. "Until Monday morning."

He kisses me before I can say anything else, add caveats or excuses or even think better of the entire stupid plan. Because it is stupid, I think as his hands slip under my sweatshirt to my hips, fingers sinking into my skin as he lifts me up and sets me on the countertop. So ridiculously and demonstrably stupid, but right now I don't care, not about how this will work or how it will end, only that he's mine. For right now, he's mine.

# CHAPTER 22

I have never spent so long in the bathroom.

Between the time we spend on the counter, and then afterward in the shower, I emerge an hour later with muscles that feel like rubber. My laundry bag is still in the corner of the living room, and I dig through it to find something to wear, settling on a pair of leggings and an oversized sweater.

Then I pile my wet hair on top of my head and steal a glance in the mirror by the bookcase. A few curls have escaped my sloppy bun, falling down the slope of my neck. My hazel eyes are clear. My freckles are more pronounced. There's none of the usual tension in my features, and I turn away before I can dissect that.

He's making coffee when I arrive in the kitchen. His hair is sticking out in all directions and his sweatpants are frayed and old. It's like he's actively resisting how attractive he is, and that somehow only makes it more pronounced.

"Grab the milk?" he says, nodding to the refrigerator as he presses a few more buttons and the machine buzzes to life.

I turn to the refrigerator and open the door. The fluorescent light illuminates the empty shelves. Well, not totally empty. There are a few beers in the back and a bottle of ketchup next to the milk on the door, but beyond that and some take-out containers, it's barren.

"Do you actually live here, or is this a fake apartment where you bring women?"

His brow furrows. "Excuse me?"

"This fridge is an abomination."

He comes up behind me and looks at the empty shelves. "I haven't had time to go grocery shopping in a while," he says as he grabs the milk.

"What the hell do you eat?"

He shrugs, pouring some into both coffee mugs, then handing one to me. "I'm usually at the office, and the kitchen there is stocked."

The information sits heavy in my chest. It's a rare insight into his life, one that feels so lonely and also so familiar.

I nod and take the mug he offers me. "So probably not the right time to tell you I'm starving."

A smug grin tugs at the corner of his lips. "Have you heard of something they call delivery?"

We decide on the diner around the corner, ordering entirely too much for just the two of us. When it arrives, we pile it all on the coffee table and curl up on the sofa, our legs tangled together as he offers me the remote control and begins picking at an order of fries. He doesn't realize his mistake until I've combed through his streaming services, found what I was looking for, and pressed play.

A synthesized pop soundtrack fills the room, and the screen fades up to reveal the glitzy logo for *The Real Housewives of New York City*.

Nathan groans, but there's a smile at the corner of his mouth, too.

I begin with season one, which I've already seen a thousand times before, so I'm barely paying attention to the dialogue or drama. I'm too busy enjoying the ease of this moment, the comfortable silence. He gets up halfway through episode five to get us beers, and when he returns, he has so many questions that I have to throw a cold french fry at his head.

It's the best Saturday I've had in a long time.

By the time season one ends, my foot has found its way into his lap, and he's massaging it lazily with one hand while he holds the remote in the other, searching for something else to watch.

I look at him and study his profile. His attention stays on the television, so I take my time memorizing the details. It always felt illicit before, like I was breaking some rule by staring at him, appreciating the features that make him up. But now it feels like a requirement before our time runs out.

My gaze finds the scar on his chin. I reach my hand up, letting my fingers run along the length of it.

"Where did this come from?"

"The scar?"

"No, the SpongeBob tattoo."

He shoots me a glare, doing his best to feign annoyance, even as his eyes glint with amusement. "A hockey stick."

"When?"

"Summer before fourth grade. My friend Taylor and I were playing hockey in the driveway with a tennis ball. Apparently, Taylor never heard of high-sticking."

I sigh dramatically. "Fucking Taylor."

He smiles. "Fucking Taylor."

His hand reaches over and traces the seam of my lips. Then he runs the back of his fingers across my freckles. "Where did these come from?"

"My dad, I think."

A moment passes. "Are you still in touch with him?"

I shake my head, an almost imperceptible motion. "He tried for a while, but then Mom remarried. So did he. I used to get cards on my birthday, but then those stopped, too."

Something in his demeanor alters, and the sardonic tinge to his expression dissolves. "I'm sorry."

"It's okay. I don't remember much about him."

"What do you remember?"

Part of me wants to dismiss the question. Change the subject and move on. But a larger part wants to tell him everything; I want him to know me. So, I let out a shaky breath and let the memory come rushing back. "Every Saturday morning, my dad would make us pancakes. It didn't matter if he and my mom were fighting or ignoring each other. Saturday he would get up early, make a huge pile of pancakes, and then blast the same song to wake me up. And I remember coming down the stairs to find him dancing around the kitchen with the music blaring, singing along as he set the table."

Nathan's gaze finally meets my eyes. "What was the song?"

I smile, hoping it doesn't look too sad. "'The Piña Colada Song.'"

He's studying my face like he can read the hidden language under my expression, the echo of the sharp pain that the years had dulled, the hurt and resignation. But the hints of joy and happiness there as well. Then he smiles, too.

After a moment I look away, and my gaze finds the bouquet of flowers on the dining table. "What about those?"

He turns to steal a glance at them. "They're from my mom."

"Your mom sent you flowers?"

"She has this whole philosophy. Says the sign of a good life is never having enough vases, because that means you're getting more flowers than you know what to do with. So she sends them to me all the time to celebrate mundane accomplishments."

I like that. "What are those for?"

He sighs. "The twenty-seventh anniversary of losing my first tooth."

A laugh bursts out of me. "Oh my God, that's amazing."

"Try telling me that in college when I would get a dozen roses delivered to my dorm room."

"At least you didn't ask her to stop."

He seems to consider. "I did once. When I was dating Rebecca."

My smile fades. I know we're dancing a fine line, toying with these cracks we've unearthed in each other. But I don't care. I'm desperate for details that will be cut off from me in just a couple days.

"Why?" I ask.

"I think she resented the fact that her boyfriend got more flowers than she did." His lip twitches with a grin, but it doesn't stick. He lets his gaze drift back to my feet. Silence envelops us again before he continues. "She was sleeping with a partner at her firm. That's why we broke up."

The shock is so acute that it takes me a moment before I remember to speak. "Nate—"

"We had been growing apart for a while. Even before my mom's diagnosis. I think since we assumed our relationship was easy, we both stopped trying. She was doing so well at work, and I was barely home, traveling between the office and my parents' house . . ."

He focuses on his lap, where his fingers are wrapped around my toes. "I took it for granted. Like we had arrived at the happily-ever-after part of the story and that was it."

"Did she tell you there was an issue?"

He shakes his head slowly. "It took me a long time to even suspect something was going on. When I finally asked her, she said I was crazy. That it wasn't what I thought. And I trusted her. It never entered my mind not to. In the end, I think that hurt more than the cheating." He pauses. "In a weird way, I think she's the reason I made partner. I started working all the time, doing anything to keep busy. To stop thinking about her. About anything."

I swallow. "I'm so sorry."

He's still staring down but his eyes are unfocused, as if he's lingering on the memory. Then he seems to shake it loose and offers me a small grin. "The worst part was that my mom thought it was her fault."

"What?"

"When I called to tell my parents that we broke up, she kept apologizing and asked, 'Was it because of the flowers?' It took me months to convince her it wasn't her fault. And I knew the minute she finally believed me, because they started arriving again."

He starts to chuckle, a deep laugh that fills the room, and I can't help joining. Even after it fades, he still has a smile on his face, the dimple dipping into his cheek, as he rubs his thumb against my arch.

"What about the 'I Hate It Here' mug in your office?" he asks softly. "I've always felt like there's a story there."

"That was a gift from Josh when I got into law school."

He nods. An odd silence descends, like we've made some sort of unspoken agreement never to discuss this area where our lives intersect. But he eventually breaks it. "How did you two meet?"

"We went to Fordham together," I say, trying to sound nonchalant. Like sharing this part of me is something I do all the time. "We have this tight group of friends that all graduated together, but he and I met first, at the beginning of our freshman year."

His thumb draws lazy circles on my ankle. "Tell me about them."

So I do. I start with those first few weeks on campus, how Josh and I met and never left each other's side for the next four years. How I tutored Travis in French and coached him in public speaking. How I met Jillian sophomore year and then introduced her to Josh. How Maggie joined us in an off-campus apartment the following year and how I convinced Travis to finally ask her out after graduation. How I helped Josh plan his proposal to Jillian, and how I organized almost all the holidays we spent at their apartment, the group hangouts before Maggie and Travis moved upstate, before the divorce became real. I tell Nathan all the mundane details, and he hangs on every word.

When I'm done, Nathan says, "So, you take care of everybody."

The way he says it, the present tense, rings in my ears. "Yeah."

A longer moment. Then, "And who takes care of you?"

My pulse bucks as I maintain his gaze. His expression is unreadable as he studies my face. It's like he sees the edit points, the scars from where I've removed the beating heart of this thing.

"What makes you think I need anyone to take care of me?" I finally ask.

Then there's that frown, the one that balances between amusement and derision. "Bea, you were evicted from your apartment yesterday while wearing the wrong day of your days-of-the-week underwear.'"

I gape at him, then I kick my foot out to free it from his grip. "I wasn't evicted! It was a temporary order to vacate!"

He starts laughing, holding tight to my ankle as I kick out my other foot. He catches that one, too.

"And I own other underwear. It's not like they're all days of the week!"

"Okay," he says through his smile, in that way that implies he doesn't believe me at all.

"God, you're such an asshole." I'm trying so hard to bite back my smile as I kick both of my legs that I only succeed in falling off the sofa onto the floor.

Nathan follows me down to the ground, still holding both of my ankles and pulling me toward him so he's kneeling between my thighs. My protests are punctuated by laughter as I buck once more, but then he leans down, kissing the soft skin where my sweater has ridden up and exposed my stomach.

"Do you want to fight, or do you want to do something else?" he murmurs.

I huff. "I haven't decided yet."

I can feel him smile into my skin as he makes a slow trail of kisses across my stomach. My muscles contract under the tickle of his stubble, as his tongue darts out to circle my navel. I twist beneath him again, but this time it isn't to free myself, but to pull my sweater over my head.

He mirrors my movement, pulling his T-shirt off. I run my hand up his chest, my nails testing the hard muscles.

God, I'm not going to get enough of this. I'll never get enough of him.

I suppress the thought as he lets go of my ankles so his hands can journey up to bracket my hips, holding me in place. He dips his head down, grazing his lips across the space between my breasts.

"We should stop," he murmurs.

"Why?"

"We haven't left the apartment all day. We should go out, do something."

"I don't want to go out and do something. I want to stay here and get as much of you as I can."

He looks up, meeting my eyes as his fingers absently caress my hips. "Yeah?"

My heart trips, trying to read his expression. "Is that selfish?"

He does a slow audit of my eyes, my lips, my freckles. "That's what this weekend is about, Bea. Being selfish."

He's not wrong. There's a stopwatch running on this weekend. And while we had spent weeks trying to avoid this happening at all, we had also somehow bypassed all the bullshit of dating. I know him and he knows me, and now it's just about being together. For a couple of days, at least.

"You didn't have any plans before I called?" I reach up and run a hand through his short hair.

"No." He places a kiss against my sternum.

I smile. "What about work?"

He hums against my skin. "Nothing that can't wait until Monday."

"That's it?"

He sighs, hands now wrapped around my rib cage as his mouth journeys up to the hollow of my throat. "I usually go for a run."

"Well, I can do that," I whisper, my breath catching as his thumbs trace under my breasts.

He licks my collarbone. "Do what?"

"Run."

He kisses up to my jaw. "Okay."

"I'm good at running."

He nips my earlobe. "That's great."

"We should go."

He finally leans back, a wry expression on his face. "You want to go for a run?"

"Sure."

"All right," he whispers. "But for now, I'm just going to give you a few orgasms. Okay?"

I close my eyes and work to sound exasperated. "Okay."

He chuckles as he wraps his arms around me, pressing his hips into mine, and the topic of leaving the apartment doesn't come up again.

# CHAPTER 23

I'm dying. My lungs are on fire and I'm pretty sure my last words will be some iteration of: "Don't invite this man to my funeral. He'll tell everyone about my days-of-the-week underwear."

"You okay?" Nathan asks as I wheeze. He's next to me, his easy canter at odds with my flailing limbs.

"You did this on purpose," I choke.

"You said you were good at running."

"Not for this *long*."

He laughs, the sound so deep it reverberates in my chest. "It's just two miles."

"It's death."

It's Sunday morning, so the running paths that line the thin track of park between the West Side Highway and the Hudson River are relatively empty. And cold. The chill dampens the smell of the water and the road, and for the first few blocks it was even pleasant. But after mile one I forgot everything that had made it pleasant. I can only focus on the skyline ahead while trying to figure out how they would get an ambulance down the footpath to pick me up when I eventually drop dead.

It's another few blocks before Nathan's easy gait slows to a walk, and I'm so happy I want to cry. Instead, I just stop, bending at the waist as I gasp for air.

He stops, too, watching me with more confusion in his expression than concern. "So, you're not a runner."

I don't bother looking at him as I shake my head.

"Why'd you suggest it, then?"

"I work out," I wheeze. "I thought I could handle it."

After a minute I stand upright again, squinting against the sun as I take a few more deep breaths. I can see that he's smiling as his gaze flits down my body, and I mentally pat myself on the back for remembering to throw my leggings and sports bra in my laundry bag.

"What do you usually do to stay in shape?" he asks.

"Yoga," I say around gasps. "What I lack in endurance I make up for in flexibility."

His smile broadens, the dimple on full display. "Well, that explains a few things."

I laugh even as a rush of heat floods my cheeks.

We cross the West Side Highway into the Village, my breath finally slowing enough that my lungs no longer hurt, and I can stand up straight without breaking into a coughing fit. Nathan, on the other hand, looks like he just stepped out of a photoshoot for athletic wear. His light brown hair is tousled in a way that looks annoyingly intentional, and, besides the sheen of sweat on his face, there's not a hint that he spent the past half hour sprinting downtown alongside the Hudson River.

As if on cue, he brings the corner of his shirt up to wipe a bit of it away from his upper lip. I watch the motion until I feel my phone vibrate on my hip. Nathan's attention is on the traffic light now, so I pull it from the pocket of my waistband, peeking at the screen.

**MAGGIE**

Are you alive?!

WHY ARE YOU IGNORING ME?

Answer or my next call is to the police.

*Shit.* I forgot that I put my phone on silent after my alarm went off Saturday morning.

**BEATRICE**

HI SORRY

I AM ALIVE

**MAGGIE**

Sorry you're alive or sorry you didn't reply earlier?

Don't answer that.

So did they fix your building?

If not you can still head up to ours.

The key is under the gnome thing next to the garage.

I instinctively hold the phone a bit closer to my chest. It's not that I don't want Nathan to see, but I still turn a bit to hide the screen as I type out my reply.

**BEATRICE**

NO ITS OKAY

I WILL CALL YOU NEXT WEEK

**MAGGIE**

If you say so.

We're not back until Wednesday so it's yours if you need it!

ps: what do you think about a floral for the bridesmaid dresses?

I send her a barfing emoji before sliding my phone back into the small pocket of my leggings. Nathan hasn't seemed to notice; he's watching the light as it changes, and then he nods for us to cross.

*Crisis averted*, I think as I take a deep breath. The last thing I want to do is bring reality into our weekend.

But I can't shake the feeling that I've just wallpapered over a substantial crack. This weekend is built off the fact that I *need* to be here, right? And somewhere in my mind that rationalized it, like the necessity of staying with him somehow makes everything else okay. Except now I don't have to be here anymore. Every second I stay is a choice. And if he knows, this all becomes so much more real.

"Everything all right?"

Nathan's voice snaps me back to the present. He's looking down at me with his signature impassive expression, one I've seen a hundred times before, but right now it feels just like the first time, when I thought he could read my every thought with that look. And all the anxiety in my chest feels like it's going to burst out.

"What?" My tone is more defensive than I intended.

"The text."

"Oh. Yeah, it's fine, why?"

"You tensed up."

I roll my eyes because I literally have no idea what to say. He's right, I did tense up. And I don't want to lie to him. I don't even know if I can. And now that anxiety feels a lot like anger because, oh my God, when did I lose all control of this?

"It's nothing," I finally say.

"Okay," he replies, in that skeptical tone I'm beginning to think he should trademark. Then he nods to the restaurant just a few doors down from us. "Want to grab some food?"

I scrunch up my nose. "I'm sweaty."

"I've noticed," he says. "But I'm starving, and there's nothing at home."

The word falls so casually from his lips that I almost miss it until it lands with a dull thud in my head. *Home.* Everything is bleeding together, and now he just called his apartment "home," like that not only meant something for him but for me, too. And suddenly my heart is racing because I realize, just as quickly, that it did. It meant everything.

So I do what I do best, what I've conditioned myself to do every time I start to feel too much—I cross my arms over my chest and fortify my armor again.

"So rather than solve that problem, you just want to ignore it?" He blinks. "What?"

"I'm just saying that if you don't have any food, maybe grocery shopping is smarter than throwing money at a restaurant."

"You want to go grocery shopping?" He's looking at me like I've suggested we shave our heads and join a cult. Any other time I would have found it annoyingly endearing, but right now I feel on edge. An odd flood of emotions is churning in my chest, and I can't decipher them.

"No, I don't *want* to go grocery shopping. But I think we *should* go grocery shopping."

"Why?"

"Because I'm not leaving you tomorrow with an empty refrigerator!" I snap, motioning wildly in the air in front of me.

It's still after that. I can feel him staring down at me, but I won't meet his eyes. I can't. I didn't intend for those words to have the weight they did, to imply exactly what I'm so scared of him seeing: that I care about him. A lot. But trying to pull it back would mean acknowledging it, so I stay quiet, staring past him at the slow line of cars passing, and let the silence expand.

"Okay," he finally says, reaching out and pushing an errant curl behind my ear. "Let's go grocery shopping."

~

The fact that Nathan knows that the store is just a few blocks away is mildly comforting. That comfort is dispelled, however, the minute he grabs a basket and heads for the frozen food section. Trying to convince him that there are other appliances in his kitchen besides the microwave is met with the same sardonic expression

I've become familiar with, so I don't even offer a biting retort as I grab his arm and drag him to the produce.

The next hour is a crash course in all things Nathan Asher. He shares tidbits about his childhood across the organic vegetables. We compare high school horror stories at the meat counter. In the dairy section, he admits that eggs are his favorite food (mostly because he knows how to cook them). He likes bell peppers (his mom used to grow them in the backyard when he was young), he hates peaches (apparently fruit should never be fuzzy), and he didn't know they still made Froot Loops, so now we're at the checkout line with three boxes. I stare down at them, conspicuous among the array of otherwise-healthy food on the conveyor belt. He sees my critical glare and pushes them closer to his side.

"Hey," he says. "Be nice or I won't share."

I roll my eyes and suppress a laugh.

The cashier finally gets to us and starts chatting with Nathan, smiling and giggling, literally *giggling*, when he tells her about the Froot Loops.

*Oh, for fuck's sake.* I turn my back on them and let my eyes wander to the front of the door. The Easter display flails in the wind every time the doors slide open. I'm considering how long it will last before it finally topples and sends chocolate eggs flying, when my phone rings. It's still stuffed in the small pocket of my leggings, so it takes me a minute to pull it out and see Jillian's name lighting up my screen.

"Hey, Jills," I answer, forcing a smile as I take a few steps away from Nathan. I just need to pretend everything is fine, signal that she doesn't need to worry. Then get off the phone as quickly as possible and call her back when I have a second to get my head around how this conversation will go.

"Hey! I saw I missed a call from you on Friday. Is everything okay?" she asks.

"Yup. Fine," I say quickly, wandering closer to the doors so she won't hear Nathan's voice in the background. "How'd the interview go?"

"Really well. I'm still up here, actually. Thought I'd take a few more days to explore the city, check out the real estate," she says, then releases a humorless laugh, and I can tell something is wrong.

"Why don't you sound more excited?"

"I know, I'm trying." Then, a moment later: "It's just, when I got back to the hotel Friday, there was an email from Josh's attorney waiting with the twenty-four-page affidavit outlining his alimony request."

It's like a punch in the gut. I'm vaguely aware that Nathan is still talking to the cashier nearby, laughing about some anecdote involving breakfast foods. He doesn't notice as I turn and walk out the door.

"He sent it to you on Friday night?" I hiss once I'm out on the sidewalk.

"Well, technically he sent it to my lawyer, and she forwarded it to me. But yeah."

My mind flashes back to that night, to the moment Nathan so casually said he had been working late before he came uptown to see me.

"What does it say?" I ask, trying to mask the growing anger in my voice.

"I'm still working my way through it. The alimony is bad, obviously. But there's also a lot that just doesn't match up. Josh's financial disclosure is here, but the numbers don't match what I thought. Like, he had worked and saved up a lot for grad school, but he dropped out after a year, so some of that money should still be here. But I'm not seeing it. It's just . . . gone."

The comment itches a deep part of my memory. This is familiar, and I hate that it's familiar. My mind races back to college, after Josh's injury when he was lying about where his money was being spent, when he was lying about everything. Thousands of dollars of his parents' money disappeared, bills went months without being paid. It had been a mess—one that hid something much more awful. But it was also something Josh had promised wouldn't happen again.

"You need to flag that, Jills." My tone barely conceals my newly stoked anger. "His lawyer needs to know if he's lying or hiding money—"

"Don't worry, I have a call with my lawyer tomorrow to discuss it. Hopefully there are enough discrepancies here to challenge the alimony. She says he can get into serious trouble for lying on these documents."

I shake my head. "Serves him right for pursuing it in the first place."

"Don't give him too much credit," Jillian says with a sigh. "He didn't come up with the idea; his lawyer did."

That bottomless pit in my stomach opens wider, pulling everything inside me down. "Nathan Asher?"

"Yeah. Apparently, all Josh had to do was mention how I have been supporting him for the past couple years, and his lawyer did the rest." Then she groans, as if she just remembered who she's talking to. "Please don't go storming into his office again, Bea. My lawyer and I just got back to a good place, and I don't want to jeopardize that."

"I won't," I say. I'm vaguely aware that Nathan has walked out of the grocery store, but the thundering pulse in my ears won't let me acknowledge him. I keep my head down and my phone to my ear.

"Thank you," Jillian says. "Okay, I should let you go. I'll call you when I get home in a few days, okay? I can finally pick up my dishes and you can help me scour Boston apartment listings."

"Sure, sounds good," I say.

Then she hangs up.

I bring the phone down to my side.

"Hey," I hear Nathan's voice ahead of me.

I look up. He's standing a few feet away, a grocery bag in each hand and a smile on his face. I don't know what to say to him. I don't know what to do with this raw feeling, this dark, ugly thing growing inside me that feels so much like anger but is sharper. Scarier. I want to hand it to someone and have them tell me what to do with it. But the only person I can ask to help is the one responsible for it in the first place.

His smile fades as he takes in my expression. "What's wrong?"

"Nothing," I seethe.

He takes a step toward me, his brow creased with concern. "Talk to me, Bea."

"Fine," I say, throwing my arms out at my side. "Everything is wrong."

"What happened?"

"Jillian just called me."

"Okay…" Nathan says it like he's waiting for the other shoe to drop.

"You remember Jillian, don't you?" I ask, my tone biting. "The woman you sent that twenty-four-page petition to on Friday right before you came uptown to help me?"

A muscle ticks in his jaw, and I hate how I see the recognition click into place. "Hey. Come on—"

"No." I shake my head, anger hitting me again. "She's spent all weekend stressed about it, trying to figure it out. Meanwhile, you and I have been pretending like everything is fine—"

"Everything is fine," he says slowly. It's his lawyer voice again, stern but tinged with annoyance.

"Oh my God, stop placating me!" I snap. "Stop pretending like you're not actively working to destroy Jillian's life."

"I'm not destroying her life, Bea,"

"Oh really? Who decided to ask for alimony?"

Something in his eyes shutters, but not before I see the guilt flash across his expression. "Listen—"

"Who?" I demand.

"They're getting divorced, Bea," he says. It comes out calmly, like he's explaining this to one of his students. "Believe it or not, I'm just trying to help them through it."

"No, you *used* to help people. But then you stopped, remember? You had to 'grow the firm' and 'focus on your clients.' That was your choice, so don't try to make yourself feel better about it by saying you're 'helping.' As if getting paid to divide up people's lives somehow makes you a benevolent person."

"I never claimed to be benevolent," he says, his expression hardening. "But my job doesn't make me a malicious asshole, either. It's just a job."

"Sorry to break it to you, Nate, but the person that walks out of that office every day is the same fucking person that walks in."

A couple of women walk by, their eyes wide as they listen to me. Then they give Nathan a sympathetic look.

He waits until they pass before he says, "Can we just—"

"No, seriously. How do you not feel bad?"

He frowns, that same frown from the first time I met him, the one that implies he's almost disappointed in my train of thought. "I thought we were past this."

"Past this?" I let out a bitter laugh, lost as to where to even begin explaining why I would never be past this. "I spent my whole childhood watching this happen over and over, and I promised myself I'd never let it happen to me. And now here I am, losing more people I love to divorce, while sleeping with the guy responsible for all of it!"

I can feel the tears burning behind my eyes but blink them away, choosing to focus on anger instead.

Nathan releases a sigh as his hands go to his hips. "You have every right to be pissed off, but don't make me the target of it. It's not fair for you to throw this in my face every time you need someone to blame."

"Well, you make it pretty fucking easy," I say, throwing my arms out at my side.

"Jesus." He shakes his head, letting his gaze drop to the sidewalk. "I know what you're doing, Bea."

I still, narrowing my eyes on him. "What am I doing?"

He lifts his gaze back to me. The sympathy is still there, but there's also a clear frankness. "You're so fucking scared of being vulnerable that you'd rather stand out here fighting for someone else's relationships than think about what you actually want, because that's easier than getting hurt, right?"

Too close. His words hit too close to my heart. Panic swells in my throat, but I swallow it down as I raise my chin. "You don't know me."

He scoffs. "Yeah, well. At least I'm trying to."

He doesn't move, as if he's waiting for me to say . . . what? That he's right? That it's easier for me to lash out than admit how terrifying all of this is? Because that's what I want to do. Right now, I want to walk those few steps forward that would bring me to his chest and let him hold me. I want to mourn what I've lost this year, what he and I could've had if none of this had happened at all. And I know he would listen; God, I can see in his eyes that he wants to.

But he's right. I'm too fucking scared.

The silence expands, stretching out like it's creating physical distance between us. After a long moment, he sighs, messing up his hair in frustration before motioning his head toward the way we came. "Come on, let's go."

We don't say a word as we walk back to his apartment. I'm a few steps ahead, and Nathan carries the bags behind me. I can feel his gaze on the back of my head, as if he's trying to decipher what I'm thinking. Except that even I can't make sense of the conflicting thoughts and worries and fears. They're all churning together in the simmering anger. But amid the chaos, I know one thing: he's too close. And that means I have to end this now.

His eyes are locked on me in the elevator. I steel my expression, keeping my gaze ahead as the car slowly climbs up to the ninth floor. As soon as the doors open, I'm walking forward, down the hall to his apartment door. He arrives a few moments after I do, unlocking the dead bolt and pushing it open for me to enter.

I pass him in silence, then hear his steps follow me inside.

"Do you want to spend the rest of the weekend not talking to each other?" he asks as we enter the living room.

I scoff. "No. That's literally the last thing I want to do."

I continue on to the bedroom and slam the door shut. I know he'll give me a few minutes to cool down before coming after me, so I take advantage of the time and tear through the room, grabbing my loose clothes strewn across the floor. Then I open the bedroom door and head down the hall.

Nathan is standing like a monolith in the center of the living room, his tall body still clad in his running gear. His head rises when he hears me coming. His expression looks tired, but when I grab my laundry bag and start stuffing clothes inside, it contorts with confusion.

"What are you doing?"

I drag the bag past him to the front door. "Going home."

His eyes widen. "Are you serious?"

"Very."

"Jesus, Bea," he growls.

"What?" I ask, turning to face him.

He's still a few steps away from me, his hands on his hips. The anger is back, sharpening the line of his brow, the angle of his jaw. "We're in the middle of an argument."

"No, you're arguing. I'm leaving."

He shakes his head. "This is bullshit. You don't just walk out the door when things get too hard."

I can't help the bitter laugh that leaves my lips as I throw my coat and backpack over my arm. "That's ironic coming from the guy who makes his money off people doing just that."

The minute I utter the words I want to take them back. But it's too late. His shoulders slump, and the mix of hurt and disappointment on his face is almost too much to bear.

I know should apologize. I want to. But the anger is still too raw, my pride too wounded. So I grab the strings of my laundry bag and drag it behind me as I leave, slamming the front door closed.

The hallway is silent, like I've just landed in a still life. Even I can't move; I just stand there, my back to his door. The elevators are ahead. Just a few steps and I could press the down button, get in one, and leave. It would be so easy. A clean break.

Easy, but not simple. Because there's some sort of admission in that first step, like I'm giving up. Like this is really over. Even the thought sends a spike of panic through my chest. I try to swallow it down, but that only seems to sharpen it, poking my heart with every breath. Reminding me of the truth: I don't want this to be done. I don't want to have to walk away from this door and never see the man behind it again. The anger is nothing compared to the abject fear of that first step.

But the alternative, the idea of not leaving, is just as terrifying. There is too much to discuss, too much baggage to work through. I had fought like we had to purge all the rot before anything else could grow, but I had taken for granted that he had more to dig out. And maybe there would be nothing left when he was done.

*At least I'm trying to.*

I don't know why those words stung; people had said a lot worse to me. But this felt different. Like it exposed some vulnerability in us both.

And he's right. I would rather lash out than acknowledge this feeling, so big and so devastating that I can't even hold on to the anger anymore. But I also know it won't go away when I get in that elevator.

It's another minute before I turn around to face the door again. My breath is shaky and so is my fist as I raise it, ready to knock . . . but I let it hover there. What if he doesn't answer? What if he doesn't—

The door swings open before I finish the thought. He's standing on the threshold, his face tired and somber and so fucking sad that I feel the last of my feeble defenses crumble and the stark reality left in its wake.

I'm in love with him.

We stare at each other, and in the silence, I try to say everything that feels stuck in my throat.

*I'm sorry.*

*I don't want to go.*

*I love you.*

But I shrug instead, swallowing back the lump in my throat and say, "The weekend's not over yet."

A muscle ticks in his jaw as he steps forward and wraps his arms around me. It's a tight, desperate embrace, like he thinks I might still disappear if he doesn't hold on. And I wrap my arms around him because, yes, I think he might just disappear, too. This rare thing could go from my life as quickly as it appeared. That fear has me clinging to him so tightly I think his T-shirt might rip.

*I'm in love with you and you're right, it scares the shit out of me*, I want to whisper in his ear. But it turns out I really am a coward, because I don't say anything at all as he straightens his back, lifting me off my feet and turning us both back into the apartment.

# CHAPTER 24

I open my eyes to find sunlight dancing across Nathan's bedroom ceiling. His sheets are wrapped around my limbs, his scent lacing my skin. It feels so ordinary, so normal, that my brain takes a few minutes to catch up, to pause and wonder if the past few days actually happened, or if they were just some lucid dream.

Then I hear clattering coming from the kitchen—metal hitting metal—and the faint chords of Miles Davis playing from somewhere in the apartment.

It's Monday morning.

I sit up slowly and run a hand through my matted curls before looking around his bedroom. The watery light illuminates the corners, revealing our clothes still strewn across the floor and furniture. After I came back inside the apartment yesterday, we spent the rest of the day in bed, a desperate attempt to fill those hours by memorizing every inch of one another—every touch, every gasp. It had been like being broken apart and welded back together into something stronger. I wanted him to feel that, too; I tried to find a way to communicate it with every kiss and lick and bite. Like I could prove to both of us that this is more than just a fling. More than just physical.

But neither of us had said anything. We'd barely spoken at all. And now the weekend is over.

The bedroom door is open, and from down the hall I can hear the shuffling of feet amid the low music. I listen for a moment longer, then stand and walk to the bathroom to brush my teeth. In the mirror I study my naked body as I brush, the faint marks from Nathan's teeth still on my hips and breasts. It sends a warm ache through my core. Which is why I walk back out to the bedroom and pull on my clothes still strewn across the chair. I need to cover it all up, like it never happened.

I make it to the kitchen doorway and see him pouring Froot Loops into two bowls. His back is to me, so I take a minute to watch the muscles as they work in tandem under his T-shirt. His broad shoulders stretch the gray cotton, his arms pull taut the sleeves. He's wearing those sweatpants again; they fall low on his hips, and I can see a sliver of skin there. The muscles in my core contract at the sight, all exhaustion forgotten as I fight the urge to come up behind him and kiss his neck.

*You can't do that anymore*, I remind myself.

"Morning," I say from the doorway.

He turns just enough to steal a glance at me. There's a soft smile on his face. "Morning."

He closes up the cereal box, then turns to face me fully, resting against the counter as he crosses his arms over his chest.

The expanse of the kitchen stretches out between us. It feels so different from the other morning, when I had barely noticed the size of it at all. Now it feels massive. And it should, I remind myself. It needs to.

"So," I blurt out after a long, tense moment. "Last night . . ."

The corner of his mouth curls up. "Yeah?"

"We didn't use a condom."

He blinks. God, I can actually see him processing it in real time. "Jesus, Bea. I didn't—"

"I'm on birth control," I barrel on. "I just . . . wanted you to know. If you were worried or thinking about it or . . . whatever."

"Okay." He tilts his head to the side like he's trying to decipher my tone. "I had my physical a few weeks ago and I'm fine."

"That's good." I fold my arms around my waist, looking everywhere but his face.

Miles Davis keeps playing in the other room, but here in the kitchen, we stand in silence for a long moment.

"I just made it weird again, didn't I?" I say, an exhausted smile starting at the corners of my lips.

He smiles back. His stubble is almost a beard now, framing his jaw. "Yeah, you really did."

I laugh softly.

"What time do you have class?" he asks.

His words hit somewhere deep in my gut. Right. Of course he wants to know what time I'm leaving. This was the deadline, wasn't it? The expiration date we both set that's now passed.

"Not until ten, but I should head home first. Make sure my building is still there."

He nods. "Right."

"What about you?"

"I usually get into work around eight."

I steal a glance at the clock on the microwave.

7:22.

I try to think of what to say, but my mind only spins. God, what is this feeling? My mouth is dry, my body paralyzed while my brain races to figure out what the hell to do next.

I feel overwhelmed. And it has been so long since I felt anything like this that I have no idea what to do with it.

"Do you want some breakfast or something?" he asks, standing upright again and turning toward the counter. "I poured you some cereal—"

"I should get going."

He pauses, his gaze suddenly sharp. "Right now?"

"Yeah." I dart my eyes away. I know if he looks at my expression too closely, he'll be able to see the truth there. "I have that huge bag of laundry, and the subway is such a mess during rush hour, so . . ." The words fade.

"I'll get you a car," he says, frowning.

"No, that's okay," I say, shaking my head. "I'm just . . . going to go."

My smile feels brittle—a superficial mask put on to keep an entirely different emotion at bay. I feel the cracks forming, and I don't have the tools to reinforce them. So I turn on my heel and start out of the kitchen.

My laundry is still by the front door, along with my backpack. The clothes that had been scattered in the living room are now folded neatly on top of it. He must have done that this morning before I woke up. It's a sweet gesture that leaves behind a bitter aftertaste. How long has he been awake, waiting for me to leave?

He's walking down the hall as I slip on my shoes and coat. Then I shove the clothes into the laundry bag before cinching it closed, grabbing the strings with one hand and my backpack in the other. I don't turn to face him; I don't think I can bear it.

"I'll see you before class tomorrow, right?" he asks.

"Yeah, I think so."

His brow furrows. "You think so?"

"I just . . . I have a lot to do, and it's just a review class tomorrow. You don't really need me there for a review, right? I have some papers I still need to grade, and I missed a whole weekend of studying for the bar, too, so . . ." My tongue darts out to wet my lips. It's not technically a lie, but it still sits heavy in my gut.

"Right." He's studying my face, those dark blue eyes working so hard to see below the surface.

My heart trips and I have no idea how to curb its manic pace. So I force another smile. "Bye, Nate."

His expression shutters. "Bye, Bea."

There's so much more I want to say, but the words stay lodged in my throat. I turn to the door before he can see my bottom lip tremble, flipping the dead bolt and pulling the door open.

Then it suddenly slams shut again.

The sound reverberates down the hall, a sharp crack that makes me jump. I look up to see Nathan's hand now braced on the door above me. When I turn, his head has fallen forward, like he's been defeated.

"I'm sorry." His voice is so low I barely make out the words.

I blink. "For what?"

His face is just inches from mine as he looks up enough to meet my eyes. "I lied to you."

"When?"

"Back in your office. When you asked me why I took over Frank's class. I lied. I told you I was doing him a favor. That's not true. He asked me to cover the class a while ago and I had turned it down."

My brows pinch together. "But then why—"

"I changed my mind when I found out that you were his TA. I took the job because I wanted to see you again. I didn't think any of this would happen. I didn't plan it, I just . . . I had to see you again, Bea. I had to talk to you and know you and . . ."

His voice fades. A heavy silence falls even as my pulse hammers in my ears, a turbulent mix of relief and shock and anger racing through my veins.

"Fuck," I mumble under my breath.

His jaw ticks. "I know. I should have—"

"Shut up." I shake my head. "I lied, too."

A moment. "What?"

"Yesterday," I say. "When I got that text after our run, you asked me if everything was okay, and I told you it was nothing. But it wasn't nothing. It was Maggie. She told me I could use the house. Told me where the spare key was and everything. So I didn't have to stay here. I'm sorry I didn't tell you, I just . . . I didn't want to go."

He stares at me for a long moment, his expression hard. "I wouldn't have let you leave."

Somewhere in the apartment, music is still playing, but I barely hear it. I'm still processing his words. It's only when I've run them through for the fourth time that it really hits me. He wants me here as much as I want to be here.

I swallow past the lump in my throat. "Technically, that would be kidnapping."

He frowns, that sardonic look. "No, Bea. That's false imprisonment."

God, he's such an asshole.

But I still kiss him. There's no thought or reasoning, only my brain wanting to claim him. *You love him. He is yours and you are his, and fuck everything else.* I lean forward and take his mouth in mine, opening his lips and sliding my tongue against his.

Nathan lets out a long groan that's more akin to a growl, a deep sound that seems to lodge itself somewhere below my sternum. Then his arms are around me, crushing me against his body as my hands dig into his hair. It's like my body melts into his, fitting perfectly against every angle and curve.

What began as lazy quickly becomes frantic, pulling and pushing and biting and kissing. It's like we're using our bodies to fight and make up and argue and negotiate. I almost want to laugh. Isn't that what we've always done? It's a language we didn't realize we were speaking until right now.

"I don't want this to be the last time I kiss you," he whispers into my lips. "I don't want this to be done."

I lean back just enough to meet his eyes.

"Me, either," I say.

The corner of his mouth turns up. "Yeah?"

I nod. "Yeah."

It's just one word but it feels so big. He rests his forehead against mine, our labored breath mingling together.

"We're doing this?" he asks.

"Yeah, we're doing this," I whisper. "Are we crazy?"

His smile broadens. "Probably."

I laugh and then let out a yelp as he kneels down and throws me over his shoulder. I try to wiggle free, but he ignores me as he heads back down the hall toward the bedroom.

"Don't you have to go to work?" I ask through my laugh.

"Fuck it. I'll be late."

# CHAPTER 25

He's late. Very late. In fact, I barely make it home in time to shower and change before I have to head back downtown to campus for class. Thankfully, the sign is gone from the front of my building, and I'm so relieved that I barely notice that the shower is still lukewarm. I stand under the spray and smile to myself.

I'm sore, that wonderful sore that aches in all the right places. The kind that keeps a stupid smile on my face as I dry off and dig through my laundry bag for clean underwear. It's only as I have it all poured out on my bed that I realize there's something missing. I reach for my phone and type out a text:

**BEATRICE**

I LEFT TUESDAY AT YOUR APARTMENT

A moment, then I see the three dots that show he's writing back.

**NATHAN ASSHOLE**

Good thing you have Wednesday through Monday.

**BEATRICE**

NOT TRUE

I AM MISSING FRIDAY TOO BUT THAT WAS A PRE-NATE CASUALTY

**NATHAN ASSHOLE**

That sounds like a good story.

**BEATRICE**

IF YOU ENJOY PETTY LARCENY AT THE LOCAL LAUNDROMAT THEN YES YOU'LL LOVE IT

**NATHAN ASSHOLE**

Tell me when you come over tonight.

**BEATRICE**

ARE YOU ASKING ME TO STAY OVER OR TO COME FIND MY UNDERWEAR

**NATHAN ASSHOLE**

Both.

My smile broadens as I put my phone down.

I'm seeing him tonight. We're really doing this.

But with each wonderful ache, there's also a nagging voice in the back of my head pointing out what this means. And what does it mean? We hadn't even gotten that far, only that we both want this. But what is this? I had been so clear about not wanting anything more, and he had agreed . . . Did he just change his mind?

Or worse, had he not changed his mind at all? When he said he didn't want this to end, was he just talking about sex?

I shake the thought loose as I file through the clothes in front of me. No, we're well past that point. Maybe if it had just been Friday night, but . . . the weekend changed that. It changed every-thing. And as incredible as that is, it also has me on edge. I'm not only worried about what that means to him, but what it means to everyone else.

Which lands me on an uncomfortable reality: I have to tell Jillian.

I manage to procrastinate for a while. I decide on an outfit—my nice suede boots and a green velvet skirt I save for special occasions—and head downtown, keeping myself busy with office hours and then with class. It's not until I finish grading assignments later that afternoon that I catch sight of my phone sitting next to me on my desk.

*Stop being a coward*, a voice says in the back of my mind.

I scowl, even as I pick up my phone and unlock it. When I do, the screen lights up. Three text messages and four missed calls. All from Jillian.

*Fuck.*

She knows.

My heart ricochets in my chest as my mind flips through every possible way she could have learned. Maybe someone saw us at the grocery store, or maybe Maggie let something slip about that first time . . .

My hands start shaking, reducing my fingers to clumsy stubs as I unlock my screen. I ignore the texts, instead going straight to my contacts and finding her number.

It rings once before it connects . . . but there's only silence on the other end.

"Jills?" I finally venture.

A soft sob.

Oh God. I slowly sit down and take a deep breath. "Jillian, I can explain—"

Jillian's soft voice interrupts me. "He abandoned him."

I blink. "What?"

"Josh abandoned Tex."

My brain is already five steps ahead and stumbles, trying to find the thread of the conversation again. "I . . . I don't understand."

"The doggie daycare called. Tex is still there. He's been there since Friday, Bea. Josh never came to pick him up and he hasn't paid for the month yet. They told me that if no one claims him today they have to list him as abandoned, and I'm still in Boston . . ."

Another soft sob.

The flood of relief that my secret is still safe is quickly over-whelmed by red-hot anger. I always knew Josh didn't care about the dog. We all did. But I didn't know he was capable of abandoning him just to get back at Jillian.

"God, he's such a dick," I seethe.

"Bea—"

"It's going to be fine. I'll go pick up Tex right now," I say as I stand and start for the door. I'll miss class, but that's fine. I'm already ahead on the reading anyway. Besides, it will be worth it for the look on Josh's face when I show up with his precious dog in hand. "Do they need a credit card or anything?"

"No, I gave them mine, it's just . . ." Her voice trails off, but I can still hear the hint of something fraying the edge of her tone. Something that sounds a lot like fear.

I pause at my office door.

"What is it, Jills?"

A shaky breath. Another sob. "It's Josh."

"What about Josh?"

"He wouldn't leave the dog like that. He wouldn't do that unless . . ."

Unless something is wrong. She can't get the words out, but I know.

Something clicks in my brain, a shift from anger to concern that is so intense that it's like I have tunnel vision. This is what I'm good at, a talent honed after years of helping my mother pick herself up after each and every breakup. The emotions can wait until this is over; right now I need to move. I step into the hallway and lock my office door, then rush to the elevator. "Have you tried calling him?"

"He's not picking up. I don't know who else to call—"

"I'm heading down there right now, Jills," I say, pressing the down button frantically until the elevator doors open and I step inside. "It's going to be fine."

∽

The doggie daycare is right around the corner from the apartment, so I grab Tex on the way. They apologize to *me* for some reason, like it's their fault his owner is a self-absorbed prick. I don't tell them that, though, and I don't answer their unvoiced questions as to why I'm there instead of Jillian or Josh. I just take Tex's leash and leave, my pace steady as I walk down Barrow Street.

I'm doing a good job of controlling the anxiety roiling my pulse as Tex and I ascend the steps to the building's front door. As usual, it's not locked, so I let myself in and climb up the stairs to the second-floor apartment. It's not until I'm standing at the door with its familiar welcome sign that I notice that it's not locked, either. It's not even closed the entire way; the latch is resting outside the strike plate. I'm about to push it open when I pause. There are voices coming from the inside. Two voices.

A kernel of something uncomfortable, something raw, sprouts in my belly. Then I push the door open.

Josh is standing there in the front hall, his hair long and un-washed, and his sweatpants loose at his waist. Beside him is a man shorter than me, with his hair tucked under a knit cap and his messenger bag open for Josh to look inside. But Josh isn't looking inside. He's staring at me, his eyes wide with dread.

It takes the other man a second to turn and notice me, too. His concern is mixed with confusion as he darts his gaze between us.

After a long moment, Josh clears his throat. "Hi, Bea."

I step forward, pulling Tex with me, and point at the man without taking my eyes off Josh. "Who is this?"

Josh's jaw slackens. "Uh . . ."

"I'm Gerald," the man volunteers.

I still don't bother looking at him. "Shut up, Gerald."

"Oh . . . Okay . . ."

I narrow my eyes on the husk of the man I used to know. "Who the fuck is this, Josh?"

I keep my gaze on him, raising an eyebrow as the silence stretches out between us.

Josh finally sighs, running a hand through his hair. "You need to go, man."

"But—"

My hand is already on the guy's shoulder, turning his body and pushing him out the front door. "Bye."

I slam the door shut before he can object, locking it for good measure.

When I turn back around, Josh is gone. I head down the short front hallway to the kitchen and find him there pacing back and forth. Tex is trailing him, too loving and forgiving to realize this is the same person who abandoned him.

"Who was that, Josh?"

"Did Jillian call you?" he asks, finally stopping to stare at me with wide eyes. No, not just wide. Wild.

"You never picked up Tex on Friday," I hiss, swallowing back my apprehension. "You know, the dog you're suing her for?"

He cringes, and I realize he forgot. The fucking dog is sitting at his feet, trying desperately to get his attention, and he still hasn't put it together.

"Fuck . . ." he murmurs, collapsing into the nearby folding chair and letting his head fall into his hands. His leg is still moving, though, bouncing, bouncing, bouncing, and goddammit, I know. I wish I didn't, but I know.

"So, what was Gerald dropping off?" I ask, glancing back at the doorway. "Just pills, or are you on something else now?"

He laughs bitterly. "Fuck you, Bea."

I ignore him. "You dropped one in that box of stuff for Jillian, you know. I found it and I tried so hard to come up with an excuse for you. After ten years, I'm still trying to make excuses for you!"

He shakes his head, still staring at the floor. "Get out."

"Oh, I'm not going anywhere. You think I'm going to leave you like this right now?"

"Why the fuck do you care?" he growls, finally meeting my eyes. God, he looks angry, unhinged. But I don't move. "You already picked Jillian, remember? You fucking hate me, so this should make you happy, right?"

I take a step toward him. "I didn't pick anyone. You're the one who decided to divorce Jillian. You're the one who went after everything she's worked so hard for, just because you couldn't deal with this like a fucking adult."

"Fine! Then just let me be the bad guy and get the hell out of my apartment."

"It's not your fucking apartment!" I bellow, waving around the room. "This isn't your life anymore! Why can't you let it go?"

He nods, his eyes dropping again. "Right."

Something shifts. I don't know what it is, but it feels like I missed a step. Before I can ask, though, he stands.

"Thanks for the pep talk. Now I need you to leave."

"Like hell I am."

"Get the fuck out, Bea." He's staring at me from under his brow. It's not the Josh I know, but it's still familiar. I remember the last time I saw this version, back when we were in college. It was only a few weeks before graduation, at a party off campus. He had been clean for just over six months, but I still noticed when the guy approached him. I saw Josh contemplate for only a minute before he walked back toward us, told us he was leaving early. Jillian hadn't suspected anything, only kissed him on the cheek and told him to call her later. But I knew. So I followed him outside, followed him until he was about to get in the guy's car, and then I confronted him.

It was a blowout. Travis would tell me later that we attracted a crowd, but I didn't see them. All I saw was Josh, huge, hulking Josh, staring at me with venom in his eyes as I yelled and screamed and told him exactly how I felt about what he was doing, exactly what it would mean.

He was livid. Worse than livid. In that moment I think he hated me. And for two people who were as close as siblings, that had hurt almost as much as the lies. But despite that look, he hadn't gone with the guy. And he didn't relapse. But we never talked about it.

And here's that look again, pinning me in place in the middle of this barren kitchen.

"I'm not going anywhere," I say, crossing my arms over my chest. "Not until we talk about this."

"Or what?" He scoffs. "What are you going to do? Tackle Gerald when he comes back?"

"Oh, I will *absolutely* tackle Gerald if he comes back."

He sidesteps me and starts for the front door. "Then I'll just find somebody else!"

"Like hell you will!" I bellow, rushing past him and blocking the exit. He is bigger than me, but he always cowers when I use that voice. "You're not going anywhere, and no one is coming in until you deal with this."

He runs his hands through his hair. "Fuck you, Bea!"

"Fuck you, too!"

He stares at me for a long moment, dark rage in his eyes that still looks so foreign there. And then he turns, bounds down the hall. Tex follows close behind, his paws offering a steady rhythm against the hardwood, until the bedroom door slams shut.

I lean back against the front door and slide down to the floor. A minute passes, then I hear my phone ding in my bag.

I reach in and read the text message.

**NATHAN ASSHOLE**

Leaving work at about 7.

Meet you at my place at 8?

God, I want to see him right now; I want him to tell me it's going to be okay, even though I know it won't. But he is Josh's lawyer, which means he either knows about this and hasn't done anything about it or that he doesn't know at all, and I have no idea what to do with that.

It's just so unfair. So fucking unfair I want to scream, but instead I sit there and text back:

**BEATRICE**

CANT MAKE IT TONIGHT

SOMETHING CAME UP

A moment. Then the three blinking dots appear moments before his reply:

**NATHAN ASSHOLE**

Everything okay?

**BEATRICE**

ITS FINE

COFFEE TOMORROW?

Those three fucking dots again, they dance on the screen for almost a full minute before his reply finally arrives:

**NATHAN ASSHOLE**

Sure. See you at 12:30.

I slide my phone back in my bag and let my head fall back, hitting the door with a thud.

And I wait.

# CHAPTER 26

There's a small puddle of saliva on the hardwood floor when I wake up next to the front door. I can hear my phone ringing, but my limbs rebel when I try to move. *No! Stop! Don't move us from this folded, inhuman position where our joints have only now given up all hope of mobility. Embrace atrophy, Beatrice. EMBRACE IT.*

But I do move. I even dare to sit up, and each muscle tightens and aches with the effort.

OUCH.

I pull my phone from my bag as I splay my legs out in front of me. It hurts so much I forget to look at the screen before answering.

"Hello," I mumble.

"What color is mauve?"

*Shit.* It's my mother.

"I'm sorry?" I ask, trying to straighten my back.

"The painters will be here to do the guest bedroom soon but I think they ordered the wrong color. I distinctly remember picking out mauve, but this one looks purple."

"I don't really have time for this right now, Mom."

She lets out an indignant scoff. "It's seven a.m. What else could you be doing?"

"No, just . . ." My voice fades, swallowed up by a pit of sadness. "I can't fix everything."

"What does that mean?"

I lean back against the door. I'm exhausted and scared and so angry I think I might burn away right here in the foyer of this apartment. But I also don't know how to tell her that.

"I can't fix paint colors. Or divorces. Or hot water heaters. Or job searches. Everything is falling apart, and I don't know how to fix it," I say. The thought of filling her in on all the details—especially the latest development—makes my stomach turn, so I just release a sigh. "And I don't know how to stop feeling so much so I can at least try."

Silence fills to the line. I think that maybe she'll start to disengage, say her goodbyes, and create distance from the mess like she usually does. But instead she stays on the line, quiet for another few moments before she says, "You know, Bea, you've always reminded me of a coconut."

The tears that had been threatening my eyes disappear as I frown. "A coconut."

"Ever since you were little," she continues, unfazed. "You know, most people are like apples. They have this protective skin, but it's not too thick. It's even kind of enjoyable. We pick them mostly because they're easy. We can get to the good stuff without too much work. But that's not you. You've got this hard shell around you. It protects you from getting hurt, but it also makes it almost impossible for anyone to break through it. In fact, I feel like once you found those friends of yours in college, you stopped letting anyone else try."

"That's not true," I murmur.

"Oh really? When was the last time you dated anyone?"

I pause to think. Nathan's face is the only one standing out to me. I had dated a few guys over the past couple of years, had pleasant conversations in the hallways with my fellow law students, but never formed any meaningful connections. And that had been the point, hadn't it?

In the silence, my mom clicks her tongue. "You're a coconut."

"So, I'm hard and hairy. Great. Thanks, Mom," I mumble, pushing an errant curl from my face.

"My point is that you're hard work, Bea. But once someone gets through that shell, what they'll find inside is sweeter and more wonderful than any apple on the whole planet. And without the bitter core."

I smile to myself and let my head fall back against the door again. "You should put that on a greeting card."

"Maybe I will," she says. Another moment passes before her voice returns, now with a comforting tone that I haven't heard in years. "I know I wasn't easy, Bea. I relied on you too much. And I know that's why you have that shell to begin with, but I never saw it as a bad thing. Because I thought it meant you'd be better protected than I was. Maybe you wouldn't get your heart broken as easily. But it also meant you had an excuse to not let anyone in. You deserve the same care and love you give away to everyone else, Bea. And at some point, you need to fight for you just as much as you fight for everybody else."

I sigh and close my eyes. "Stop making sense or I'll hang up on you."

"Oh, don't worry. I was planning to hang up on you anyway. I need to figure out who replaced my mauve paint with purple."

I smile. "Mauve is purple, Mom."

She hums, like she's not listening at all. "All right, I'm going to go yell at someone. Love you," she says.

"I love you, too."

I hang up, then stand and hobble to the kitchen, praying that the coffeemaker is one of the things Josh insisted on keeping, but the countertop is empty. I begin opening the cabinets in case it's hidden somewhere. To my utter dismay, all I find a lone jar of instant coffee.

A door creaks open somewhere in the apartment. There's the steady beat of Tex's paws followed by slow, lumbering footsteps that make their way down the hall. I turn just as Josh arrives at the doorway to the kitchen. He's still in the same sweatpants from the day before, but he's taken off his sweatshirt so I can see his bare chest. He's skinny, too skinny, and his face is slack with sleep the same way I remember from college. His hair is jutting out in all directions and he's itching his head in a familiar way, too. Relief floods my chest because there, for a moment, between the cracks, is the Josh I know, the Josh I remember.

It takes a second for him to look up and see me, but when he does his eyes widen, as if the entire night comes back to him all at once.

"You twisted fuck," I growl. "Who the hell drinks instant coffee?"

He stills. It's like he had been mentally preparing himself for something else to come out of my mouth. Then his shoulders relax, and he offers me a weary smile. "I broke the coffeemaker."

"And you never thought to buy a new one?"

He runs a hand through his hair. "I've had other things on my mind."

*Right.* I sigh, taking the jar of instant coffee from the shelf along with two mugs.

Silence envelops the room as I make us each a cup. He watches me microwave the water and stir in the granules. It isn't until I push his mug in front of him that I say, "How long?"

He stares into the depths of his coffee for a long moment.

"Two years," he finally murmurs. He catches my shocked expression and winces. "I know. At first I thought it was manageable. I mean, it was . . ."

I frown. "Josh . . ."

He knows what I want to say. Because these were the excuses before, the insane idea that it was okay, the pills and the lies were okay, until the moment when they weren't.

He hangs his head. "Yeah."

I stare at him, letting a moment pass before I ask, "What happened?"

"Grad school was . . . rough. I know you thought it was a fucking joke when I quit my job and applied, but I thought it would give me some direction, you know? Or at least give me time to figure out what the hell I was doing with my life. But it was hard—too hard. And trying to balance that and Jillian, it was just . . ." His hand rakes down his face. "So I dropped out. Started doing temp work. That was hard enough, but then Jillian got promoted. And she was working late, and I had to go to these stupid parties with her, and it felt like everybody knew. Everybody was looking at me like I was a fucking failure. Like I was living off my wife. And I know it was all in my head, but it didn't make it untrue, either. And I just . . . I had to get away from the stress and the expectations and . . ." His voice trails off and he shakes his head. "You don't just stop being an addict, Bea."

I let out a long exhale. "Why didn't you talk to me?"

He laughs bitterly. "Right. Should I have called before or after you sent me all those STD notifications?"

I force a small smile onto my face. "I don't know what you're talking about."

He laughs again, this time with a bit of humor. It fades quickly. "Jillian started to think something was wrong, but I never let her find out what. That's when the fighting got bad. Really bad." He swallows, and there's a new sheen to his eyes. "I didn't tell her I was filing for divorce. I don't even know why I did it. I was just so pissed, and it felt like we were already done . . ." His voice fades, and silence replaces it.

Something tightens in my chest, a vise made of fear and sadness, but it doesn't stop me from leaning forward.

"Does anybody else know?"

"No. I think Travis suspects, though. He texted me a few times, but I avoided answering. And Jillian moved out before it got really bad."

"What about your lawyer?"

Josh scoffs. "God, no. Can you imagine?"

My heart drops. "But—"

"Bea. I can't tell him. I probably could have in the beginning, but it's too far gone now."

"He needs to know, Josh." It sounds like I'm pleading, and I realize I kind of am. "This affects the case. If it comes out later and you're not the one to tell him, it compromises both of you. His career is on the line."

"Why do you care? I thought you hated him."

I swallow, even though my mouth is dry. "Josh . . ."

He shakes his head. "If I told him, then it's out there. He could drop the case. I'd lose everything; I'd be fucked."

"You don't know that."

"Neither do you."

I run a hand through my knotted hair. I get it; Josh likely did a lot of lying to cover this up for so long, which means that any financial disclosures were probably covering for it, too. But that also means Nathan was likely the one who submitted those documents to the court. The thought sends a spike of anxiety through my chest.

"If you tell him, then at least it's protected under attorney–client privilege. He can help you work through this without anyone knowing. Because if Jillian finds out about this . . ."

His expression changes, like a wave of guilt hits him, and his eyes dart away from mine.

I pause. "Is that what you're worried about? Jillian finding out?"

He looks around the room, as if that will help him organize his thoughts. "It's not just Jillian; it's everybody that helped me before. If they find out . . ." He finally meets my eyes, and I can see he's close to tears. It clicks into place then, the desperate logic behind his shame that got us to this point.

I reach across the counter and put my hand on top of his. "Then they'll be there to help you recover again. Simple as that."

He looks up at me, and for a moment I'm not sure he's heard, if he processed what I've said. But then his face crumples and he's sobbing; great, heaving sobs that bow his shoulders as his head falls into his hands. I envelop him in the tightest hug my arms are capable of, letting wave after wave pass through him.

I don't know how long we stay like that, but it's long enough for his sobs to subside, for him to take a few deep breaths and lift his head, eyes swollen. "I need help."

I give him one more squeeze. "Then let's get you some."

We spend the next couple of hours online researching rehab facilities, emailing counselors. It's laborious and exhausting, with discussions about in-patient versus outpatient, treatment goals and methods, location—everything—until we finally find the right fit: an in-patient facility in California near his parents.

I book him on a flight Friday afternoon to Sacramento.

It's only then that I look at the clock and realize the time.

"Shit. I have to get to campus soon," I murmur, closing his laptop and running a hand through my matted hair. Sleeping on the floor has not done it any favors. "Can I steal the shower?"

"Yeah, sure," he says, staring down at the countertop.

I pause. "Are you okay?"

He looks up at me and offers me a watery grin. "I'm okay. Freaking out a little, but okay."

"Do you want me to stick around?"

"No, no, it's fine." He lets out a long breath. "Just realizing all the conversations I have to have this week."

I understand. He already texted his parents to tell them he was coming out, but he didn't tell them why. That still leaves our friends.

"I'll call Jillian," he continues. "See if she can take Tex and watch the apartment."

"Do you want me to tell Maggie and Travis?" I ask.

He nods. "Yeah. That would be great."

I let a moment pass before I ask, "What about your lawyer?"

He closes his eyes briefly. "Bea . . ."

"Josh," I say, my voice laced with warning. "You have to tell him."

"I will. I just . . . I just don't know when yet. Maybe before I leave. Maybe when I get back." A thought occurs to him then, a realization as he lifts his head and stares at me. "You can't say anything, Bea. Promise me."

My eyes go wide. "What?"

"I know how you get when you're pissed, and you already stormed his office once about the alimony. You said it yourself, if he finds out about this from anyone else but me, it's going to be awful. A fucking disaster. So just promise me."

I nod, even as a knot tightens in my gut. "Fine. I won't say a thing. I promise."

He sighs. "Thank you."

I reach up and pull him to me again, holding him in a tight embrace. It's a long moment before I pull away, but even as I do, I hold his hand tightly and maintain his gaze. "You're going to be okay, Josh."

He nods, the grateful smile on his face slowly becoming a grimace.

"What?" I ask.

"You've got some dried spit on your chin."

I frown. "You're a dick."

"And holy shit, your breath, Bea—"

"I'm going to take a shower and steal all your hot water," I mutter, tossing my so-called coffee in the sink and heading down the hall to the bathroom. His laughter follows me until I slam the door shut.

I turn on the shower and use my finger and some toothpaste to brush my teeth while it heats up. By the time I step in, the water is scalding, and I stay under the hot spray longer than I need to—partly because it's a novelty, and partly because I really do want to steal all his hot water. It's not until I'm out and have found a clean towel, a mint-green one that is entirely too small to be considered a bath towel, that my mind begins to race. I wrap it around my body and begin combing out my wet curls, trying to focus. All I can think about is Nathan.

I don't want to lie to him; I don't even know if I can. But is not telling him about this really lying? After all, this isn't my information to share. It needs to come from Josh to protect them both, so all I have to do is wait for Josh to tell him.

That's it. I just have to wait. I let out a long breath, a knot of anxiety loosening in my chest. I can wait.

I'm just stepping out of the bathroom to grab my clothes from the bed when I hear the doorbell. Its familiar, disjointed version of Beethoven's Fifth echoes through the hollow apartment, and I perk up at the sound. It's not quite nine o'clock in the morning. Who would be stopping by? But even as the question forms, it's replaced by the realization that it's probably the same person I kicked out only yesterday: Gerald.

Anger rolls through my chest as I storm out of the bedroom, holding the little green towel around me as I march down the hall to the front door. I have to get there before Josh, before he's tempted.

It's the only thought in my head as I throw open the door.

Nathan is standing on the threshold.

A stuttering jolt goes through my body, paralyzing me in the doorway. All I can do is stare up at him and blink. He stares back, his expression marred with confusion.

"Bea?"

My mouth opens—to say what, I have no idea—but then I hear "Nate!" from down the hall, followed by the thump of Josh's footsteps.

When I left him in the kitchen to take my shower, he had still only been wearing his sweatpants, and with each step I send a silent prayer out into the universe: *please let him have put on a shirt, please let him have put on a shirt, please let him have put on a shirt* . . .

But when he stops at my side, smiling and still bare chested, with his sweatpants low on his hips and Tex dancing at his heels, I realize the universe hates me.

"What are you doing here, man?" Josh asks.

Nathan is still looking at me, his eyes traveling down my wet hair to the tiny towel wrapped around my chest. And then, slowly, recognition clicks into place.

"Did you want to come in?" Josh offers. "Grab a cup of coffee? Fair warning, it's instant. Bea hates it, but I don't think it's so bad."

Oh God, I think I'm going to be sick.

Nathan's gaze is locked on me, and I try to communicate everything I need to say through my eyes. *It's not what you think! Please don't look at me like that! Wait for me downstairs and let me explain!*

But then Josh throws his arm over my shoulder and Nathan looks away.

"No, thank you," he says. "I didn't mean to interrupt. I was hoping to talk to you before work."

"It's okay. Bea's taking off in a sec."

"No, that's all right," Nathan says, already taking a step back. "It can wait."

Josh nods. "No worries. I need to talk to you about a few things, too."

Another step back. "I'll let the office know, so we can set something up."

"Sounds good." Josh says.

Then Nathan turns around to start down the stairs without saying goodbye. He doesn't even look back.

# CHAPTER 27

It takes approximately forty-seven seconds to throw on my clothes—the short pleated skirt and suede boots I had worn yesterday when I had planned on seeing Nathan—and fly out the door. He's not outside the building, and the sidewalk is empty. I go left, toward the avenue, my mind racing as fast as my feet. Even if I find him, what do I say? If I tell him the truth, not only would I be breaking a promise to Josh, but none of this is covered under attorney–client privilege. He could be obligated to tell the courts about Josh's financial documents, how his client covered up his addiction and then Josh's secret will be out there.

But in the end, it doesn't matter that I don't know what to say, because by the time I reach the corner, Nathan is gone. Some small part of me hoped that he would be there somewhere, that he knew I would follow him so he decided to wait. But no. The sidewalks are filled only with the usual commuters darting back and forth, none of them noticing my dejected expression as I stand alone on the curb.

I pull my phone from my bag, typing out a quick text to him.

**BEATRICE**

> DID YOU GO TO WORK? CALL ME.

Then I see the time: 9:29 a.m.

Shit.

I have class in twenty minutes, a two-hour seminar that requires all phones to be on silent. Then I have to go up to Frank's office for my weekly meeting with Nathan.

That's good news, I tell myself as I head to campus. Even if I miss his call, I'll still see him today so I can explain. Exactly how I will explain still gnaws at my gut, though, anxiety that distracts from the crowds of students and faculty and tours as I maneuver my way to class. I go through the motions: put my laptop on my desk, silence my phone. Ignore the fact that there are no text messages waiting when I do.

At exactly 12:29 p.m., I head up to the fourth floor of Vanderbilt Hall. The hallway is empty when I step off the elevator, and I do my best to ignore the growing sense of dread puddling in my stomach as I walk down to Frank's office. I unlock the door and step inside, putting my bag down next to my usual chair before sitting down myself. I glance at the clock on the far wall.

12:32.

I try to swallow back my anxiety. He could just be running late. A meeting at work ran over or something. I pretend the thought settles my pulse.

It's another few minutes before I hear the elevator ding. Then I hear his footsteps, an even gait as he comes closer. But my relief dissolves when he walks in. He's wearing his suit again, and he has that impassive expression on his face that I remember from the first time I met him. I hate it.

He doesn't sit down like usual, just leans against Frank's desk, his arms on either side of him, gripping the worn wood finish. Maybe it's because he doesn't want to crease his suit. Or he's not planning to stay long. My heart lurches with the thought.

"Hi," I say.

"Hi."

He doesn't offer anything else. It's so quiet that I'm positive he must hear my pounding heart.

"Why didn't you call?" I finally ask.

"I was at work," he replies. "Why didn't you?"

His voice is low and biting and I can't help but bristle. But then something in me cools with the realization that he's right. I didn't call. I was in class, yes, but that wasn't an excuse. Fear never is.

"Why were you at Josh's apartment today?" I ask, raising my chin as if the act will give me courage.

"You told me that it was a conflict of interest to be with you while I was also Josh's attorney. I was there to tell him that I'm handing day-to-day responsibilities of his case to an associate."

"First thing in the morning?"

"I wanted to do it in person and outside the office so he didn't think I was charging him a fortune just to admit that I was sleeping with his best friend."

The words sound sharp enough that I almost wince.

He stares at me for a long moment. "What were you doing there, Bea?"

My mouth falls open, but everything I want to say is stuck in my throat. I don't want to lie to him, but I don't know how to do this and keep my promise to Josh. I have to protect them, even when withholding information will end up sounding like a lie anyway.

"You need to talk to Josh."

"I'm talking to you." He somehow makes it sound like an accusation.

"I get that, but I can't—"

"I'm talking to you," he repeats.

My eyes narrow.

"Then talk to me," I say defensively. The door of the office is open, and a couple of students pass, their eyes darting toward us. I immediately lower my voice. "Sit down and have a conversation instead of standing there like you're interrogating me."

He doesn't move, but I swear I see a crack in his stoic expression.

"I know what it looks like, Nate," I continue. "But I promise, it's not what you think . . ."

God, it's such a cliché. I can tell he thinks so, too, by how his head falls forward and he lets out a long breath.

"I've heard that before, Bea."

I blink. And then I realize that it's not just a cliché. It's what Rebecca told him when she was lying about her affair.

*Fuckfuckfuuuuuuuuck . . .*

"It's not like that," I say, my voice betraying a bit of panic. "I mean, I stayed there last night, but we didn't sleep together or anything. It's just . . . this is between you and Josh, and I can't . . ." My brain is doing somersaults and it's coming out as an amalgamation of dissociated words.

"You can't what?" It's not a question. It's the statement of a lawyer taking a deposition, a means to garner information and nothing more.

Another group of students meander by the doorway. They must hear us before they pass, because they immediately lower their voices, as if trying to glean a few details as they walk by.

*Damn it.* Even if I was willing to implode Josh's possibility of using attorney–client, I couldn't tell Nathan anything right now. This is too private for student gossip.

"I can't talk about this here," I say, lowering my voice to barely a whisper. "Just call Josh, and then we can discuss everything. Trust me."

"Right." He nods, an absent gesture. "I've heard that before, too."

His voice is back to the same tone from when I first stormed into his office. Aloof. Unbothered. It's like he's already done. Like he made up his mind before he even showed up here.

And that's when it hits me: he probably did. He knew exactly how this was going to go the minute I opened Josh's front door. Nathan has donned his defenses again, that familiar suit of armor that I have myself, and I'm left with the man I met all those weeks ago. Except this time I don't have my armor to match. He destroyed it, leaving me naked and vulnerable. A sacrifice on the altar of self-preservation.

"I'm not Rebecca," I seethe. I want to say more, but a dull ringing stops me.

Nathan reaches into his jacket and pulls out his phone.

"Nathan Asher," he answers. He listens and nods. "All right. I'll be there in twenty." He hangs up and puts the phone away. A muscle in his jaw ticks as he clears his throat. "I'm going to cancel class today. I have work to finish up at the office. Please send an email out to let the students know."

My mom's words come back to me—*at some point you need to fight for you just as much as you fight for everybody else*—but what seemed tangible only a few hours before, now feels impossible. This isn't my story, and putting myself in the center would be selfish. No, it's worse than that: it would hurt the people I love. And I can't do that.

Staring up into Nathan's cold eyes right now, it already feels too late anyway.

"So that's it?" I can already feel the anger rising up inside me, ready to swallow the pain.

"Unless you have something else to say."

There's a vicious part of me that feels vindicated. It's like I somehow always knew this would happen, that no matter how good it seemed, it would end. Because everything always does. I was so stupid to ever think this could be the exception. All that's left to do is leave before he sees how close I am to falling apart, and hope I survive it.

"I guess not," I say, gathering my things back up and walking past him to the door. I pause on the threshold. "I take that back. When you do finally talk to Josh, don't call me. I won't pick up."

Then I turn and walk away. And he lets me.

I get off the subway at 168th Street an hour later. The subway entrance is crowded, and I forget to watch out for where the top step is broken. The heel of my boot catches and snaps off, rolling away until it stops next to a half-eaten piece of pizza by the trash can on the corner.

I love these dumb shoes. I bought them on sale almost two years ago and had barely worn them since, too precious to even consider exposing them to the dangers of New York City sidewalks. But I had put them on yesterday, back when I raced home to my apartment after leaving Nathan's—showering and shaving and ripping my closet apart to find the perfect outfit to wear—because I thought I would see him. I had worn these shoes for him.

Stupid, stupid girl.

I hobble to my building, broken heel in hand, and find my apartment just as I left it, clothes strewn across the floor and furniture, a half-finished cup of coffee on the countertop. It's a still life that captured a perfect, fleeting moment filled with so much fucking hope. My stomach twists and I feel sick, a perverse motion sickness as if the world has turned too fast and my brain can't catch up.

I close the door behind me, drop my keys on the hardwood floor, and shuffle to my bed. It's unmade, but I don't care. I perch on the edge and stare straight ahead at the blank wall, at the crack making its way across the plaster. And for the first time in what feels like hours, I let out a breath.

*You should have told him*, a voice says somewhere in my head—a nagging, taunting hiss that I ignore. I can't deny that for a moment I considered it. When Nathan stood in front of me, I was so scared of losing him I almost told him everything. But then I caught that look in his eyes, the resignation before I had really said anything at all. And I realized I had lost him before I even showed up there today. Guilty until proven innocent.

It hurts—a deep, sharp pain in my chest. My hand comes up to rub it out, but only seems to bury it deeper. This is exactly what I was so desperate to avoid. I didn't want to get hurt. I didn't want to show that vulnerable part of me and leave it exposed to someone who could do this.

But I thought he was worth it. I thought he was different. Stupid, stupid girl.

After a moment I realize my phone is vibrating from somewhere deep in my bag. I want to ignore it, but apparently there's still some small part of me that's refusing to give up on that hope, because I lean down to where my bag sits at my feet. It takes a few seconds to find it, and when I reach for the glowing screen, I hate that I want to see Nathan's name across it.

I see Jillian's smiling face there instead.

I squeeze my eyes together, forcing back the tears and answer.

"Hey," I say weakly.

"Hey, how did it go? Did you get Tex?"

"Yeah," I say, letting out a shaky breath. "He's fine. He's with Josh."

"Oh, thank God." There's a relieved sigh before she continues. "I was so worried. You have no idea—"

"I have to tell you something." I force the words out, my voice so loud that she falls silent for a moment.

"Okay," she finally says.

My mouth falls open. I want to tell her about Josh. I want to ask her if she knew, or at least suspected why we've all been navigating this battlefield with only partial information. But right now, none of that matters. The only thing I can control is the one thing that could hurt her even more. And I have to be honest about it.

"Nathan Asher," I say.

"Josh's lawyer?" she asks. "Oh God, did you go back to his office? Bea, if you—"

"I was with him this weekend."

A moment, and I can almost hear her trying to connect the dots. "You ran into him this weekend?"

"No, I was with him. At his apartment," I say as a tear rolls down my cheek. "I stayed with him."

Silence. Painful, deafening silence. Then: "Bea. How long has this been going on?"

"Since I stormed into his office." A moment passes, and I know she's counting the weeks. I choke back a sob. "Jillian, please let me—"

She hangs up without another word.

# CHAPTER 28

I cancel my office hours the next day. I tell the faculty coordinator it's because I don't feel well and I tell myself it's because I have to study, but a small voice in the back of my mind whispers the truth: I'm a coward. I don't want to hear any students coming in to talk about Nathan Asher. I don't want to be reminded of him at all.

So I stay home, ready to spend the morning on my sofa watching a new season of *The Real Housewives of New York City*, even though it seems like an odd moniker now since none of the new cast members ever seem to be home. By episode three it feels like a conspiracy and I'm deep in my online search—*How often do women have to be home to be considered housewives?*—when my cell phone rings beside me.

I know it's not Nathan, since I blocked his number—a pathetic attempt to avoid looking to see if he ignored me and tried to call—but the sound still sends my heart to my stomach, my pulse into a free fall. I wait until the second ring before I reach for it and find Maggie's face on the screen. I think I'm relieved. Or maybe I'm just numb. I don't take time to figure it out before I answer.

"Hi."

"Okay, so you have to go to Miami," she says by way of greeting. "There's this restaurant where you're eating in, like, the middle of a club. Or it's a club where you dance around people eating. Whatever, it's amazing. I'm so bummed to be back. The closest thing we have like that up here is the grocery store obsessed with playing eighties power ballads."

Dammit. I totally forgot that Maggie and Travis were coming back today. Yet another detail of my life that's fallen through the cracks.

My head falls back onto the pillow, and I mute the television. "I'll have to check it out sometime."

"Get on that," she says. "So, did everything work out with your apartment?"

"Yup," I say. My voice is so flat that it's almost convincing.

"Good, because I need your full attention on wedding planning for at least the next six months."

"Okay."

A moment passes, and I can actually feel her frowning at me. "What's wrong? I just mentioned wedding planning and you didn't yell at me."

"It's nothing," I say, forcing some levity into my voice even as tears begin to prickle my eyes. "Just tired. This bar prep is really intense and—"

"Your voice is doing that weird high-pitched thing."

*Shit*. It totally is.

I was hoping to delay this conversation until I knew that Josh was checked into the facility, or at least on the plane. But I had also promised to tell Maggie and Travis, relieve Josh of that one burden.

"I went to see Josh on Monday," I reply. "He forgot to pick up the dog and Jillian was worried, so I went to the apartment."

"And?" Maggie asks.

"We were wrong about that pill."

There's an awful gravity in the silence that follows. A beat of understanding. And then a mumbled "Shit."

"Yeah."

"Travis has been trying to nail him down for weeks to ask him about it. We thought it was weird that Josh kept avoiding him, but we've all been so busy, I didn't think . . ."

Her voice fades under all the familiar words we've said before. *How did we miss this?* Instead, she asks. "What did you do?"

"I yelled at him for a while, and he stormed into the bedroom. Then I slept in front of the front door to make sure he didn't sneak out." I say it with a small smile, and she laughs softly. "It was better in the morning, though. We talked. Did some research and found a good in-patient treatment center near his parents' house. We lined everything up. He leaves Friday."

"God, Bea." She sighs. "I can't believe you did that."

"He needs help, Mags. He wants it."

"Good. That's really good," she says, and lets it sit for a moment before she continues. "How are you doing?"

I sit up and push the curls away from my face. "Honestly? I don't know."

"You did everything you could, Bea," she says reassuringly. "There's nothing more—"

"It's not that."

"Then what?"

I squeeze my eyes shut, hoping to keep the tears at bay. "I did something epically stupid."

"Again?"

I don't want to cry, but I also don't think I can hold it back anymore. So I stop trying and let out a heaving, miserable sob. "I think I fell in love with Nathan Asher."

There's movement, like she's up and walking to a different room. Then the distinct sound of a door closing before she speaks again, her voice solemn. "Tell me everything."

So, between the sobs, I do. About my apartment, how I had tried to get ahold of her before texting Nathan. And then everything else pours out, every detail of the weekend, unvarnished and raw. It feels good to say it out loud, like it makes it real somehow, and not something that would forever live in my memory. Proof that it wasn't a dream.

"It was only supposed to be the weekend." I sniff, wiping away some errant wetness from my nose with a nearby take-out napkin. "Get it out of our systems, you know? But I think we both knew it was more than that."

"I think you both knew it was more than that weeks ago," she murmurs.

"Maybe. But I didn't think I was going to fall in love with him."

She makes a sound like she doesn't believe me, but she doesn't push it. "So why are you upset? Don't tell me he's shit in bed."

"No. Definitely not. That was . . ." I let out a shaky breath. "That was amazing."

And then I start crying again. The ugly kind that makes me glad I never hung a mirror in this room.

Maggie listens for a moment before she softly prods, "Talk to me, Bea."

I let out a long sigh as the memory floods my mind again. "By the time Josh and I finished getting his tickets and everything, I didn't have time to go home before class, so I just jumped in the shower at the apartment. And as I was getting out, I heard the doorbell. I thought it was Josh's dealer, so I ran out in only a towel and answered it. But it wasn't the dealer. It was Nathan."

"Oh," she says, and then I hear a sharp intake of breath as understanding clicks into place. "OH."

"Yeah."

"So now he thinks you and Josh are sleeping together or something?"

"Pretty much," I say, swallowing back another sob.

"So why don't you just tell him the truth?"

"It's so complicated, Mags. The truth doesn't just involve the pills. Josh also used some of the divorce documents to cover up all the money he's spent on this. And Nathan is the one that submitted them to the court. Josh needs to be the one to tell him, so this is all protected under attorney–client privilege."

"Then tell him that," she says. "Even if you can't tell him everything, you can tell him about this whole attorney–client thing."

"I tried. But I promised Josh not to mention the pills to Nathan, so there was only so much I could say."

"So what happens when Josh finally tells him and he tries to call you?"

"He can't. I blocked his number."

"Bea—"

I shake my head. "He didn't trust me, Mags. That's the worst part of it. And I understand why, but that doesn't make it hurt less. So this is for the best. It was never supposed to last, and now it's over. A clean break. This way no one gets their heart broken."

She scoffs. "Oh really? Then what do you call this?"

I swallow around the lump in my throat. "Surviving it."

For a long moment there's only silence. I know Maggie is trying to find a way out of this, using the rational part of her brain to work it all out, but the longer the silence goes on, the more I know she understands.

She sighs. "So, it's over. Just like that."

I trap my bottom lip between my teeth and nod. "Just like that."

There's so much more she wants to say that I can feel the weight of it through the phone, but she stays silent for a bit before finally asking, "And what about the job interview?"

My brow furrows. "What?"

"Didn't he introduce you to a woman you were hoping to work for?"

I squeezed my eyes together. *Shit*. I had forgotten.

"Marcie Land," I say with a sigh. "Yeah, I'm supposed to have lunch with her today at one. I'm going to have to cancel."

"Why? It's only ten."

"Because Nate and I aren't together anymore?" I say, as if this answer should be obvious.

"But you weren't together when he introduced you, either."

"Well, no . . ."

"And he didn't make the introduction because you were going to sleep with him, right?"

I roll my eyes. "Definitely not."

"Then why wouldn't you pursue it now that you're back to not sleeping with him?"

My mouth hangs open for a moment before I slam it shut.

"If this was never supposed to be anything other than business, then make sure you at least get the business thing out of it,"

Maggie continues. "Otherwise, you're screwing yourself. And not in the *amazing* way you did this weekend."

"Great pep talk," I mumble.

She doesn't say anything for a minute, and I can tell she's weighing her next words carefully. "You're going to be okay, Bea."

I nod, more tears suddenly springing from my eyes.

"How did you get so wise?" I ask, a small smile pulling at my lips.

She sighs. "Day drinking."

# CHAPTER 29

The restaurant is in Midtown, just off Seventh Avenue, in an office building that I'm sure thousands of people walk by every day and never notice. The tinted windows hide the interior, while the steel-and-glass exterior looks like every other skyscraper in Midtown. That's what this part of town was designed for, I suppose. A race upward rather than attention to the world below.

I let out a nervous breath as I walk through the revolving door. The huge space of the restaurant opens before me, a sea of creams and golds crowned by a huge crystal chandelier. Marcie's assistant picked this place, and I can see why. The dining room is filled with the same type of people who had been at the bar association event just a couple of months ago: men and women in suits who all appear more interested in how they look than what their companions are saying.

I'm early, but the hostess has my name and shows me to a table near the windows. I sit down and try to calm my pulse, reviewing the script in my head that I had fumbled together on the train ride here.

*Thank you so much for this opportunity, but I have to be honest about the circumstances of—*

"Bea."

I look up to see Marcie approaching, a smile on her face as she confidently walks by the other tables until she reaches ours. She leans down and gives me a kiss on each cheek. "So good to see you again."

"You, too," I say, and I mean it. There's nothing fake about her smile or subdued about her vibrant red suit. She gives off the impression that she's entirely herself, a woman who does exactly what she wants, when she wants to do it. Which only makes this entire thing so much harder.

The waiter comes by and Marcie orders a drink, then sighs and leans back in her chair. "I feel like I need to apologize for the restaurant."

I look around at the towering ceilings, the white tablecloths, the linen-upholstered chairs. "It's gorgeous."

"It's pretentious," she replies. "Every lawyer within a ten-block radius comes here for lunch because they think all this impresses people. Unfortunately, it's also the only restaurant across the street from my office, so convenience wins out."

I try to smile. It feels like a grimace.

"I'm glad you were able to meet today," she continues, still smiling, but her gaze is astute. As if she's sizing me up. "We just had a meeting about some staffing opportunities, and I thought of you."

My mouth goes dry. "That's . . . incredibly flattering."

She laughs. "Not really. A lot of grunt work, to be honest. And the position would be contingent on you passing the bar. But in the meantime, we have a big class action case coming up, and it's going to require a lot of research into individual states' medical malpractice statutes. Considering your background, it could be a good fit." She must notice how my eyes light up, because her smile grows. "We'd have to talk a bit more, of course. I'd need information about what you've been doing at school. But I'd like to start that conversation if you're interested."

"I am," I say, because yes, this is exactly the type of thing I'm interested in. This is what I've worked so hard for, what I've been dreaming of. That's why my chest hurts as I add, "But . . ."

One eyebrow cocks up her forehead. "But?"

"I feel like I should be honest with you about this situation."

She brings her fingers to her chin, waiting for me to continue.

I take a deep breath. "Nathan and I were . . . we were together. Or, at least, we almost were. I mean, not when he introduced me to you. To be honest, I'm not sure we were even really together after, since we didn't get a chance to have that conversation before everything . . . happened . . . but regardless, we kind of were, and . . ." God, I'm rambling. Every practiced word has dissolved in my mind.

"And?" she prods.

"And . . ." I let the word hang there, even as it leaves a fresh tear in my chest. "And I feel like you need to know that, so you don't go out of your way for me on his behalf."

She leaned back slowly, arms crossing over her chest.

"On his behalf," she repeats.

"Yes."

She nods then, surveying the room for a long, excruciating minute before she speaks again. "Do you know how I started Land and Associates, Bea?"

The non sequitur is so unexpected that I pause. "No."

"I was with another firm before this one. It was founded by my first husband years before he met me. Needless to say, he was older and more established, so it was his name on the door. And because his name was the first thing people saw, they assumed I was there because of him. That he had done me a favor. And after a while, I started to believe that, too." She pauses on the memory for a moment, then shrugs. "Obviously, when we got divorced, I left the practice. He told people he was glad, because I was a pain in the ass." She smiles. "He wasn't wrong. He just never realized that was a good thing. It's what made me a good lawyer. And what prompted me to start my own firm a year later. It was terrifying, of course. I didn't know if I was smart enough, if I had only been successful for all those years because of him. But do you know what? All the clients I had at my husband's firm followed me to my new one. Every single one. They didn't do that because he had given me the opportunity. They did that because I'm good at what I do."

She finally turns to look at me, her gaze sharp and her lips pursed. "I appreciate your honesty, Bea. And I understand it. But I also need you to know that it's bullshit. Nate wouldn't go out on a limb for you just because you were sleeping together. People's reputations have been ruined for less. And there's no way in hell I would hire someone simply because they were sleeping with him, either. I don't even hire the people I'm sleeping with."

I can't help but smile.

"Nate is a smart lawyer," she continues. "He introduced you because he thought you were smart, too. And I'm sitting here right now because I agree. Whether you're with Nate or not doesn't affect that. Okay?"

I nod, the knot of unease slowly loosening in my chest. "Okay."

"Good. Can we order now? I'm famished."

We spend the next hour talking, and for a little while I forget to feel sad. Between our salads and entrées, she tells me about her current caseload, about the direction the firm is moving in, and what sort of areas she sees potential growth. During dessert and coffee, I give her an overview of my time in law school, about balancing my course load and my TA position. She listens and nods; a few times I see her dampening a smile, as if she relates to my struggles with the petition against the Haun donation to the school.

"Yes, Frank mentioned that," she says.

I still. "You talked to him?"

"Nate gave me his number," she says offhandedly. "Frank also mentioned that you've known you wanted to pursue healthcare rights law since your first year."

I nod.

"He also didn't know why."

She leans back in her chair again, one hand still resting on the table as her red fingernails tap a lazy rhythm. She's waiting for an answer to her unvoiced question, like she knows there's more there than just a passing interest and is ready to give me the time necessary to confess it.

I never have before. Not to anyone. But here at this pretentious restaurant with Marcie patiently waiting, I find myself taking a deep breath and saying: "My best friend has a substance use disorder."

Something in her expression softens, but she doesn't say anything, only waits for me to continue.

"Before his injury, I had never witnessed addiction before," I say, my tongue nervously darting out to wet my lips. "I had stereotypes in my head of what that looked like, how it affected someone. I think everyone does. Then I witnessed it firsthand. I saw how it swallows a person up. And how it leaves its mark, even after they tell you they're better. And now . . . I think those stereotypes exist to make people feel better about ignoring it, as if this awful thing that will destroy a person's life and their relationships exists outside of their world, that it can't easily find a way in with a minor injury, a single prescription. Because the minute you realize that? It's terrifying. But we need to acknowledge that. Fully understand that the stereotypes exist to keep the people who have profited off these addictions safe, not us."

Silence then. She watches me for a long minute, studying my expression, and I let her. Then, finally, a slight smile. "I can see now why Frank told me I'd be a fool not to bring you on board." She pauses, angling her head to look at me from under her brow. "That is, if you're still interested."

I nod and try to temper a grin. "Absolutely."

$\sim$

We leave the restaurant a few minutes later. Marcie explains the next steps in the hiring process as we walk to the curb—how I will be getting a call from her assistant in the next few days to set up a time to meet with her partners—and I'm trying to absorb every word but can barely hear her over the sound of my pulse in my ears. By the time she says goodbye and I start walking to the subway, I'm struck by what just happened: I might be working at Land and Associates in the fall. This is happening.

And then my heart drops when I realize that the only person I want to tell is Nathan.

# CHAPTER 30

When my alarm goes off at 8:00 a.m. the next morning, I consider just turning it off and going back to sleep, which sounds so much more inviting than office hours at nine, followed by a two-hour seminar at noon. But I'm sick of my apartment, of the same four walls staring back at me, of how much I now know about housewives in California. So I throw on an old pair of sweatpants and a sweatshirt, grab my bag, and head to campus.

Clouds clog the sky when I emerge from the subway at West Fourth Street, a rolling amalgamation of grays and whites and blacks. They mute the new bursts of green punctuating the trees along the block. It's supposed to storm today, and I begin to feel the rain as I make my way to Vanderbilt Hall. Big, heavy drops pelt my coat and mat my hair, but I manage to get inside the lobby before it really starts coming down. By the time I make it upstairs to my office, it's pouring. Water cascades down my small office window while the wind makes the nearby tree branch play a staccato against the pane.

The floor is otherwise quiet, so the squeak of my chair seems to reverberate through the small room as I slump into it. My bag falls to the ground beside me and my head lolls to the side to look at my desk. I should open my laptop, check my email for the first time all week, and attempt to make this a normal day.

Or I could just make a cup of coffee.

I grab the handle of my "I Hate It Here" mug and shuffle down to the lounge, filling it to the brim before making the slow trek back to my office.

But when I get there, someone is standing outside my door.

For a split second my heart drops, but it's quickly followed by a dull ache when I realize it's not Nathan underneath the trench coat. It's Jillian.

"Hi," she says as I approach. Her voice is strained, and for the first time in years, I can't see any makeup on her face.

I want to give her a hug. I want to cry and tell her I'm sorry again and again, but instead I just say, "Hi."

She smiles meekly, like she's grateful that I've said anything at all. "I remember you saying that you had office hours Thursday mornings, so I thought I would stop by."

I take a step forward. "Jills, I'm so sorry—"

"Josh called me last night," she interrupts. I can see the new sheen in her eyes before she darts her eyes down to look at her feet. "He's signing the papers. His lawyer told him to drop all the petitions, too. Including the alimony. I even get to keep Tex. We agreed this just needs to be over."

A vise I didn't even realize had been gripping my chest loosens.

"I'm glad," I say.

She looks up to meet my eyes again, a tear escaping out of the corner of one eye. "He also told me where he's going. And what you did."

I have played out this conversation a million times in my head, worked out every excuse I can give her for the fact that I bent over backward to help someone who had hurt her so much.

"He needs help, Jills," I reply quickly. "And I couldn't—"

"I'm not mad, Bea." She shakes her head. "I'm so glad you did it. I just . . ." Her bottom lip begins to tremble. "I should have seen it. I should have known. All the signs were there, but I just . . . didn't want to even consider it. But if I had . . ."

She's crying now, and I don't let her finish before I reach out with my free hand and wrap her up in a hug. She buries her face in my coat, and her shoulders quiver.

"I'm sorry," she groans into my hair.

I laugh weakly. "What do you have to be sorry about?"

"You were trying to be honest with me and I got so angry and hung up on you when I should have listened."

"I'm sorry, too," I say softly, squeezing her tightly again. "I should have talked to you about it sooner."

She releases me just enough to meet my eyes, a warm smile on her face despite the tears still on her cheeks. "Do you want to talk to me now?"

We go into my office and close the door. I don't worry about work or class. I lay out everything that has happened since that first day I stormed into Nathan's office. It tumbles from me, and I let it, enjoying the catharsis of not having to censor myself anymore.

My coffee is almost empty by the time I'm done detailing the moment Nathan confronted me in Frank's office, how cold his demeanor became and how quickly it ended. A moment passes, then Jillian lets her eyes drift to the rain falling outside my office window.

"There's only so many lives this divorce should be allowed to ruin," she murmurs.

"Yeah, well . . ." I let my voice drift off and shrug.

She catches the motion, her expression softening. "Well, what?"

"It doesn't matter," I say. "Nathan and I were never going to work anyway."

"You don't know that."

"I do, actually."

"Bea—"

"I've never been good at the whole love thing, Jills," I say, throwing her a flat expression. "You know this."

She sighs. "Bea, of all of us, you might be the best at it."

"How can you even say that?"

Her head tilts, like she's considering. "Remember when Maggie and Travis almost broke up?"

I blink. "Right after graduation?"

She nods. "They had only been dating for a few weeks and Maggie invited him to Chicago to meet her family. It was just for a weekend or something, but he freaked out. And instead of talking to her about it, he started to pull back, setting the groundwork for a breakup. So, you went to his apartment."

I smile. I do remember it. Travis was on the sofa, watching *Heat* for the hundredth time, and wearing a hoodie with a week-old ketchup stain on the front. I sat with him and listened to his worries and fears for more than an hour. When he was done, I calmly stood, picked up the remnants of some pizza from the coffee table, and threw it at his head. It pissed him off, but that was the point: snap him out of his spiral long enough to talk some sense into him. And it worked.

"To be fair, I think they would have stayed together regardless," I say.

She shrugs. "Maybe. But maybe not."

The words sit between us for a moment.

"You loved Travis enough to make sure he didn't mess it up with Maggie," Jillian finally continues. "And you love Maggie so much that you'll wear whatever god-awful bridesmaid gown she picks out." I snort and Jillian smiles. "And you love me. You've spent months pretending to hate Josh for me, even though I knew it was only pretend." Tears prick my eyes again. I try to blink them away, but I can tell Jillian sees them because her eyes start to glisten again, too. "You love Josh, too. You loved him when it was hard to love him. That's not easy, but you did it."

*Not easy, just simple.*

I close my eyes and let out a long breath. "I miss us."

I want to say more, but I know she understands. Our group had been our family. For years, we had been together for all the ups and downs. For the good and the bad. And I had tried so hard to hold on to it, to keep change at bay. But in the end, nothing I did mattered because it was all fractured now. The different parts were drifting away from where I stood, trying to balance on my own.

"We're still here, Bea."

I shake my head. "It's not the same."

She lets out a soft laugh. "Of course it's not. It was never going to be. Change is inevitable. You can't protect yourself from it or you'll just keep getting hurt."

"But I don't know how not to," I say. There's a familiar lump growing in my throat. "And I don't think I can get hurt again."

"I understand," she says. "But did it occur to you that maybe Nathan is somewhere thinking the same thing?"

The words hit a chord in my chest, their hint of truth resounding through my limbs. I want to ask her what that even means in the grand scheme of things. If it even matters anymore. But before I can, there's a knock on my door.

Blake enters before I can invite him in, stopping in the doorway and leaning against it. "I will pay you a hundred dollars to check our voicemail box even once."

I groan and let my head fall into my hands. "Go away, Blake."

Per usual, he ignores me. "I'm serious. It's full, and not one of them is for me. You're killing my social life."

"What's going on?" Jillian asks, looking between us.

Blake barrels on, undeterred. "Or at least let me change the outgoing message so Nathan Asher knows you're not the only one who uses it."

My eyes snap open and lock on him. "What are you talking about?"

"He left like a dozen messages on there this morning. There probably would have been more, but we ran out of storage," Blake replies.

Jillian's eyes widen. "Wait. Nathan Asher called her?"

He looks over at her like she's missed a step. "Obviously."

"What did he say?" I ask.

But Blake isn't interested in answering questions. "Why is he even calling our voicemail? Doesn't he have your cell? Then he could at least text you and—"

"Blake," I practically yell. "What did Nathan say?"

His head cocks to the side as he seems to think about it. "Something about a guy named Josh. He talked to Josh? He knows about Josh? Then something about Josh and Sacramento. Then there were a few where he was really insistent that you call him, his voice got all gruff. Actually, those were great. I saved those. Then the last couple sounded kind of desperate."

"Desperate how?"

"You know, the usual. 'I'm sorry, please call me, I love you.'"

The words land heavily in the middle of my closet-like office. A dozen different emotions roar to life in my chest as Jillian lets out a sound that lands somewhere between a gasp and a shriek.

I stand up, keeping my movements slow like it's the only thing that will prevent me from exploding. "He left that on our *voicemail*?"

Blake catches my expression, and he looks almost confused. "What is that face? Did you honestly think nobody knew you two were together?"

Jillian looks like she's fighting a smile as she answers for me. "I think she did, yeah."

Blake rolls his eyes. "Oh please. You two weren't fooling anyone."

I open my mouth, but it snaps shut again. Because up until that moment, I had thought we were fooling everyone. I thought if I pushed him away just enough, no one would see what I was too afraid to acknowledge: I'm in love with Nathan Asher. I have been for ages. Weeks of pretending, and it had still been blatantly clear to everyone except me.

Embarrassment and anger and sadness swell from somewhere deep inside me, and I want to scream. But I don't. I grab my bag and head for the door.

"Bea . . ." Jillian says, her voice calm and soothing.

I ignore it as I storm past Blake, who looks at me like he's confused as to why I've suddenly gone murderous. "Are you okay?"

"Go away, Blake," I yell over my shoulder as I head toward the stairwell and throw open the door.

It's about to close behind me when I hear Jillian yell, "Be nice!"

# CHAPTER 31

I spend the elevator ride up to the law offices of Hayes, Patel & Asher daydreaming about nailing Nathan Asher's balls to the side of his office building. Literally. I want to nail them to the stone facade of this skyscraper. I had been contemplating it since I stormed out of my office and into the rain that was coming down in sheets outside. I had forgotten an umbrella in my office; I had forgotten almost everything as I marched to the subway, took it to Midtown, and got out at his building. I didn't even stop as I stalked through the lobby, just mumbled to the wide eyes of the men at the security desk that I was going up to Hayes, Patel & Asher, and got in a waiting elevator.

The reflection in the mirrored doors shows the aftermath—my soaking-wet sweatshirt, my matted hair, the mascara running down my face. But I barely notice; I am solely focused on the mission at hand.

Of course, it's only once the elevator doors open onto the wall displaying the law firm's name in giant gold letters that I remember that I yet again forgot my hammer.

The woman at the front desk blanches when I emerge. Her phone is to her ear, and I can only assume security already called up to warn her about my arrival. She's probably calling Nathan right now. But I don't care. My attention is zeroed in on the closed office door ahead. I keep my steps even and my chin high, a Herculean effort considering the rage coursing through my body.

There's another woman sitting at the desk outside Nathan's office, and her eyes widen when she sees me. Her mouth is agape and her phone to her ear, but she doesn't try to stop me as I walk past and throw open the door.

Nathan is sitting at his desk when I enter. And damn him, he looks good. Really good. Calm, composed, his suit untouched by the rain, and his short hair perfectly combed away from his beautiful face.

"Thanks, Vanessa. Yes, let me know when he's downstairs," he says, and hangs up the phone.

"What part of 'do not call me' do you not understand?" I screech. And it really is a screech. My voice is so loud and so high that I should be embarrassed, but I'm too close to tears to care. "I don't care if Josh told you everything, I didn't want to hear from you! I blocked your number for a reason!"

He slowly stands. "Bea—"

"And then you leave a message like that on my work voicemail?" I take a step closer to his desk, close enough that my flailing arms send droplets of rain onto the papers in front of him. "That's like cc'ing the entire faculty! You can't air your dirty laundry in front of my colleagues like that just because you feel like it!"

A little voice in the back of my head is whispering about the irony of the situation right now, but I ignore it, letting my anger swallow up every other emotion in my body. I need it to; I can't let myself feel even an ounce of the pain or the love or the hurt that's trying to break through, because I know I'll crumble. A blubbering, pathetic mess lying in the middle of Nathan's pristine marble floor.

He frowns. "Listen—"

"That's not okay, Nate! Why did you think you can do that?"

"Because I love you, Bea." Nathan's voice booms through the room, and I hear a dozen bodies turning to look at us through the door behind me. "I think I've loved you since that first moment you burst in here and called me an asshole." Nathan's blue eyes stayed locked on me while someone in the office behind me laughs, and a handful of people shush them. "I love you so fucking much that it scared me to death. And if you were going to hurt me . . . I couldn't survive it. So I left first. And I'm sorry for that. I don't need you to forgive me. I just needed you to know."

He's staring at me, waiting. And I don't know what to say, because the anger is now battling against an entirely new emotion: regret.

"You know the worst part?" I say, my voice suddenly cracking. "I love you, too. So fucking much that *I* wanted to run, *I* wanted to find a way to cut you loose. Because I knew I would get hurt. But you made me stay. And then it happened anyway!"

"I know," he replies.

His tone is flat; his face is unreadable. That's when I'm struck with the realization that despite the declaration, he didn't say he wanted me back. He didn't even ask. He only apologized. And I realize I may have gotten this situation all wrong.

I swallow, working to dislodge the lump in my throat, when the phone on his desk rings. The sound feels like the thunder outside, so loud and unexpected that my heart jumps. But then it plummets through the floor as he picks up the receiver. *I'm pouring my heart out to you and you're taking a phone call?* I want to scream. But the words are caught in my chest, and I know if I claw them free, tears will follow. Endless, endless tears, and those have to wait.

"Yes?" he answers. He listens for a moment, his attention down on his desk. "Thanks. Yes, just have him wait down there."

He hangs up and brings his attention back to me.

I let out a bitter laugh. "Oh, I'm sorry, am I keeping you? Do you need to find a way to get rid of the belligerent woman before your next meeting? Well, don't worry about it. I'm leaving. Wouldn't want to interrupt all those billable hours, right?"

He doesn't reply. I expect him to protest, to offer some explanation, but he simply looks sad. So . . . broken. And I hate how I want to go and hold him and make that broken thing go away.

Instead, I shake my head again. "Goodbye, Nate."

And I turn and leave.

The office is absolutely silent as I stalk back down the hall, a dozen eyes watching me press the call button for the elevator and wait an eternity until one arrives. When it does, I escape inside as if it's a lifeboat. And maybe it is, because right now I definitely feel like I'm drowning.

I want to stay angry at Nathan; I grasp at the threads of it, trying to hold on, but those threads break under the weight of the pain.

I press the lobby button again and again and manage to hold it together until the doors close. As soon as they do, I let go. The tears burst forth, rolling down my cheeks as I let out an ugly sob. My whole body shudders under the force of it, and I brace myself against the wall. The anger is gone, a Potemkin village that folds under this wave of pain and grief and regret.

I'm vaguely aware that the elevator doors open on the third floor, that an older man is there waiting to enter the car, but when he sees me—mascara running under a mess of matted curls, wiping my nose on my sleeve—he slowly takes a step back into the hallway and lets the doors close again.

The elevator continues down and finally opens on the lobby. I step out, ignoring the men at the security desk again, who are eyeing me with concern. They don't stop me, only watch as I make my way to the glass doors that lead to the sidewalk.

It's storming even harder than it was when I arrived a few minutes ago. Sheets and sheets of rain billow in the wind as cars speed past, as thunder rumbles in the distance. I stand just outside the doors, letting it envelop me. I know I need to go back to my office to get my bag and keys before I go home. But I can only stand there as the truth hits me.

It's over.

The knowledge should make the next part—the leaving—easy.

But it doesn't feel easy. This feels like the hardest thing I've ever done in my life. Especially when it would be so simple to stay.

Not easy, just simple.

"Fuck," I mutter, letting my head fall forward into my hands.

"Ms. Nilsson?"

The voice comes from my left, just as an umbrella appears above my head. I turn to see one of the men from the security desk, now at my side. He has a brass name badge that says Gary, and he's holding the umbrella so it covers me completely, sacrificing half his body to the rain.

My brain can't compute the moment, so all I say is "Hi."

His expression becomes more concerned as he takes in my blotchy skin, my bloodshot eyes. "Are you all right?"

*Oh, Gary, where do I start?*

"I'm fine," I manage to say, my chin beginning to tremble again.

He smiles like he doesn't believe me at all. "Are you ready to go?"

I blink. "What?"

"Your car is parked at the curb," he says, nodding to the black Suburban just ahead that I hadn't noticed before.

I look at the car and then back to Gary. "What?" I repeat dumbly.

"Mr. Asher called down and told us to escort you. The driver will take you wherever you need to go. Do you want—"

I shake my head. "But . . . why would he do that?"

"The driver?"

"No. Nathan."

Gary shrugs. "Well, he probably wants you to get home safe."

My mouth falls open, the words faltering on my tongue. "I . . . I thought . . ."

I thought he was done with me. The way he had looked at me upstairs, how he hadn't said anything, the phone call . . . I had assumed he didn't care anymore.

And there it is. The punch in the gut that takes the breath from my lungs. I had assumed. Been so concerned with not getting hurt that I had come to a conclusion and run with it. I had assumed the worst to protect myself. Just like he had.

Gary watches my expression and nods. "Yeah. Love's a bitch like that."

I let out a long breath. *Shit*.

∼

The entire floor is humming when I step off the elevator again, a cacophony of phones and keyboards and conversation. But as I march back down the hall, a wave seems to pass over each row of desks, a systematic silencing of every sound as all eyes follow me until I reach the end and throw open Nathan's office door.

I know the receptionist has called down to him, probably warning him that the crazy woman is back, because he still has the phone to his ear. He stares at me as I march toward him so my hips are flush with his desk.

"What the fuck was that?" I say. My clothes are dripping wet, and I know there's a pool of water growing at my feet, but I don't care.

He puts down the phone slowly, like any sudden movement might scare me away. "I didn't want you out in this storm."

"That's none of your business! You can't just put me in a car when you feel like it! Or worry about how I'm getting home! You can't care about me anymore, and . . . you can't . . . you can't . . ."

I can feel the eyes watching us from the hallway behind me. Watching him as he stands, a soft expression on his face.

"Yes I can, Bea," he says. "It's simple."

The hard line of my lips begins to tremble, and just like that, the last of my armor is gone.

I don't know how he got around the desk, only that he's in front of me in an instant, picking me up and crushing me to his body.

"I love you, Bea. I love you so fucking much," he murmurs into my hair, my skin.

My arms wrap around his neck, holding so tight that there's no space left between us. "I love you, too, you stupid asshole."

Cheers and clapping erupt from the hall, but I barely hear it as his lips find mine. I never thought I would feel this again, and I need to soak in as much as I can. To keep him close and never let go.

The applause continues, and Nathan curses under his breath as he turns us just enough to kick the door closed with his foot. Except when he tries, it suddenly feels like we're off-balance. It's only as he stumbles back that I look down to see the huge puddle at our feet.

He tries to catch himself, but he keeps slipping forward and then back again, and then suddenly we're falling.

"Shit!" he bellows.

I yelp and reach out for something, anything, but only manage to take a chair with us; it crashes down next to the desk, making the floor tremble.

A moment of stillness follows, with Nathan flat on his back and me straddling him, my sodden hair dripping rainwater all over his pristine suit.

"OH MY GOD! Mr. Asher!" someone blurts out, and suddenly the cheering is yelling, people running, someone asking if they need to call 911.

But I can't move. The laughter bubbles up before I can stop it, taking over my body so I can barely breathe.

Nathan is looking up at me, an eyebrow cocked and a grin teasing his lips. Then he reaches up to brush a few stray curls from my forehead.

"So, is this romantic?" he asks, his smile broadening to reveal his dimple.

I nod. "Absolutely."

"Thank God," he says. And then he pulls me down to kiss me again.

My body relaxes into him, and I forget to notice the chaos swirling around us. The people yelling or the wet floor or his now-sodden suit. It's just him and me, arms around each other as we hold our breath and fall.

# EPILOGUE

## Eight Months Later

"This is bullshit." I lift my phone higher, staring up at the illuminated screen. "What kind of hotel doesn't have Wi-Fi?"

"The kind that has a rotary phone as their landline," Travis murmurs, the receiver of said phone to his ear. He's seated on the edge of the bed in the center of the room, his tuxedo bow tie loosened. "Yes, Josh. I'm talking to you on a rotary phone," he says into the receiver, then listens for a moment. "No, I didn't get married in 1985. Shut the fuck up."

Behind him, Maggie is standing on top of the green-and-pink quilt covering the bed. She's practically scaling the antique headboard in her ivory chiffon wedding dress, holding her own phone up near the ceiling. "Oh! I think I've got one bar! Yes! Wait . . . never mind."

"Maybe if we walk down to the road?" Jillian interjects from the far side of the room. She's holding her phone out the open window with one hand, while keeping the front of her green taffeta bridesmaid dress intact over her chest with the other.

"I'm not walking down a dirt road in the middle of nowhere," I say, getting up on my tiptoes. "That's the beginning of too many horror movies."

"We're in Vermont, not the middle of nowhere," Travis interjects, phone still to his ear.

"Classic horror movie line."

He shakes his head and curses under his breath. Josh must hear it on the other line because Travis murmurs, "No, not you."

When Travis and Maggie told us they had decided to get married at a bed-and-breakfast in Vermont—the one they were modeling their own after—we were all thrilled, not only because the website made the place look idyllic, but because it was also within driving distance of the city. Jillian was only too happy to get out of Boston and headed up with the happy couple to help set up, while Nathan and I left a few days early to stay with his parents in Great Barrington beforehand. Contrary to popular belief (i.e. Travis's opinion), Dan and Pat Asher love me, and after spending a week with them when they came to the city to visit Nathan this past summer, they were only too happy to host us. And Pat is a fan of *The Real Housewives*, too, thank you very much.

The only one who isn't here for the nuptials is Josh, but he had told us that he wouldn't be able to come, long before the location was confirmed. In addition to just starting a new job out in Sacramento, he's also enrolled in an intensive outpatient program that requires him to attend meetings a few times each week. He could have requested a few days off, but he knew it was better for his recovery if he didn't. When he told us, I think even Jillian was impressed.

Of course, I have no such consideration for my own mental health, because despite promising myself not to check the bar exam results that were supposedly sent out today, here I am, cursing every cell tower in New England as I try to connect with my email. And like the incredible family they are, my friends are here with me for support. And approved access to my inbox so I can exploit their data plans.

"Why would the bar association send out test results on a Saturday? Who does that?" I ask, reaching my phone a bit higher.

"Sociopaths," Maggie whispers.

"Can we go downstairs and enjoy our wedding reception now?" Travis asks.

"No," Maggie, Jillian, and I reply in unison.

The door to the room opens then, and we all turn as Nathan enters. I take a moment to appreciate the view: the tuxedo that he apparently already had in his closet cuts a crisp line across his shoulders, his waist. He even brushed his hair before the ceremony. That was hours ago, though, and now it is back to a disjointed mess atop his head.

He's carrying two glasses of bourbon, and as he walks forward, he hands one to Travis. I didn't think it was possible for Travis to idolize him more, especially after they first met, when Nathan mentioned that he could get them box seats to a Rangers game, thanks to one of his former clients. But from the awestruck look Travis gives Nathan now, the mouthed *thank you* as he cradles the drink in his hand, apparently, I was wrong.

"Any luck?" I ask, smiling hopefully as Nathan stops at my side, hooking one arm around my waist.

"The woman downstairs thinks they have a dial-up modem somewhere. She's going to look in the barn."

My smile flattens. He has the gall to look mildly amused.

"I wonder if anyone has ever tried to use dial-up with an iPhone," Travis muses. Josh must answer because he sighs into the receiver. "It was a rhetorical question, dumbass."

Nathan glances up at my phone's screen. "How about you?"

"I can't feel my arm anymore," I answer.

"I can work with that," he murmurs, taking a sip of his drink.

I turn enough to send him a sharp glare.

"Oh! I think I've got it!" Maggie yells from where she's perched on the headboard. "Yes! Bea! I have two bars!"

"Don't move!" Jillian shrieks, scrambling off the windowsill. She's on the bed in an instant, standing beside Maggie and squinting up at the screen.

"Is it there?" Travis asks, leaning back to look up at them.

"Hold on, hold on," Maggie says. "It's reloading."

Jillian lets out a strangled groan. "Oh my God, why am I so nervous? This is awful."

I should go up there, too, squeeze between the two of them to open the email myself, but I can't move. My legs are frozen in place as my heart leaps into an erratic staccato in my chest.

I look up at Nathan, panicked and wide-eyed. "Distract me."

One corner of his lips turns up, as if he anticipated this.

"Distract you," he repeats, like he's mulling over the words.

I don't reply; this is not the time to be cute.

His smile broadens, and then he reaches into his pocket. A moment later he pulls out a small box. A small velvet box. The kind you put jewelry in. The size you might get for a ring.

My heart stops. Time stops. For a moment, I don't even breathe.

"What is that?" I whisper.

"Open it."

"No."

"Open it, Bea."

My hand is shaking as I reach up and brush my fingers against the soft black velvet. I take it gently from his palm and test its weight in mine. It's substantial enough that I know something is inside.

My gaze snaps back to his blue eyes. There's a commotion happening around us—Jillian and Maggie arguing about the connection, Travis translating the scene for Josh—but right now the only thing I can concentrate on is the man with a wry grin on his lips standing in front of me.

Nathan nods to the box in my hand. I take a deep breath before clicking it open.

Inside is a key.

A mix of relief and confusion knits my brow. "What is this?"

"A key."

I narrow my eyes at him. "A key to what?"

"My apartment."

My pulse spikes and I'm not sure I even know how to breathe anymore. He takes the opportunity to take a step toward me, so close that I can feel his breath in my hair.

I blink. "What's happening?"

"I'm about to ask you to move in with me." His smile broadens so his dimple now teases his cheek.

"But . . ." I swallow. "Why?"

"Because I'm in love with you. And most of your stuff is there now anyway."

I want to argue, but the statement is fair. There has been a slow pilgrimage of my things over the past few months: a toothbrush, some books, a couple of drawers in the closet. It wasn't even a conscious choice, just the natural thing to do. Nathan splits his time between the firm and Safe Harbor now—Marcie put him on the board of directors a few months ago, but he also does pro bono work when he has time—while I spend entirely too much of my week at Land and Associates, doing research for their latest class action lawsuit until I get my bar results. We're both so busy doing the things we've worked so hard to do that it only makes sense to simplify our time together.

It's a good excuse, I tell myself. But it's flimsy, because in reality, this is so much more than that. I love waking up next to him in the morning. I love arguing about movies and books and weekend plans. I love how he knows when to push me and when to let me curl into the crook of his arm that seems made just for me. I love this life we've built with one another, and I'm suddenly so worried that something as small as a key could throw it off-balance.

"But . . ." My voice trails off. "What if you get sick of me?"

His eyebrows knit together. "What?"

My tongue darts out to wet my dry lips as I scour my brain for the necessary words. "You're going to figure out that I eat peanut butter out of the jar with a spoon and how I'm awful when I get sick and that I paint my toenails on the floor without putting anything underneath so eventually you'll have little spots of five different shades of red on the hardwood and . . . and . . ."

His smile returns. "I already know about the morning breath, Bea. We can only go up from here."

I stare down at the key. The worry has dissolved and I'm waiting for fear to rise up and take its place. It doesn't, though. There's only the sound of my pulse in my ears and an eager giddiness growing in my chest.

My hand slowly rises to trace the key's crooked edge. It looks so ordinary. Like any other key on any other ring in the city. But this one is mine.

"Move in with me, Bea," he murmurs, his voice so deep it vibrates in my marrow. It's warm and comfortable and safe. It's home. Nathan is home.

I open my mouth to answer, to say yes and throw my arms around him, but I'm cut off as Maggie and Jillian scream.

"You did it, Bea!" Jillian squeals. My gaze darts across to where they're both jumping up and down on the bed, Maggie's glowing screen between them. "You did it!"

Together their cheers make a deafening sound that dissolves into laughter as Travis stands and joins in.

"She did it!" Travis yells into the phone. "Our girl's a lawyer!"

I did it. I passed the bar.

I turn back to Nathan, expecting to see elation and surprise on his face, too. Instead, there's just that same wry grin on his lips. A look that suggests he isn't surprised at all. That he knew exactly what he was doing.

My mouth falls open. "Oh my God. Did you do this right now because you knew I would need a distraction?"

He shrugs one shoulder. A lazy admission of guilt.

I narrow my eyes at him. The anger is right there, ready to be wielded. But it's dwarfed by so much else now. Happiness, pride, contentment . . . but most of all, love. A fierce and devastating love that I stoke and stir until it's white-hot. All-consuming. And I let it overwhelm me as I smile. "You're such an asshole."

He laughs, then leans down and kisses me, soft and lingering before pulling back just enough to whisper, "I love you, too."

# ACKNOWLEDGMENTS

This book has lived a thousand different lives, and I'm so thankful to every person who was there for the long (and, at times, agonizing) journey that brought it into your hands. From my family and friends to my publishing team to the woman at the grocery store who gave me a hug when revisions brought me to tears in the self-checkout line, thank you.

First and foremost, to Tom: Your endless love and support are the reason this book exists. I could write a thousand stories and never come up with a romantic lead as good as you. I love you so much. And to Poppy and Henry, the two most incredible human beings I have ever met: It is such an honor to be your mom—I love you more.

I could not have asked for a better cheerleader for this project than my fabulous agent, Joëlle Delbourgo—you knew what this book could be, and for that I am eternally grateful.

Before being published, I don't think I appreciated how much a good editor can help shape a book. Imagine what it's like to have a *great* one. Molly Gregory, you are a gift of a human being. Thank you for your patience and expertise and unwavering love of Nathan! And to the whole team at Gallery, especially Jennifer Bergstrom, Sally Marvin, Matt Attanasio, Lucy Nalen, Tianna Kelly, Christine Masters, and Stacey Sakal. And to Jonathan Karp: thank you for loving the original title so much!

Endless gratitude also goes out to Rupert Holmes and his entire staff, particularly Teresa Jennings, for their patience and enthusiasm for this project. From the start, I wanted "Escape (The Piña Colada Song)" to play a role in Bea's story, and they worked so hard to make that dream come true—thank you all so much.

This book has gone through so many iterations as I tried to get it right, and I don't know where I (or Bea and Nathan) would be without those friends/beta readers who offered feedback in its early stages. Thank you to Erica Orloff for reading that very first draft and knowing exactly what this needed to be, to Thomas Cummins for telling me what was working and what definitely wasn't, and to Borbala Branch, for reminding me why I love this story so much.

And to my friends and family who have been there from the beginning: my parents, Kevin and Joan, Conor, Joowon, and Harper, thank you so much for the support and love and bottles of wine! To my transatlantic family, who are always cheering me on even when I feel like I have no idea what I'm doing. To Melissa, who has believed in me ever since she let me sleep on her sofa after I moved to NYC with nothing but a negative balance in my bank account: thank you for being there for all the biggest milestones. To Audrey, the best writing partner and friend I could ever ask for—you're a superhero and I love you so much. And to our crew, Zoran Zgonc, Nicole Page, Jessica Winchell Morsa, and Jenna Helwig: How did I get so lucky to have such incredible friends? Thank you for being there through everything and then some.

And finally, to you, the readers, especially my fellow angry girls: you're fucking perfect and don't let anyone tell you otherwise.

**B**eatrice Nilsson is a lot of things: feisty (to those who love her), combative (to those who don't), but most of all, she's the kind of person who will always fight for those she cares about. So when the marriage of her two closest friends falls apart, Bea storms the office of attorney Nathan Asher to tell him exactly what he can do with his divorce demands. Unfortunately, what should end with a few choice words soon spirals into uncharted territory when Nathan shows up at her NYU Law office a few days later as a newly minted adjunct professor—and her new colleague.

Bea still hates Nathan, of course. But between weekly meetings and networking events, walks around Washington Square Park and late-night pizza, that hate begins to feel a lot like something else. And as uncomfortable truths emerge about the divorce that started it all, she's faced with the impossible: choosing between her friends or, for the first time, her own happily ever after.

© MONIKA NORMAND

**EMILY HARDING** is one-half of the writing duo behind the For the Love of Austen series, including *Emma of 83rd Street* and *Elizabeth of East Hampton*. She lives in Dallas with her husband, two children, and an incredibly spoiled Texas heeler.

FICTION

ISBN 978-1-6680-8274-4  **$18.99 U.S./$25.99**

SimonandSchuster.com
@GalleryBooks

GALLERY
BOOKS

COVER DESIGN AND ILLUSTRATION BY SARAH HORGAN

9 781668 082744